CHASM

James Bruno

This is a work of fiction. Names, places, characters, and incidents are either the product of the author's imagination or are used fictitiously, and any resemblance to actual persons, living or dead, business establishments, events, or locales is entirely coincidental.

CHASM

But when to Mischief Mortals bend their Will,
How soon they find fit Instruments of Ill!

- Alexander Pope
  Rape of the Lock

CHAPTER ONE

When he awoke at dawn, slaughtering his family was not on his mind.

Polishing up his speech to the Yale Club was. *Let's see now. Refugees. Ah, yes. Will have to dig into the refugee issue. Don't know squat about refugees, even though the State Department says I'm an expert. Time. Time. Time. Not enough. And the deceit . . .*

One thing that really, really got William Winford Ferret's goat more than anything else was the way his wife threw his socks into the dresser drawer willy-nilly. Browns and blues and grays and greens and whites all mixed up together. But tossing the argyles into the mélange got to his craw. Argyles, already incorporating a mix of colors, simply did not belong with the rest of them. Any fool knew that. He would talk to her later about it. *Calm, Win. Be calm. Old blood Connecticut Yankees kept their cool. Sign of a good diplomat as well as a good husband.*

He closed the bathroom door tightly, yet silently. He tried to lock the door. But the lock was jammed. *Why*

*don't they tell me when things need to be fixed? Lynette
must be told once more. And the boys too. And mother.
Mother . . .*

He reached down into the cabinet below the sink
and retrieved that can of Edge -- the extra tall one for tough
beards that said "25% free!" Connecticut Yankees loved
bargains. He pulled out one new Schick razor from a crisp
cellophane bag. He looked around, out the window. Then
breathed easily. He wet his face and applied the lather.
Refugees. *Must look good before my fellow alumni. These
folks are as smart as they come. You can get away with
winging it before the Raleigh Rotary Club. But not before
Yalees in Washington, D.C. Cream of the cream. Power
elite and all that. They can spot a phony a mile away.*

A rivulet of blood sprang from his flesh, just below
the chin. He froze and stared at himself in the cabinet
mirror. The crimson trickle poured effortlessly down his
neck. A tiny, serpentine current progressing without
hindrance, aided by wet skin and gravity. How fascinating.
Life's essence oozing forth with the ease of a spring brook
in a virgin wood. How horrifying. Unlike a brook, its
content was finite. If enough escaped the confines of a
body, that body would cease to function, would die. An
athletic man, not yet forty, a healthy man with so much to
live for, could expire if the outflow were not stanched.
Women and children, smaller and weaker than men,
presumably would die faster.

The door burst open with a violent bang. The rat-a-
tat-tat echoed off the tiles and exploded into his head. A
nebula of primal emotions erupted from his innermost core,
uncontrolled, spectacular forces that instantly devoured and
neutralized his humanity. Except for one overriding
instinct: survival.

Rat-a-tat-tat-tat-tat. He saw nothing. He felt nothing. He was subsumed in a brilliant mega-burst of light. It guided him. Told him what to do to survive. The all-encompassing white light held him, steered him, empowered him. At this moment there was no thinking, no morality, no yes, no no. Only survival.

All fell silent. The violent nebula ceased. A painful cold replaced the powerful, blinding light. A child stood before him laughing. No. Cackling. Mocking. Sneering. At him. At the instant when the urge to survive was to be transmogrified into counteraction, overwhelming counterforce, it stopped. His heart pumped like a piston in a racing engine. The sweat pouring from his brow entered his eyes and blurred his vision. Rat-a-tat-tat was replaced by this cruel, little child's squeal. A gleeful, high-pitched squeal which, coupled with his bent-over position and flushed face, broadcasted, "I am the victor at your expense. You stupid, unproud adult fool!"

Reason returned, yet the blunt force of survival lingered. He had to do all he could to calm it, direct it inward, always inward. Anger supplanted it. His firm grip on the boy's shoulders and vigorous shaking broke the five-year old's mirth. The child's plastic "Terminator" machine gun dropped to the floor.

"Rup! Rup! Rup! Rup!" The Golden Retriever hopped around them. He sensed the tension. A dog's barking in such circumstances can signal the need for help or simply its own hysteria.

"Jeremy, What is WRONG with you!! Are you trying to give me a heart attack?! Don't ever do that again!"

The boy scrunched his face up and began to wail. Tears streamed down his freckled face. "Whaa! Whaaa!!" The crying only fed Ferret's anger. And it got louder.

"RUP! RUP! RUP!" The dog barked more loudly. It nipped at Ferret's pant cuffs.

"All right! All right!" The matron appeared at the top of the stairs. She was wiping her hands, wet with soap suds, with a dish towel. She gathered the boy into her arms and comforted him. "That's okay. There's my boy. Aww. Don't be frightened. Daddy didn't mean any harm." She shot a reproving glance at Ferret.

"Mother, he scared the living day lights out of me."

"We'll talk later." She lifted Jeremy in her arms and carried him downstairs with the pet in tow. He could hear Lynette's voice. "*What* did Daddy do? . . . My heavens . . . come here little one . . . Mommy will take care of you."

Ferret shut his eyes. *Too much. Escape. I must . . ."*

"Win, are you all right?" Lynette's face was the definition of wifely concern. Her neat blonde hairdo accentuated the proper good looks of a generic Midwestern, all-American girl.

"Yes . . ." He shook his head. "I'm fine. It's just that Jeremy . . ."

"Have you taken your medicine?" she asked in a hushed voice. She reached into the medicine cabinet and took out a small plastic bottle, opened it and looked inside. "Time for a refill. I'll do it this afternoon on my way to art class." She shook out one capsule, filled the bathroom cup with water and offered both up to her husband. "Here. Only one gulp and it's done. Come on."

"I really don't think I need--"

She popped the pill into his mouth and pressed the cup against his lips. "Let's do a-l-l gone. Like a good boy." He swallowed it and washed it down.

"That doctor. I feel he's got it wrong. I'm fine. Really, I'm fine."

She placed her hands around his waist. "Darling, he knows what he's doing. He's one of the best. Been treating half of Bethesda for years. And forget your male pride and that damn Yankee stoicism of yours. Depression is no shame. Lot's of people have it. And it's treatable." She kissed him, then smiled. "Come on, hon'. Breakfast. Your mother's making blueberry pancakes and bacon. Your favorite."

Ferret hated his job. But with a wife, three kids, his mother, a mortgage on a suburban ranch house and two cars to support and maintain, he didn't have the luxury of dreaming about a radical change of careers.

But during the 30-minute commute between the Bethesda neighborhood of Carderock Springs and the State Department, Ferret would dream of what might be or have been. Above all, he'd wanted to be a news reporter. He had developed fact-gathering and writing skills from his three years as an Army intelligence officer. And he had the language skills to qualify him as a foreign correspondent. "This is Win Ferret reporting from Jerusalem." "And Baghdad braces itself anxiously as the bombs claim scores of innocent victims. Back to you, Brian." He would practice aloud newsmen's sign-offs with a dramatic flurry as he drove the 1999 Dodge Caravan down River Road. Then reality would take over again.

The Office of Special Admissions, Bureau of Population, Refugees and Migration, occupied a suite of offices in the basement of Main State -- the headquarters building housing the Secretary, his senior staff and the regional bureaus. Just three blocks from the White House, Main State had all the flourish and charm of a Soviet ministry of mines. The *Washington Post's* architectural critic once described it as "modern Mussolini office building minus the grandiosity."

"D" Street entrance interior, like all the building's entrances, hadn't changed -- except for the electronic, I.D.-reading turnstiles -- since the structure was completed in 1954. Ferret, clad in a gray-beige London Fog raincoat, trudged in lock-step with all the other gray-coated, attaché case-bearing bureaucrats reporting for work at 8:15 on an overcast November morning. The walls, exterior as well as interior, were also gray-beige. Only glass doors and aluminum trim on the stairwells and chronically malfunctioning elevators detracted a bit from the scheme of common-denominator non-colors. The overall effect was of conformity. People blended easily into the walls. A homogenized universe of unremarkable lost souls.

The Office of Special Admissions was tucked away in a rear corner. What set it apart from other State Department offices was a security door which opened after one pressed the correct combination on the electronic access box just to the right. As with all employees who had to deal with such devices, Ferret quickly tapped the code by habit; he wouldn't be able to recall the actual numerical combination if his life depended on it.

Inside the door, there was a second security check: a human being in the form of a pleasant African-American receptionist named Gerrie. "Good mawnin' Mr. Ferret," she drawled. "How's Lynette and the boys?"

"Oh, just fine. Fine," Ferret mumbled. He forced a courteous smile.

"Ambassador Goldman wants to see you," she added.

"Uh, sure." Ferret felt a headache coming on. He preferred to ease into his work in the mornings. Being confronted with immediate demands while still shaking off vestiges of sleep wreaked havoc on his nervous system.

"Hey, Win. Those boys still cleanin' up at the swim meets?"

"Yeah. You bet," Ferret answered security chief Pete Boyar.

"You can be proud of those--" Boyar went into a spasm of coughs. His last overseas tour, three years as head of embassy security in Bogotá took a heavy toll on the former athlete. Recurrent malaria, chronic hepatitis, an assortment of parasites and three months as a hostage of the guerrilla group M-19 claimed thirty pounds, his health and the remainder of his youth.

"Get some rest, Pete."

"Can't." *Cough, cough, hack, hack.* "Outta leave. Besides, I'm fine. A Washington tour is just what the doc ordered. Heh, heh." He managed a cheery grin on his sallow face.

Ferret liked the security man. But he had an uneasy feeling, the queasy feeling one gets when staring at death directly in the face. Boyar's complexion was grayish-yellow. He was losing his hair. Dark circles framed sunken eyes. They said that he'd lost two-thirds of his liver

to the hepatitis. An M-19 torturer cleaved off two of his
toes and one pinky. But better to have been a hostage of
political guerrillas. The Medellín druggies were worse. A
captured DEA agent several years back was flayed and
slowly dismembered over a week's time before being
thrown into a crocodile pit.

As he did every morning, Ferret hung his coat and
set his brief case on the corner of the desk in his modular
cubicle. He switched on his computer. "You have unread
item(s)," blinked the screen. Ferret checked his email.
"Please see Ambassador Goldman at OOB," it read. He
closed his eyes and rubbed his temples. *Escape. Escape.*

A metallic noise made him snap to. A little man
was adjusting the venetian blinds on the single window in
this corner of the suite. "Gotta keep these shut," exclaimed
Boyar's deputy, Leonard Crudd, in his nasally voice. The
diminutive man stood on the window sill. With a flick of
his hands, he shut the curtains tight, thus blocking all
natural light. Like the final, supercharged rays of an
expiring star, the overhead fluorescent lamps now reigned
supreme in the sterile office space.

Ferret looked around him, his eyes flitting in all
directions as if searching for an emergency exit. They
rested on a terra cotta pot on the window sill. He picked it
up and studied the brown stem and desiccated leaves of the
near-dead coleus. "Ah Yorick. I knew him Horatio," he
said.

"How's that, Mr. Ferret?" Crudd asked.

"No life," Ferret murmured.

"Huh? Oh, right. Yeah, plants don't grow good in
here. But security comes first. Gotta keep this place tight
as a drum. That's my job. Mr. Ferret, please drop by to get

your new safe combination and sign new nondisclosure forms. Just routine."

In the innermost recesses of his brain, a furious eruption was taking place. Blood was displaced by something much more potent. In his mind's eye, Ferret saw lava, brilliant, blinding, cosmically hot, spewing skyward in a ballet of savagery, directed only by the forces of nature.

"Hey, how's Mrs. Ferret, anyway? Everybody loved her pictures at the art show last week."

"Huh?" Ferret struggled to mentally resurface.

"At the Foreign Service Family Art Show. Remember?" The security man eyed Ferret worriedly.

"Uh, sure. Of course."

"You got a great gal there, Mr. Ferret. Pretty, talented. She can cook good too, judging from her Christmas pies."

Ferret regarded Crudd carefully. The stooped, balding nebbish of a man became transformed into an ogrish figure from a Bosch painting. Grotesque and malevolent. A minor keeper of the Gates of Hell.

Crudd dismissed himself after once again reminding Ferret to report to the security office.

Ferret took three deep breaths. He then marched back across the suite to the Front Office. He automatically returned the "Good mornings" and "Hi Wins," though not fully conscious of doing so.

Brenda Hitz greeted Ferret with a curt smile. "Ah, Mr. Ferret, just in time." With a freshly sharpened No. 2 pencil, she checked off a notation in her desk calendar. A Clairol redhead in a discount-house power suit, Brenda Hitz was Goldman's "executive assistant." As computers displaced more secretaries, those survivors fortunate to

have landed jobs with senior officials got their titles
changed. Typical of great bureaucracies everywhere, this
form of title inflation served simultaneously as ego
gratification and faux job protection.

"Please have a seat. The Ambassador will see you
in a moment." Brenda lowered her eyes, pretending to read
a terse, overclassified cable on a topic that was of great
interest to several dozen government functionaries and a
handful of outside academics. As an "executive assistant,"
she had to stay on top of the issues, a quest of those who
made their existence inside the Beltway, just as recovering
the Holy Land was for their forebears.

As Goldman shook hands with Ferret, he gripped
the latter's upper arm with his other hand and kept direct
eye contact. American power purveyors, both real and self-
styled, possessed a peculiar form of assertive and perky
business manner developed over centuries of selling and
trading land rush domains, all manner of bovines, and
slaves.

With his graying temples, Oleg Cassini suit and
studied casual air, Goldman was typical of his breed, the
soon-to-be retired successful professional still hoping for
that one last grab at the brass ring.

"How's Cloris?"

"Mother's fine."

"And the kids? Fine boys you got there. Tell
Lynette that she should be working on Broadway or in
Hollywood. Her Halloween costumes are the best. We
really enjoyed seeing the boys dressed up." Goldman had
no idea the boys' names, having seen them all of two
minutes on his stoop soliciting Halloween treats.

"Yes. Great family." Ferret stared at his shoes.
"Don't know what I'd do without them."

Brenda Hitz entered and placed a pile of papers neatly stacked in Goldman's empty in-box.

He winked thanks to her. "Most of it is cable traffic from Conakry. I just can't let go. Thought that maybe I could be useful should the Administration want my advice . . ."

Goldman had reached the pinnacle of his thirty-year diplomatic career as U.S. ambassador to Guinea, an African country which slid unnoticed into oblivion after the end of the cold war. That he thought that anyone cared about the place or would seek his counsel, no less, underscored the self-importance cum self-delusion that characterized the Washington apparatchik. It was a trait that became especially pronounced in pre-retirement, swan song assignments in the bureaucratic backwaters.

"Well, Win. Back to business. The Dayton Agreement may be history, but much of the responsibility falls on our shoulders to make sure it holds. And we're doing our part -- unheralded and completely behind the scenes, of course. The Secretary has expressed personally his view that Special Admissions has been crucial, that, without us, the whole agreement would've been stillborn from the outset."

The hypocrisy! Midwives to evil! It's wrong! It's wrong!! Ferret betrayed no emotion. On the surface, he took it all in. His honest Yankee's face remained impassive. Take all of life's challenges calmly and deal with them. That's how the Ferrets have survived and risen since they first stepped off the *Mayflower,* his father used to tell him.

But the volcanic forces inside began to churn again.

"This just came in." Goldman handed Ferret a cable.

TOP SECRET ULTRA
FROM EMBASSY BELGRADE
TO SECSTATE WASHDC NIACT IMMEDIATE
INFO CIA WASHDC
    THE WHITE HOUSE
    JOINT STAFF WASHDC

SEXTANT CHANNEL
DISTRIBUTION: CHASM

NOFORN WNINTEL
SUBJECT: RESETTLEMENT OF BOSNIAN
SERB LEADERS

1. TOP SECRET ULTRA - ENTIRE TEXT.

2. FOLLOWING BOSNIAN SERBIAN
REPUBLIC (BSR) PERSONNEL TO BE
TRANSPORTED VIA C-141 DEPARTING
FRANKFURT/MAIN NOV. 30 AT ZULU 2030.
ETA ANDREWS ZULU 1130:

ZINOVIC, BOGDAN; COL. BSR ARMY.
DEPENDENTS: MARISA (WIFE), JOZIP (SON),
RATKO (SON).
BAJIC, BRATISLAV; LT. COL. BSR ARMY. NO
DEPENDENTS.
VROZ, ZIVORAD; CIVILIAN, BSR INTERNAL
SECURITY SERVICE. DEPENDENTS: LINA
(WIFE), DUBRAVKA (DAUGHTER), KATRINA
(DAUGHTER); ALIZIA (DAUGHTER).

MLAVIC, DRAGAN; COL. BSR SPECIAL OPS.
NO DEPENDENTS.
RAZNATOVIC, ZELJKO; COL. BSR MILITIA.
NO DEPENDENTS.

3. REQUEST CHASM PERSONNEL MEET AND
ASSIST. REQUEST CONFIRMATION OF
ONWARD PROTECTION DESTINATION.
SUBJECTS HAVE BEEN GIVEN STANDARD
SECURITY AND LOGISTICAL BRIEFINGS.

4. SPECIAL REQUIREMENTS: RAZNATOVIC
LOST LEFT EYE TO MUSLIM ASSAILANT IN
AN ASSASSINATION ATTEMPT. REQUIRES
PROMPT SURGERY AND THERAPY UPON
ARRIVAL. MRS. LINA VROZ REQUIRES
PSYCHIATRIC TREATMENT RESULTING
FROM EXTENDED SHOCK. MLAVIC HAS
VIOLENT OUTBURSTS AND DISPLAYS
CRIMINAL TENDENCIES; SUGGEST
PSYCHOLOGICAL EXAMINATION UPON
ARRIVAL.

KINCAID

"As you can see, this is a particularly sensitive lot.
Important too. Big troublemakers. Couldn't disengage,
adjust to peace and have been in hiding since the end of
hostilities. The authorities there told us nonetheless that
they were out of control, a threat to the accords. Just
couldn't keep them in line. So, they fall into our lap."

Ferret read and re-read the telegram. He slowly lifted his head. "These people are bad. I mean, they're as bad as they come."

"Win. You needn't tell me what kind of people they are. Our job is to take them in, debrief them, subdue them, hide them, whatever. That's the program, after all. CHASM undergirds peace. We're the widget in the mechanism that makes these things work but nobody sees. Without us, the world stays a more dangerous place. We've got a role. The President relies on us—"

"The risks to ordinary folks who live near them. Anything can happen. Have we thought about that?"

Goldman cocked his head and pulled a face in a gesture of impatience. "Win, we've been through this already. If you had any doubts about the program, you shouldn't have signed on--"

"I was dragooned into it."

"No you weren't. And you know it. The prospect for a double shot at promotion is quite appealing. No other office can offer that. As it turns out, we've got some of the best area specialists in the Department. You happen to have fluent Serbo-Croatian, not to mention German, Spanish and Russian. You're a genuine asset to CHASM. We all undergo pressures in our jobs. You can look forward to moving on next year. In the meantime, you've got a terrific wife and kids to support you. Spend more time with them."

"But, my God. Look who's on this list. Ratkovic. 'Arkan' is his *nom de guerre*. He's a butcher. He slaughtered 600 Muslim men at Nova Kasaba alone--"

"Win! That's enough. Just do your job. Be there at Andrews day after tomorrow, in the morning at 6:00 sharp. Make sure it goes smoothly. Like you've done before."

CHAPTER TWO

Andrews Air Force Base is little different from other airports. Big expanses of concrete are marked by control towers, hangars and utility vehicles that dart between idling aircraft and squat, gray terminal buildings. The air is unnatural, infused with the burnt odor of jet fuel exhaust; indoors, it is stale and thoroughly inorganic. The argument could be made that, since God did not intend for man to fly, nothing associated with flight should fit comfortably into nature. Andrews is no different. Famous for hosting Air Force One and a fleet of government VIP aircraft, and as the arrival and departure venue for the President, the sprawling base lies, like a blotch on a toad's back, smack in the middle of prime suburban territory.

Ferret stood on the edge of the west tarmac at dawn, bundled in a winter parka, and stomped his feet to ward of the zero degree wind chill factor. An Arctic front blasting in from Canada brought winter early to the nation's capital.

Also bundled in winter coats and jerking their limbs to keep the blood flowing were three others. The four figures, standing forlornly amid acres of flat landing areas, silhouetted against a timid sun on the eastern horizon, staring heavenward, resembled modern Druid priests awaiting a divine sign, or perhaps even a god.

The woman saw it first. She pointed at a black dot approaching from the south. The C-141 came in fast, the bright landing lights resembled not the eyes of a god, but rather of a huge bird of prey delivering its young to a safe place.

The plane's wheels made a thud and spewed smoke as they hit the runway. The aircraft shuddered and then screeched as the flaps were lifted. Like a bird of prey. Big, dark, ominous. Unlike other Air Force planes, this one sported USAF insignia on the camouflaged body and horizontal stabilizer that were so small as to be visible only up close. Aircraft on special ops missions were dressed up this way. And they took off and landed at night. Their cargo, whether made of steel, rare elements, or flesh, were almost always lethal.

A small bus pulled up behind the Druid sky gazers. A dozen beefy MPs piled out and formed a neat line, winter frocks flapping in the wind, riot sticks at the ready.

The virtually windowless aircraft taxied halfway back down the runway, turned right into the parking area and came to a halt. After several minutes, the infernal roar of the engines fell silent. The shivering greeting party waited patiently for the starboard hatch to open. A crew member's head stuck out just as the ground crew wheeled up the ramp stairs.

The reception party formed a semi-circle around the front of the aircraft. Two crew members scampered down.

Out of the hatch appeared a stocky, middle-aged, blond man. He was holding the hand of a little blond girl.

He paused a moment to survey the environment, filled his lungs with the frigid air, then sauntered down the steps, careful that the girl did not make a misstep.

Next appeared a thin woman in a bulky wool coat and kerchief on her head. Another crew member assisted her and two more girls down the steps. These were followed by four more men, one woman and two boys.

The last man to disembark also paused at the top of the steps. Unlike the others, he did not huddle against the cold. Dressed only in a gray, open-collar, wool shirt and jeans, this man took his time. The wind whipped his shock of straight brown hair, but he remained unfazed. Where others were cowed, indeed intimidated by the premature winter tempest, this man appeared to soak it in. His stubbly face cracked a smile, but it was not benign. He was in his element, this man. He may have been in the storm, but the storm was within him as well. He gazed upon the terrain as a victorious general looks upon a new conquest. He looked down. His eyes caught Ferret's and held them.

There was a connecting of souls between the two men. Ferret felt suddenly powerful, yet also vulnerable. He knew this man's face. He knew Dragan Mlavic's reputation as an effective, yet ruthless soldier. Colonel Mlavic's three companies of elite fighters called themselves *Narodna Obrana* -- "National Defense," after the terrorist gangs which, in the struggle for Serbian independence, carried out guerrilla attacks against the Austrian Hapsburgs before World War I. Mlavic's men wore black uniforms and fought fiercely. They also slaughtered Muslim and Croat civilians just as fiercely.

The bus pulled up to the plane. The MPs took their positions parallel on each side of the ramp. Ferret hesitated. He was to lead his counterparts from Defense,

CIA and the Joint Chiefs of Staff to the ramp to greet the newcomers.

An Air Force major in his flight suit clambered gingerly down the ramp. At its foot, he looked around impatiently. Ferret's other-agency colleagues looked at him expectantly, not wishing to make the jump on the lead agency representative.

Ferret stared at the sun, the cloud-streaked beams of which fought vainly to burst through the winter sky. Again, the ballet of savagery began to play in his soul. Rage vied with the urge to flee.

"Mr. Ferret," the man from Defense hissed. "Mr. Ferret!"

Ferret's trance was broken. He looked at Menard, from DoD's CHASM unit. Menard jerked his head toward the ramp and the Air Force major, whose impatience was now turning to anger. Sarah Bramley, the CIA rep, looked at her shoes, then at the sky above in a display of impatience and scorn.

Ferret saw the major and the huddling Serbs. He still did not move. The major strode toward him in broad paces. He stopped and saluted smartly.

"You in charge here? Are you the State rep?" he demanded.

"Yes," Ferret replied simply.

"You got a name?"

"Yes. It's Ferret."

The Air Force officer pointed to his passengers without breaking eye contact with Ferret. "I'm Major Donald Bennett. They're yours now, Mr. Ferret. Delivery accomplished, Free on Board. Sign these. I've got other things to take care of." He thrust a ream of papers at Ferret.

Major Bennett waved for the group to approach. Obligingly, they did. Except for Mlavic, who lingered behind while smoking a cigarette.

"Hey! Shithead!! Get the fuck over here and I mean now!" Bennett shouted. "Whaddya want, a formal invitation?"

An MP promptly knocked the cigarette out of Mlavic's mouth and yanked him over by his collar.

"This dude thinks he's something special. Acted like our Starlifter was his personal VIP jet and the crew his servants. Watch him closely," Bennett said.

"His name's Mlavic," Ferret muttered.

"His name's mud to me, pal. I've got two teenage daughters and I shudder to think that we're turning scum like this loose in this country after what they did over there. You got kids, Mr. Ferret?"

"Uh, yah. Three boys."

"You love 'em?"

Ferret stared blankly at Bennett.

"I said, do you love your kids, Mr. Ferret?" The major was in Ferret's face.

"Why, uh, sure. Of course."

Like most of his fellow officers, Bennett just couldn't brook wishy-washy civilian bureaucrats. "Aw hell. Just take them off my hands, Ferret."

Ferret quickly signed the documents and signaled for the group to get on the bus. Six MPs also boarded. He and the other officials entered a small van. The vehicles, with a Humvee in the lead, sped off. Ten minutes later, they arrived at a squat, bunker-like building surrounded by a high, razor wire topped cyclone fence in a remote cul-de-sac overlooking the golf course in the southwest sector of the base. Four sentries, batons on their belts, stood waiting

at the front gate. They took positions flanking the door of
the bus containing the Serbs and the MPs. Each adult male
disembarking the bus was escorted by one MP. The
women and children were taken off last. The little girl of
the blond man and dark-haired woman clung to her
mother's coat as she stared with fright at the gargantuan
MPs. In single file, they were marched into the cinderblock structure. Wafts of heat enveloped them as they
walked through the door and past a plexiglass-enclosed
security cubicle manned by a Marine. It was a world of
white. Too many fluorescent lamps illuminated hospital-
bright walls. A perky female Navy lieutenant greeted them
with a smile.

"Hi! I'm Rachel. Welcome to America. Would
you please follow me?" A short, dour Army corporal
translated into Serbo-Croatian. With the smile still fixed
firmly, Rachel sashayed down a corridor cuddling a
clipboard to her chest. She could have been a guide at
Disney World. She led them to a small, bare-walled
conference room. They took seats around a table. Ferret
and his counterparts sat facing them.

Rachel jauntily handed a packet to each Serbian
adult. "These are your welcome kits. You'll find
information on all fifty states -- including vacation spots --
our currency and measurements, an English phrase book,
American food, tipping as well as a copy of our
Constitution."

Ferret looked at Rachel in disbelief. He spoke up.
"Lieutenant uh . . .?"

"Patterson, sir."

"Yes. Um. Can we dispense with the travelogue?
These people aren't here care of Thomas Cook. These

people are . . ." He fell silent as they looked at him,
waiting for him to complete his sentence.

"Well, they're tired. You can leave the packets in
their quarters for perusal at their leisure, okay?"

Menard leaned over and whispered, "Be easy on the
girl. She's new to the program, Win."

Ferret would not make eye contact with his charges,
except for the little girl. Her innocent doe eyes were
identical to those of countless Bosnian Muslim girls who
lost their childhoods or lives to the fathers and brothers and
uncles of Serbian lasses just like her. He kept his gaze
alternately on the far wall and on the conference table.

"My name is Ferret, from the State Department.
With me are Mr. Menard, Department of Defense, Ms.
Bramley, of the CIA and Lt. Col. Jones, Joint Chiefs of
Staff. Our mission is to resettle you in this country and to
monitor your well-being and behavior. As you know, you
may not move from your new homes unless we give you
permission. You may not return to the former Yugoslav
republics for any purpose without the explicit permission of
the governments of the United States and Serbia. In fact,
you may not leave the U.S. for any purpose without
receiving advance permission from us. A team will oversee
your settling into your assigned communities. Should any
questions arise of an emergency nature, call me or Captain
Rasheed." Ferret gestured toward a tall, young black
Marine officer.

The Serbian men took notes, except for Mlavic,
who sat back, ankle across a knee, and glowered at Captain
Rasheed.

"This week, we will conduct intensive debriefs with
you--" Bramley began.

"When can we go back home?" Col. Zinovic blurted.

Ferret made eye contact for the first time. "I told you, not without the explicit permission of the U.S. and Serbian governments," he replied stiffly. "It was deemed by the policymakers that your absence would make the peace more viable."

Zinovic pointed to his two young sons. "I want them to grow up in their own homeland as Serbs, not as Americans. Your country is powerful, but your society is immoral."

Vroz quickly added, "I have three beautiful daughters." He caressed tenderly the blonde tresses of two of his pre-pubescent girls. "In Serbia, they respect their parents. In America, we hear about drugs and teenage pregnancy. Runaway kids and gangs."

A thermal storm roiled inside Ferret. His face flushed and his heart raced. He leaned forward on his elbows and looked straight at Vroz. "You were stationed in Prijedor, weren't you?"

"Why, yes," he said uncertainly.

"You were in charge of secret police operations there."

Vroz blinked nervously. "I was chief of law enforcement."

"Let me ask you this. Does 'law enforcement' involve mass rapes? Does your so-called law mandate sexual molestation of young girls just like your daughters? Of slaughtering innocent civilians and unarmed soldiers?" Ferret's eyes, wide and agitated, blocked out everything but the Serb sitting in front of him. Sweat glistened on his face. His breathing accelerated.

Vroz's daughters became petrified. One, then the other two began to cry.

Bramley braced Ferret's forearm with her hand. "Win, calm down. We've got work to do," she said through clenched teeth.

Ferret gathered himself and took a deep breath. "We'll now break up for debriefs and resettlement counseling."

The session broke up and the Serbs were escorted out of the room to meet individually in smaller rooms. The children were taken to a small child care facility on the premises.

Bramley turned to Ferret. "Do you know what you're doing?! These people are nervous enough as it is without you turning on them."

"We're letting war criminals into this country and placing them into law-abiding communities," he shot back. "Don't you see?!" Fists clenched, eyes focused somewhere inside his soul, Ferret looked desperate, like a man about to lose everything and helpless to do anything about it.

It was clear to Bramley that Ferret was overwrought. In a gentle voice, she said, "Win, calm down. You know the score. This is the price of peace. Remove them from the scene. Keep them under wraps under new identities. They're a fount of valuable intelligence. A gold mine of information."

"Like Wernher von Braun and those other Nazis we took in after the war."

"That's history. The White House, CIA, Pentagon and your State Department find CHASM useful. At the very least, what these tell us can save the lives of NATO troops."

"What about Mr. and Mrs. Joe Blow back here? These terrorists move into their neighborhood and they're none the wiser. Pederasts get reported. Alien mass killers don't. Jesus." He ran the fingers of both hands backward through his blond hair in a gesture of utter confusion and frustration.

Bramley watched him carefully. "All I can say, Win, is get
with the program, or get out," she said in a low, even tone. She grabbed her purse and attaché case and left the room.

Ferret interviewed each Serb individually. The last was Mlavic. They sat in a tiny, windowless room with only a small table and two folding chairs. The ambience too was fluorescent white.

Ferret reviewed the special ops colonel's dossier. "You've got marketable skills. Should be easy to place you with a pharmaceutical firm or lab somewhere, what with a graduate degree in chemistry."

Mlavic sat back relaxed. A smirk creased his face, which was covered with a week's growth of dark stubble.

"Did you think I was some kind of uneducated barbarian?"

Ferret did not lift his eyes from the file. "I've long known of your reputation as well as your background. We have good information," he stated evenly.

"Yes. Your CIA. They have spied on us for decades. And now they help the Muslims kill our people."

"Tentatively, we plan to place you in one of the Rocky Mountain states -- Idaho, perhaps Montana."

"I wish to go to New York, or San Francisco."

"Impossible."

"Why impossible?"

Ferret looked up and, in a weary voice, said, "So that we can keep a better eye on you."

"Am I a child--?"

"And to keep you away from other ex-Yugoslavs."

Mlavic leapt to his feet. He slammed the table with one hand. "I demand to be treated properly, as a military officer!"

"You're nothing but a killer!" Ferret scowled. "How many did you murder at the Omarska camp alone? Five-hundred? A thousand? Two-thousand? It was your men who dug the mass graves and filled them with slain Muslims. And somebody gave the orders. Now, sit down!"

Mlavic retook his seat. He snickered. His fingers toyed with a paperclip. "You Americans just don't know." He shook his head. "You are all so naive."

Ferret put the folder down. "We sent 20,000 troops to your country to do what? To save you from yourselves. I thought we did it out of idealism, but, come to think about it, we must be naive."

"My country is sorely misunderstood, Mr. Ferret." Mlavic jabbed his chest with his right thumb. "We, we Serbs have saved Europe from being overrun by Muslims, from becoming enslaved. Now we fight a blood war -- against the Muslims -- and a political war: against the international conspiracy to undermine Serbia, led by the United States. We Serbians love freedom and we will survive. Can you grasp that? Freedom and survival. We will do anything -- *anything* -- to achieve these. And so would you."

Ferret's eyes widened. He listened intently to his ward.

"A man is not a man unless he has complete freedom and the means to survive. It is a primal urge. It is in our nature, Mr. Ferret. You and I, we are the same. You carry out the instructions of your government, and I mine. In the name of idealism. Am I therefore so bad? If I were, then your precious America would not allow me to come here, to make my livelihood here, to raise a family. Just like you, Mr. Ferret. Just like you."

Ferret kept his eyes fixed on Mlavic, but his brain was far away. "Freedom. Survival," he muttered. "Family."

"I believe you do understand," Mlavic said.

CHAPTER THREE

Mike Gallatin's path never crossed that of Win Ferret. His liaison for resettling refugees was the smiling do-gooders of Catholic World Services, the non-profit organization under contract with the U.S. government's legitimate, overt refugee program to resettle Bosnians in American communities.

"Dad, I'll be gone Saturday night."

"I beg your pardon, young lady?" Gallatin dropped his newspaper and half rose from his easy chair.

"I'm staying over at Nura's."

"You ask first, sweetheart. Maybe you're getting confused. Your age is one-three as in 13, not three-one as in 31."

"Oh Dad!" she harumphed. Lauren was the picture of her mother's beauty and verve.

Active in her church, Mike's wife heeded the call to sponsor and assist refugees. Following her death from ovarian cancer two years previous, Mike continued to heed the call, as much to honor her memory as to help fellow human beings. Besides, keeping busy was a partial antidote to grief and loneliness. And working as a senior investigator for a big insurance company and raising a thirteen-year old daughter on his own guaranteed that he indeed would be busy.

"I'm teaching Nura cool English."

"Cool English?"

"Yeah, how to talk like the rest of the kids at school."

"God help her." He resumed perusing the headlines. "You two have really hit it off, haven't you?"

"She's a great kid. And she's lived through really awful things over there. Some things she talks about. Other things she just, like, falls silent."

Gallatin knew some of them. After her village was captured by the Bosnian Serbs, Nura Suleijmanovic, was taken with all the other women to a holding camp called Trnopolje in northwestern Bosnia where most were repeatedly raped by Serb soldiers over a month's period. Eventually reunited with her parents, the family was brought to the U.S. to put their lives back together.

"She misses her two brothers a lot. One is in the army. The other one was captured by the Serbians. She doesn't know if he's even alive. He was only 16."

Gallatin also knew that Kemal Suleijmanovic was one of 12,000 Bosnian Muslim troops who were intercepted by Serb forces near Srebenica in July 1995. Virtually all were massacred and dumped into mass graves. It would be a miracle if Nura's brother had survived.

"Nura's parents think you're the greatest. He loves his job."

"You mean being heating and a/c mechanic at Erie Mutual Insurance, Inc. is the answer to his prayers?"

"I didn't say that. He's just grateful that you got him
a good job. And Mrs. Suleijmanovic -- I shouldn't say
this." Lauren covered her mouth with one hand.

"Hey, kid. You're on a roll. Why stop now?"

"Well, she thinks you're very handsome and says
you should get married."

Gallatin didn't respond. He had that thousand-yard
stare that hit him every time Celeste's memory returned to
him.

"Dad? I'm sorry if I said something wrong. It's just
that . . ."

"I know honey." He embraced her with one arm.
"It's not easy for either of us. And you need a mother.
Let's just take it one day at a time, huh?" He kissed her on
the cheek.

"Dad?"

"Yes, Lauren." Gallatin answered somewhat
impatiently.

"So, is it okay if I stay over at Nura's?"

"You bet. But don't overstay your welcome, and
call Sunday morning."

Adnan and Leah Suleijmanovic rented a small,
single-story house in Brookpark, near the airport. The
neighborhood of faded brick buildings and plain clapboard
houses, was home to an aging population of Slavs and other
East Europeans. Gritty, dingy, gray, yet neat, it hearkened
back to an earlier America -- industrial, immigrant
America. Small groceries, bakeries, shoe shops and dank,
blue collar bars still lined its streets. On a good day, wafts

of kielbasa, cabbage, freshly baked bread, and old folks speaking in their native tongues, resonated the past. With the downfall of communism, the area received a small infusion of fresh immigrant blood.

Adnan moonlighted as a plumber. After her eight-hour job as a cleaner-upper at a factory cafeteria, Leah worked as a night cashier at a local convenience store. They hoped to scrape together enough money in two years to purchase a tire dealership from a Croatian-American who was looking toward retirement in Tampa. Friday evenings, however, the family unfailingly attended services at the mosque.

Lauren and Nura spent hours talking about their classmates, their favorite rock band – The Ataris, as well as TV and movie hunks – Jamie Johnston and Chad Michael Murray, and flipped through gossip magazines that they sneaked by Nura's parents.

They complained about teachers and giggled till they were red in the face. On one subject, however, Nura fell conspicuously silent: boys. Whenever Lauren and other girlfriends talked about cute so-and-so, or shared the titillating revelation that one had actually kissed a boy, Nura would shut down. An invisible veil would descend across her face and she would hug herself as if she had a chill. They knew that she was receiving counseling.

Nura talked freely of her nightmares, flashbacks to the times when she huddled with her family in cellars as Serb rockets and artillery rained down, of classmates and their parents being blown to bits by bombs in the marketplace, of grandmothers cut down in "sniper alley." But at other times, she just shut down. Lauren became sensitive to these moments and would be quiet and hug her new best friend.

They watched *The Gilmore Girls* and *My Name is Earl*, then were instructed to go to bed by Adnan and Leah, both of whom were off work that night. Under the covers they giggled and teased each other. Leah cracked the door open and released a torrent in Serbo-Croatian.

"Yes mama," replied a now quiescent Nura.

"What'd she say?" Lauren whispered after the coast was clear.

"She said, we must go to sleep. Stop fooling round," Nura whispered back.

"I can't sleep yet. I'm having too much fun. What about you?"

"Yes. Me too. We are good friends, no?"

"You bet. The best. We'll be best friends for ever and ever and ever." Lauren sat up on her knees and told her pal to do the same. She donned a face of grave solemnity.

"Nura, in our country best friends for life make the Indian Oath."

"Indian Oath? What is that?"

"Just follow me." Lauren knelt ramrod erect on the bed and raised her right hand. "Come on, do like I do."

Nura followed suit.

"Repeat after me. 'I, Nura Suleijmanovic, do hereby sullenly swear.'"

"I, Nura Suleijmanovic, do hereby suddenly swear."

"That . . . that I and Lauren Anne Gallatin will forever be best friends, in thick and thin, in everlasting love and respect, with truth and justice for all . . . so help me God,"

". . . with truth and just yeast for all . . . so held my God."

Lauren spat in her right hand. "Go on. Do it."

Nura spat in her hand. Lauren grabbed it in hers and proceeded to perform a conscientious approximation of the soul handshake.

"Indians cut their palms and mix the blood, but an old guy told me that spit will also work. Now do this." She scrunched her eyes shut. With her thumb, Lauren drew an X on her chest. "Cross my heart and hope to die."

"But I do not wish to die."

"Don't worry, you won't. It's part of the ritual stuff. *Just do it!*"

Nura did it.

They lasted till midnight. Their biological batteries having finally run out, the two conked out and fell into deep slumber.

Leah and Adnan checked on the girls before themselves retiring. Standing in the doorway with their arms around each other's waist, they smiled.

"Leah, what do you see besides two beautiful angels in repose?"

"I see our only remaining child with her newfound sister."

"Yes. But I see something more. I see a Muslim girl sleeping with a Christian girl, who is her best friend. Just imagine how unthinkable that was, before we came to this country."

"And it is so natural. Why shouldn't it be? In this country it is possible. Back home the devil had the people by the throats."

"The devil is everywhere, Leah. Even here. The difference is that in America the devil is kept in check most of the time."

"Oh, but I miss home, Adnan. I miss Srebenica as it used to be. I miss our family. I miss the village feasts and picnics by the Sava, and . . ." She buried her face in her husband's neck and wept. Adnan closed the door.

The Suleijmanovics' bedroom lay just a few feet opposite their daughter's. Whether their dreams were of angels or devils or picnics on the Sava, will never be known. Just as their sons were torn from their midst, their humanity stripped, and their little girl pitilessly violated, their dreams that night were robbed from them, snatched and killed as a hawk preys on a young robin.

The explosion ripped through the outer wall so fast that the couple made the transition from deep sleep to death without having awakened. A fury of flames engulfed the room with the power of a tornado. Like forces of hell unleashed, they whipped through the old wooden structure with a satanic vengeance, devouring the sparse furniture, incinerating the few family photos to have survived the Bosnian holocaust, turning to smoke Nura's homework on the kitchen table.

The roar of explosion and fire set Lauren instantly upright in the bed. *Roooooooossh!* The wind of flames soared through the hallway. *Baaamm! Crash!!* Windows were blown from their frames, the glass splintering and spraying into ten thousand lethal shards. *Creeaak! Smash!* House beams and ceilings collapsed.

She wanted to scream, but could not. A panic seized her, but was quelled, subdued in an instant by a counterforce present in all human beings. The instinct to survive is a powerful one, even in pre-adult, middle class girls from Cleveland. Smoke emitted from under the bedroom door. The intense heat bearing down on it radiated across the room and against Lauren's face.

"*Wake up!* Nura!!" She shook her still slumbering friend. Nura instantly sensed the danger. She hopped out of the bed and went for the door.

"No!! Nura, no!!" Lauren lunged at Nura and tackled her to the floor. "We gotta escape. Now!" She dashed to the window facing the small yard. "Nura. Come! When I open this, the fire will come in. We've got to jump out fast."

"I must get my parents first."

"You can't, Nura. The fire is everywhere." She shook Nura with all her might. "Help me!" Lauren tried to pry the window open, but it stuck. "Nura. You said you don't want to die. *Please* help me." Tears rolled down Lauren's flushed cheeks.

Nura broke from her hesitation and rushed to the window to help Lauren. It went up with a bang, leaving only a screen between the girls and the outside.

The bedroom door snapped lengthwise in half, the determined fire plunging into it like a battering ram. The dresser caught fire, then the curtains, and the bed.

"*Eeeeeeeeeeh!!*" they screamed in unison.

A lick of flame touched Nura's pajamas and flashed upward to her curly brown hair.

Lauren was horrified. The person to whom she felt closest, after her father, was on fire, waving and jumping frantically, like a mechanical doll with an overcharged battery. Nura fought vainly to extinguish the flames with her hands, only to intensify the death struggle.

A wave of intense warmth traveled from somewhere deep in Lauren's core to her head. With wide eyes of fright, she checked herself to see if the fire had now gotten to her. It hadn't. Another force consumed her, fed by a rush of adrenaline.

Lauren grabbed a blanket and threw it over Nura. She then leapt at Nura, knocking her to the floor. Kneeling over her friend, Lauren beat the flames out with the blanket. With tears streaming down her face, Lauren drew on a might she theretofore had never experienced. She hefted Nura, wrapped mummy-like in the blanket, and flung her feet first against the window screen. Nura went flying out of the house, landing softly on a snow drift six feet below. Lauren dashed to the window and dove through it headfirst like a champion swimmer. As her body exited, the unsatiated flames whooshed out as if in chase. They lapped the clapboards above, setting that exterior side of the old house afire.

The American Dream became a vision straight out of hell. The little suburban house burned to the ground, the hopes and expectations of its murdered occupants turned to ash.

CHAPTER FOUR

Ferret got news of the Suleijmanovic's immediately. CHASM's Cleveland senior coordinator, Chaim Glassman, called him late that night. Adhering to security protocol, Glassman simply stated, "A Bosnian refugee's home was firebombed this evening, Mr. Ferret. I thought the State Department might want to know. My name's Glassman," and he gave his number.

Ferret sat up in bed and froze. He clenched his teeth, and shut his eyes as hard as he could. Elbows bent, he tightened his fists at chest level and shook.

Lynette turned on her bed lamp. "Win! Win! What's wrong? Win!" Tentatively, she reached out to touch him.

Ferret raised his head, still with his eyes shut tight, and continued to tremble.

"I'm calling Dr. Berman," Lynette muttered frantically. As she reached for the phone, Ferret broke from his trance.

"No. Don't. I'm fine."

Fear and consternation marked her face. "Win, you aren't fine. You're not well at all. The medicine's not working. And you've been under a lot of stress. Let's see Dr. Berman."

"I said *NO!*" With lightning motion, he grabbed the radio alarm clock and sent it hurling across the room where it smashed against the bedroom wall. Ferret darted from the bed like a raged beast let loose from its cage, and began pacing the room frenetically, as if in a panic search for an exit. His breathing was as if he'd just run the marathon. Sweat poured from his forehead.

Lynette froze in fear, her eyes unblinkingly wide, her mouth half open. She'd never seen her husband in such a state.

"You're against me. All of you. I'm trapped," he hissed. Ferret then raced out the door, went into the bathroom and slammed the door shut.

Sleepy-eyed Jeremy shuffled into his parents' bedroom. Seeing his mother in tears, the five-year old went to her and quietly embraced her. "Mommy, don't cry. I love you. What's wrong with Daddy?"

Through her sobbing, Lynette said, "Oh, baby. Daddy's not feeling well lately. Everything will be all right. Don't fret, sweetie." She ran her fingers through her boy's blond hair and kissed him on the forehead.

Brothers William Winthrop III and Brandon appeared. "Mom, what's with Pop?" the older boy said. "You guys having an argument?"

"I'm scared Mommy," ten-year old Brandon blurted.

"Boys, there's nothing to be scared about. It's just that Dad . . . Dad's been under a lot of pressure in his job lately. He--"

The bathroom door opened. Ferret put out the light. Re-entering the bedroom, he stopped in his tracks and just stared at his family. His hair and face were soaked with water.

"Win?" Lynette said cautiously. "Are you okay, honey?"

Ferret's eyes focused briefly on her, then flitted about nervously. He went to his dresser and commenced to remove socks from the top drawer. "I've got to go to Cleveland first thing in the morning. Something's come up. Uh . . . everybody get back to bed. Get back to sleep. You boys need to catch the bus early too." His voice was flat and deliberate, as if he were reading a text.

His sons marched carefully out the door and returned to their rooms.

Lynette got up and placed her arms around her husband. "Win. Did you take the Serax?"

"Yes."

"Are you feeling all right now?"

"Yes."

"Can we talk about it later?"

"Yes."

She kissed him on the cheek.

"You mix the browns and blacks," he said.

"What, honey?"

"I said, you mix the browns and blacks. And what's more, the argyles are scattered just everywhere." There was an edge to his voice.

She took his left hand and pulled him back to the bed. "Come, husband dear. Come to bed. I'll pack your bags a little later. Come into my arms and sleep. Sleep."

Ferret rested his head on his wife's breast and sobbed. "The evil. The evil," he whispered.

From Hopkins Airport, Ferret took a cab to the Flats, whose old bridges, warehouses and slag heaps were fast being offset by yuppie bars and upscale restaurants and shops. "Glassman Printing and Engraving", flanked by a Navajo jewelry store on one side and an latte bar on the other, was one of the few old establishments that had survived the yuppification.

The elderly proprietor was hunched behind the counter when Ferret entered. He was scrutinizing a stamp with a large magnifying glass under a halogen lamp. The light glinted off a gold Star of David on a thin chain around his neck. The old man barely flinched as Ferret approached.

"Do you collect stamps?" he asked, dispensing with greetings.

"Er, no. But I used to collect coins," Ferret replied.

"Not the same," Glassman said in his pronounced German accent. "Here, take a look at this." He handed Ferret a sheet of paper which held the stamp. "It is the Black Honduras. See how exquisite it is. Remarkable. So much art in so little space."

To Ferret, one old stamp looked like any other. "It must be valuable."

"This little slip of paper, Mr. Ferret, would buy several BMWs. But a BMW's value declines by a quarter once you drive it off the lot, and even more thereafter. The Black Honduras only increases in value. But its beauty is immeasurable, priceless."

"Chaim, you retain a lively and interested mind when your contemporaries are off retired in Florida." It occurred to Ferret that this old German had acquired a considerable fortune during the sixty years he had resided in the United States.

"Florida. Bah! I'd sooner be sent back to the Russian front. Florida is a vast boneyard for those waiting to die. I'll work here until I fall dead, I'm afraid."

The secret irony of "Chaim Glassman" never failed to make Ferret shudder. A protegé of Operation PAPERCLIP, Chaim was known until 1945 as Gruppenführer Rolf Schleicker, a rising young star in the SS. An Austrian by birth, Schleicker had lived and traveled extensively in Yugoslavia with his businessman father as a youth. He spoke native Serbo-Croatian. Later, the SS assigned him to Yugoslavia to take part in the Reich's efforts to subdue the Yugoslav partisans. With the war's end, Paperclip valued his expertise on the Yugoslav communists, particularly his intimate knowledge of Tito the man and his leadership structure. Hence, he was recruited by the OSS, the CIA's precursor, and, through Paperclip, resettled in the U.S., initially bypassing all immigration formalities. Fearful that he would one day be found out, he changed his identity to that of Chaim Glassman, a "non-practicing Jew," in his own words. What better cover for an ex-SS man than being a Jew? Who would ever suspect? And it worked, lo these past six decades.

Glassman left the store in the charge of a clerk and bade Ferret to join him in his private office in the back of the shop. He pulled a bottle from behind a row of accounting notebooks. He took two small glasses from his top desk drawer and placed one in front of Ferret.

"A little *slivovitz* before business makes it all go a bit easier." He filled both glasses. He then raised his glass.

"*Prost!* -- or I should say, *Lachayem!*" Glassman gulped the contents. Ferret did the same. He hated the potent plum brandy. It smelled to him like burning tires and tasted worse.

Glassman offered a second shot. Ferret declined.

"So, this business of last evening. Nasty." He shook his head.

"I've traveled all the way from D.C. So, what happened?"

"The Branko boys. They are the worst. I couldn't control them. So filled with hate. So . . . so beyond the pale. You should not have brought them. Let them stay in Bosnia. Somebody would have killed them. I am sure of it." Glassman poured himself a third *slivovitz*.

"Branko boys. You mean the two militia guys."

"Hah! They are *Ustashi*. Croatian thugs. Nothing more. I know. We fought with the *Ustashi*. Only interested in murdering people. Not winning the war. Skorzeny and I almost nabbed Tito, but the *Ustashi* blew it. You know, if we had had three more divisions in Yugoslavia--"

"I don't have time to talk about old times, Chaim."

"Ah, yes. But you know that I knew Waldheim."

"Yes. I'm aware."

"I knew that man would go places one day," Glassman said, referring to the former United Nations Secretary General who for decades had hidden his Nazi past. The old man broke into a hoarse laughter. "Well, yes, ah, the Branko boys. Cousins from Banja Luka. They were democratic killers."

"Huh?"

"They murdered Muslims, Serbs, Albanians -- when they could find some -- even fellow Croats who crossed them. They killed everybody equally -- democratically, you see. They would be killing NATO soldiers today if they were still back there. Anyway, last night, they planted an incendiary bomb at the home of a Bosnian family. Killed the man and his wife instantly. Their little girl is in critical condition. Over half her body is burned. Terrible tragedy. Terrible." He shook his head again and stared into his empty glass.

"How do you know they did it?"

"They told me! The older one, Milan, phoned me at midnight. He told me to listen to the local news in the morning. I asked him what he was talking about and he laughed. 'Ten little Muslims. Two down, how many more to go?' he told me in a kind of sing-song. Then he hung up. Of course, in the morning, I turned on the TV and there it was. Top story. Bosnian family attacked. Naturally, I was shocked. Shocked." The last sentence he stated flatly, as if feigning deep emotion, but without success.

"But, why? Why them?"

"Mr. and Mrs. Suleijmanovic were leaders. They built a mosque, encouraged more Bosnian Muslims to move here, set up a foundation to help Bosnian refugees. They were sought out by the news media for interviews. Very sympathetic people. The Serbian community here felt slighted and slandered."

"Chaim, but you were responsible for those two Croats. Where are they?"

Glassman looked down and shook his head. "I don't know. They have disappeared. Did not show up at their jobs at the brewery. They are now probably off in a stolen car to create mayhem elsewhere. Two more American road warriors. I'm too old for this. But these people you are bringing in now. They are . . . barbarians." The last word, he enunciated in a hushed voice.

Ferret could feel his heartbeat accelerate, each quickening palpitation marking the expiration of time like a countdown to mortality. He bolted up from his chair and confronted Glassman. "You've got to find them, Chaim. They must be brought back. Do you hear me?!"

Ferret's cracking voice and throbbing temples reflected his teetering on the edge of a steep emotional precipice. Glassman had seen a lot in his lifetime. Nonetheless it unsettled the old man.

"Sit down, Mr. Ferret. Be calm. Now tell me, what do I do with them when I find them? This is unprecedented."

"You have friends . . . friends with special abilities."

Glassman studied Ferret's face gravely. "What would you have me do then?" he said in a low voice.

"They are evil. Evil. And evil must be stamped out. By . . . by whatever means."

"Let me tell you about 'evil,' Mr. Ferret. When you are in the grip of others, men who, in troubled times, can manipulate you, make you believe anything, you are capable of *anything*."

Ferret re-took his seat. "What do you mean?"

"In Germany, we were desperate, prostrate. We yearned for a knight on a white steed to rescue us. And Hitler knew this. He was a master of manipulation. I was a young man. He captured my brain and my soul, along with those of millions of other Germans. We would do his bidding to save ourselves as a nation, yes, even as a race. These Yugoslavs are no different. Each people sees its struggle as one for survival."

"You became the evil that Hitler conjured."

"Yes, we became the evil. Good *bürgerlich* people. Not guttersnipes. It can happen, in the right circumstances, to anyone. Even in America."

"And yourself?"

"I . . . I was . . . misguided."

Ferret looked quizzical. "Misguided?! But you were in the Deathshead Division of the SS. They did horrible things. Slaughtered whole populations. How can you say--?"

"Mr. Ferret. When it happens in America, then you will understand."

Ferret's eyes were locked onto Glassman's face.

A torrent of emotions was raging inside the younger man. Glassman looked worried. "Mr. Ferret, you need to move on. To something else. Otherwise, this program will consume you. Believe me. I know."

But Ferret wasn't listening. His eyes were distant. "We became the evil . . . Survival," Ferret, lost in thought, muttered in a barely audible voice.

CHAPTER FIVE

Gallatin wanted answers. That which he cherished more than anything else, his daughter, barely escaped violent death at the hands of unknown persons for unknown reasons. He struggled for answers.

As an investigator, Gallatin had come to know the Cleveland police force extremely well. Fires, theft cases, criminal vandalism, fraud. They cooperated closely and helped each other out in resolving cases. Senior Detective Ray D'Angelo was more than a colleague. He was a best friend. The two men stood up for each other's wedding, became godfathers to their respective children. Ray was good. Very good. He'd been offered supervisory detective jobs in Chicago and Seattle, but he'd turned the offers down. Cleveland was his home town. He took care of his aging mother and his wife and kids liked their suburban life there just fine. The veteran police detective was as shocked as everyone else over the Suleijmanovic's' murders. Firebombing was just not the kind of crime that afflicted Cleveland.

The two men met at their favorite pub, Shaughnigan's, on the edge of Murray Hill, Cleveland's Little Italy. They had struck a compromise early in their friendship. Since the Irish had the best bars and the Italians the best restaurants, they would conduct their off-duty carousing anywhere where an Irish pub and an Italian eatery were within five blocks of one another. A beer at Shaughnigan's, therefore, was often followed by linguine at Nostri Amici, two blocks down on Mayfield Street.

What distinguished Shaughnigan's from its counterparts was not the old, long, curving oak bar with brass rails, nor its ecumenical clientele, nor its tolerance of a small, unassuming clique of gay dart throwers. It was its restrooms. A clever artist had fashioned around the ladies' room toilet a distinct likeness of Britain's Queen Elizabeth, and around the men's room john, that of Prince Phillip. The toilet seat formed a gaping mouth and lips, so that the effect was of the monarchs' swallowing a patron's feces. It was one of the many little touches that gave the establishment a cast of jolly bawdiness. Otherwise, musty, dark, reeking of stale alcohol and decorated with the usual Irish kitsch -- the de rigeur "Erin Go Bragh!" sign, green leprechauns and shamrocks -- it was just another neighborhood bar.

"How can you drink that shit?" D'Angelo inquired of his pal.

"It's called a Black 'n' Tan by the Queen's Ass, or Her Majesty's Royal Butt, for short," Gallatin responded. He diluted soupy, black Guinness with Michelob draft, using the mixture to wash down a shot of molasses-dark Irish whisky.

"I won't ask why. I'm sure there's a lot of history behind it."

"You got it."

D'Angelo tried his best to lift his pal out of the
doldrums in the two years since Celeste's death, but to little
avail. Gallatin still had a boyish face which, when he
smiled, gave him a dimpled, little-boy mischievousness that
made him irresistible to women. D'Angelo's own black
hair sprouted twice as many grays as Gallatin's sandy
strands, and the latter, at 6'2", retained a muscled physique.
But Gallatin was self-destructing inside. And a potent
antidote to such a process, female companionship,
remained absent from his life.

"You're hittin' the sauce pretty serious these days."

"I'll let you criticize my drinking when I start
calling into question your eating habits, Mr. Salami and
Provolone."

"Hey. Sorry! Excuse me all to hell and back!"
D'Angelo caught himself. "Mike. I didn't mean anything--"

Gallatin waved him away. "No sweat. Forget it."
He took a long gulp of the beer.

They sat silently, though the communication hardly
stopped. One of the vestigial traits that humans possess,
and share with animals, is being in mental synch with one's
mate, one's best friend, one's children. Nothing is spoken,
but much is understood.

"How's Lauren?" D'Angelo asked.

Gallatin grunted and took another swallow of his
concoction. "You know, every time I look into her baby
blues, I see Celeste. But she has this . . . this granite mask.
No sign of life. Just an empty shell. Funny. She pulled
Nura out of a snowdrift, verified that her pal was alive, then
went into shock. Could've been from seeing Nura's
disfigured face. The doctors don't know for sure. And I
. . . I--" He choked up and looked away.

"Mike," D'Angelo said softly. "I hate to see you like this. Anything I can do, I will. You know that. But you've got to pick yourself up. Move on. If you don't, you'll just destroy yourself. And the way you're drinking, you're well on the way."

"Yeah, well. Remember how when we played football, they used to call me 'Let 'em Go Gallatin'? Again, I was too late to save Celeste. Now Lauren." He hit the table with his clenched fist. He fought back tears. "So, what about it then, Ray? You guys got any leads?" he demanded.

D'Angelo studied his friend's face, then said, "You know how it is. We poke around. Talk to people--"

"Cut the bullshit, Ray."

Ray looked at his friend and thought for a moment. "I don't know if we got any leads."

"But you do have some information."

"Some. But it doesn't necessarily mean anything. We need to develop it further."

"Time, Ray! Time!" Gallatin exclaimed. "It's running out. And every day that the perpetrators are on the loose, my daughter drifts further away. I could've saved my wife. I didn't act in time. I'm not going to lose my daughter. Not!" He banged his fist on the table.

D'Angelo nodded sympathetically. "This is what we've got. First, it wasn't an accident. Six gasoline-filled pipe bombs detonated electronically blew away the bedroom and quickly ignited the rest of the house. Low-tech stuff, but very effective. It's a miracle that the girls weren't killed instantly like Mr. and Mrs. Suleijmanovic. ATF told us that it was definitely a professional job. Most likely by someone with military training."

"Like anti-immigrant militia crazies?"

"Don't know. But we've asked the FBI and state police to look into it. Meantime, we've been checking out the ethnic angle. There it gets interesting. Seems there's been some tension among some of the newcomers."

"That's nothing new. Remember when the Irish and Italian boys used to go at it with their fists on the ballfield? Then, when there was a standoff, they'd go after a Bohunk." Gallatin chuckled.

A buxom, forty-something waitress replenished their glasses. "Noraid'll be collectin' tonight, boys. Just thought you'd wanna know," she said in a brambly brogue.

"Shit." Gallatin surveyed the blue-collar types bellowing jokes and singing drinking ditties at the bar, the old men huddled in a corner recollecting old times, the klatsch of smart, young yuppies debating politics and business cycles at another table. "Look at 'em. Searching for their roots in the wrong places. In bars that could've come straight out of some Hollywood studio's prop department. These dumb fucks give to Noraid so they can blow up school kids and Christmas shoppers if the peace there ever falls apart again. So, are the Serbs, et al. taking lessons from the crazy Micks?"

"Maybe something like that. We looked into all the hate incidents within the Bosnian-Serb-Croat community over the past couple of years. Oh, there's been a couple of scuffles, one barroom fistfight, a lot of complaining to the cops that Mr. or Mrs. So-and-so-ohvic called somebody names. Crap like that. We narrowed down to six individuals, though, who've made repeated threats. Three Serbs and three Croats. Not all the threats have been directed against Muslims, mind you. They go after each other and folks within their own group. Everybody seems

to be after everybody else. They're *pazzo*, if you ask me."
D'Angelo tapped his temple.

Gallatin leaned forward on his elbows. "So?"

"One Croat dude's clearly a nut case. Sixty-eight years old. He marches up and down Ontario Street with a placard scribbled with all kinds of crazy shit about saving the world from the Muslim hordes. Two of the Serbs were definitely out of town the day of the bombing. They were in Chicago visiting their girlfriends. The alibis stick. Mean SOBs, though. One took his kids out of school because it had Bosnian, Arab and Somalian kids. The other wrote a couple of hate letters to the *Dealer* praising the guys responsible for genocide over there. So, that leaves one Serb and two Croats."

A trio struck up a rendition of the "Black Velvet Band." The patrons began to clap and stamp to the beat.

"Anyway, the last Serb's a 39-year old loner who's been fired from two jobs for picking fights with Bosnian co-workers. He's on probation for carrying around a handgun without a license."

Gallatin's interest was piqued. "He sounds like a good prospect to me. Have you questioned him?"

"You bet. One problem. He's got no legs. Apparently, they were blown off by a Bosnian mine. He can't forgive and he won't forget. But the guy's confined to a wheel chair. Strange dude."

"No accomplices who might've done it for him? Like that Arab who ordered his followers to blow up the Trade Towers in New York? He was just a blind, old fart."

"Not likely, Mike. As far as we can tell, this Serb dude's got no friends at all. What I don't get is why we let people like that into the country, legs or no legs."

"Yeah. Okay, so the occasional bad apple gets in.
Can't avoid it. Anyway, so he's out of the picture. What
about the two Croats?"

"Now, I'm not saying we've got anything hard here,
but they definitely fall into the category of scumbags. Two
cousins named Branko. Shortened it from Brankovic.
Been here nine months. From the minute they arrived,
they've been trouble. A Croat woman, wife of a green
grocer, accused the older one, Milan, of attempted rape
three weeks after he arrived here. But the charges didn't
stick. At about the same time, the younger one, Zlatko,
punched out a *muezzin* -- a Muslim clergyman -- on the
sidewalk after Friday services at the mosque. Milan got
fired from the Goodyear plant for petty theft. Meanwhile,
Zlatko busted up a bar down near the docks. They both got
fired from jobs they got in a packing plant after the
manager, a Jew, found them trying to recruit members for
something called the Cuyahoga Militia. They're into guns.
We found gun catalogs, bullet casings and rifle oil in their
apartment."

"Where are these guys now?"

D'Angelo shrugged. "They're gone. Left their place
a pigsty. According to the grateful landlady, they haven't
been at their place since--"

"The night of the bombing."

"Exactly."

"What else do you have on them?"

"It's funny. There're several things about these
clowns that don't add up."

"Like?"

"Like how come they always seemed to find jobs
after getting repeatedly fired. And how come they always

seemed to have plenty of cash. And why there are no detailed records on them."

"What do you mean, 'no records'?"

"We went to your buddies at Catholic World Services. Not only don't they have anything on the Branko boys, but they've never heard of them. And they're responsible for resettling all the Yugos here."

"What about Homeland Security? Have you tried them?"

D'Angelo threw his hands up. "That's the most screwed up agency in the government. They couldn't find a bus ticket in their pocket much less a file on a particular immigrant. I spent three hours at their Immigration and Customs Enforcement district office. I never saw so many semi-literate bozos with their thumbs stuck up their asses. Even the FBI guys give up. They call ICE 'The Land of the Living Dead.' And they're supposed to be working together -- for chrissakes."

"Hmm. The Cuyahoga Militia, huh?" Gallatin said.

D'Angelo looked up from his beer. "Yeah. Mike, stay away from them. Leave the militia crazies to the FBI, ATF. They're nutso." He turned a forefinger at his temple. "And dangerous."

The music turned decidedly political, with the lead singer, a young woman with straight red hair and a sad face, giving a forlorn rendition of *Patriot Games*. Three deadpan-faced men positioned themselves on the perimeters of the audience, each eyeing the listeners carefully. A fourth looked about furtively, then waded into the crowd with a large Tam O'Shanter which he extended in patrons' faces as if it were a collection plate at church. "For the lads," he said quickly. People unhesitatingly tossed in fives, tens, twenties -- grocery money, car payment money.

When he reached Gallatin's table, the latter shrugged the man off, not setting eyes on him. The man paused and shook the hat. "For the lads, I said," he repeated insistently.

Gallatin turned his head slowly toward him, cracked a half-smile and said, "Fuck off."

"You're an Orangeman then," the collector retorted.

"I'm a human being."

"So are the lads in Belmarsh Jail."

"At least they're alive!" Gallatin erupted. "Unlike the poor, innocent slobs they've murdered!"

The collector dropped the note-filled hat and lunged at Gallatin. He was stopped cold in his tracks with a large fist planted like a brick on the man's nose. There was a commotion as people diverted their attention from the music and toward Gallatin. A barman the size of a mid-sized refrigerator rushed over clenching a baseball bat in his hand.

"All right! That's it. Get outta here. All o' yuz. Now." He stood menacingly over an agitated Gallatin, a stunned D'Angelo and a prostrate Noraid fundraiser.

Restraining his buddy with one arm, D'Angelo held the other up in front of his chest palm outward and said, "Hey, no problem. Really. We'll go." They got up. D'Angelo pulled some cash out of his pocket and placed it on the table.

"One recommendation though," Gallatin said. "Stick to being a restaurant. There're too many phonies out there."

The barman stood impassively, as stolid as a marble pillar. The other three Noraid men checked their buddy out and glowered at Gallatin as they would a marked man.

D'Angelo pulled Gallatin toward the door. But Gallatin had locked his sights on the Noraiders. The unspoken message between the men was that this wasn't the end. They'd finish it later.

Out in the cold street, D'Angelo put his arms on Gallatin's shoulder. "Hey! Cool down, goombah. C'mon, I'll buy you a latte and cannoli up the street."

Gallatin rubbed his face with both hands and nodded.

CHAPTER SIX

Gallatin admired the folk in Ohio's hinterland.
Hard-working, upstanding, fine citizens all. They lived in
small towns, as neat and plain as their inhabitants. Dairy
farms, hog farms, cash crop farms, small industry. Very
nice. Very boring. He rarely ventured south of Cleveland,
especially in winter. And little Coshocton, 12,000-strong,
normally held as much interest for him as, well, milking
cows.

He pulled off Interstate 77 to Route 36. Soon a sign
announced, "Welcome to Coshocton - Home of the Hot Air
Balloonfest." As an investigator, Gallatin valued diners,
crossroads of information, as he liked to refer to them. He
pulled into the first one he saw, "Stan's Diner," on
Whitewoman Street.

Stan's was a relic from another age. All aluminum
and glass, its linoleum-top counter and red plastic-covered
booth seats with chrome jukebox selectors evoked the era
of Ike, Elvis and the Edsel. Gallatin ordered coffee and
rhubarb pie.

He studied the waitress behind the counter, a forty-something who could easily pass for a fifty-something. Her eyes were sad, reflective of a harsh life of early marriage, several children, grunt work and a life long devoid of dreams.

"Some weather, huh?" Gallatin murmured as he sipped his coffee.

"I hate winter," she said. The woman gazed lingeringly out the window, her eyes focused somewhere beyond the fields of stubbled, brown corn stalks poking through the thin layer of snow which extended to the horizon. Somewhere beyond, somewhere warm, maybe Florida.

He asked about business. She said it was slow this time of year. Mostly truckers and traveling sales and service people. The busiest time was between the Balloonfest and the Canal Festival, June through August. She tidied the pies under glass on an elevated holder.

"What do people do for fun here this time of year?" Gallatin asked.

"Well, not a hell of a--" She perked her ears at the distant gun shots. "Deer huntin'. Every male with a gun -- and they *all* own guns, mind you -- goes out deer huntin' up till just before Christmas." She again focused on the distant horizon and said, almost absent-mindedly, "So much killin'."

Gallatin tipped his cup for a refill.

"Where you from, mister?" she asked, as she poured.

"Cleveland."

"What brings you to Coshocton?"

"Come to hunt. What else?" Gallatin answered nimbly. "I'd like to link up with some guys who know the terrain, though. Any suggestions?"

The waitress thought a moment. "Well, they just formed something called the Coshocton Hunt Club." She looked side-to-side, leaned toward Gallatin and whispered, "But rumor has it that they're into more than huntin'."

Gallatin jerked his head back and grimaced. "Like what?"

"Oh, Jerry Spencer, the Magruder boys, a bunch of others, they've been spoutin' off about the federal government's no good, out to get us, sellin' the country out to the Yew-nited Nations. Claptrap such as that."

"No kidding," Gallatin said. "But does Jerry Spencer hunt?"

"You bet. And shoots. Him and his buddies love nothin' better than to load up on cases of beer and haul off into the boonies and shoot up a storm. Lord knows what they've got. All these big guns everybody's been buying. My word. My daddy had a shotgun and a twenty-two. That was plenty to get meat on the table for us."

"Well, I'll check with him anyway on hunting prospects. Where can I find him?"

"At his garage. Right on Route 16."

Gallatin thanked the woman, finished his pie and left a fat tip.

Gallatin was grateful that Jerry Spencer wasn't out hunting that afternoon. Bent over the engine of an '85 Malibu, under a sign, "Jerry's Auto Repair," in amateurishly daubed black and white cursive letters, he appeared anything but a crazed, gun-mad, apocalypse-obsessed political maniac.

"Afternoon," Gallatin said as he approached the mechanic amid a jumble of auto carcasses and barely resurrected used vehicles for sale crowding the small lot.

Spencer peered upward. He wore his Penzoil cap backwards. His face was smudged with grease. "Hiya," he said, his hands continuing their battle against an uncooperative manifold.

Gallatin tried to engage the man in small talk. About the weather, about business. Just trying to break the ice.

"What's your problem?" Spencer asked.

"Oh, uh, no problem with my car. I'm down from Cleveland. Got some time off. Wanna do some huntin'. Been told you're about the best when it comes to finding the big bucks in this area."

"Big bucks?" Spencer asked skeptically.

"Oh, I mean deer. Ha, ha."

"Yeah. Well. Maybe I do. Trouble is. Man's gotta work or hunt. Huntin', it's fun. But it don't bring in the bucks, if you know what I mean," Spencer replied with a snicker.

"Yeah. Yeah. I get it. Play on words," Gallatin chuckled. He extended his hand. "Mike Gallatin's my name."

Spencer displayed a greasy right hand without holding it out. "Jerry. Jerry Spencer." He capitulated to the manifold and stood up, crossed his arms and looked at Gallatin expectantly.

"Whaddya use for big bucks?" Gallatin asked.

"Well, that depends on what you mean by bucks. If you mean deer, I used a twelve-gauge. If you mean money, well, I'm still workin' on it."

"Well, I could be talking about both."

"Yeah?"

"Firepower. The right amount can get you big bucks -- both kinds," Gallatin said.

"Yeah?" Spencer was guarded, his eyes revealing nothing.

Gallatin looked around him. "You know, some people, they like to upgrade to more sophisticated weapons."

Spencer remained passive, but receptive.

"Ever hunt with an AR-15?"

"Fine weapon."

"Well, I've gotta bunch for sale, at the right price," Gallatin said with a low voice.

"You don't say? Well. A single bullet from a thirty-odd-six will kill a deer as good as any other," Spencer replied. He turned around to resume his struggle with the Malibu's manifold.

"These are different. They just keep on shooting," Gallatin said. "Fully au-to-mat-ic," Gallatin enunciated carefully.

Spencer rose again from his labor. He squinted. "Maybe I'm interested. Maybe I'm not. My question, mister, is how do I know you ain't an ATF agent out to entrap me?"

"I'm not. Just a businessman out to make a buck. That's all," Gallatin said.

Spencer eyed him warily. "A bunch of us . . . 'hunters' . . . congregate over to the Tuscawaras Inn at around 8:00. You're welcome to join."

"I'll be there."

The jukebox blared Reba McEntire's latest hit. The draft beer flowed. Men hovered around the two pool tables in the rear. Work caps, jeans and protruding bellies marked this as a blue-collar watering hole. Facial hair and shaggy manes predominated among the younger males.

Gallatin felt almost at home. A pinball repairman, bartender and construction worker in his younger days, and son of a railroad man, proletarian playgrounds such as the Tuscawaras were as familiar to him as pie and coffee, a boiler-maker after work and swapping dirty jokes on the job.

Spencer was sitting on a bar stool hunched over a bottle of Bud. Shed of his overalls and grease, the president of the Coshocton Hunt Club, was a hulking, fit ex-Marine in his mid-30s. He sported a pair of reflective sunglasses popular with the State Trooper set. He smiled as Gallatin approached and promptly made introductions.

"This here's Hank, that's Jeffrey, Al, Dave and Whore." The men ranged from mid-20s to late-50s. They shook Gallatin's hand in turn.

"Whore?" Gallatin felt compelled to ask.

"Oh yeah. Whore'll work for anybody doin' anything. You name it. Real name's Clarence."

The other men gaffawed. Whore was not amused.

"Sort've a Boy Named Sue syndrome," Spencer said good humoredly. He raised his bottle to Whore, the youngest, and Gallatin surmised the dumbest, of the lot.

"I take it then that this is the famous Coshocton Hunt Club?" Gallatin asked.

"Give or take," Spencer replied.

"Dr. Jekyll and Mr. Hyde'll be here presently," Jeffrey, a jolly, red-cheeked, young farmer, said.

Jose Cuervo, you are a friend of mine . . . the female crooner sang from the juke box.

"I love this song," Hank, a barrel-bellied, middle-aged man with an Abe Lincoln beard, said, shaking his head.

Spencer gestured for the group to retreat to a secluded booth in the rear.

"So, Mr. Gallatin, why don't we just get right down to business," Spencer said as he cast a challenging gaze at the newcomer.

Gallatin nodded. "Well, like I said. I'm an independent salesman and I offer special products. AR-15 being one of them."

"What's the big deal about them?" Dave, a surly construction worker in his early 30s, demanded. "Get 'em anywhere. Probably can get 'em at Wal Mart by now. Big fuckin' deal."

Spencer signaled Dave to put a lid on it.

"Fully automatic," Gallatin added. "I'm selling them off paper. No records."

"What makes you think a hunt club would have any interest in automatic weapons?" Spencer said, plumbing Gallatin for suspicious signs.

"What's a hunt club doing mouthing off about the evil U.S. government, the United Nations conspiring to take over the country--"

"I get your point, Mr. Gallatin. Hard times are comin'. Citizens got to be on the ball. Just like during the Revolution."

"No Waco woulda occurred back then. Not with the likes o' Paul Revere an' Patrick Henry!" Dave blurted.

"I said, shut the fuck up!" Spencer ordered. "Who's commander of this militia anyway?"

Dave fell silent and angrily swigged his bottle of Pabst Lite.

Spencer switched from hot to cool. "Mr. Gallatin, we've got problems with the Brady Bill. We've got problems with the way Big Government is trampling on the Constitution. And, yes, we've got problems with the United Nations. Honest citizens've got to defend themselves for the day when they declare war on the American people. So, you have any samples?"

"In the car."

The heads of the Coshocton Hunt Club's members turned collectively in the direction of two men who had just walked through the door.

"Dr. Jekyll and Mr. Hyde," Jeffrey announced.

They were in their late twenties, disheveled, and they swaggered in their matching, studded, black leather jackets. The taller one wrapped an arm around an unsuspecting young waitress. She threw his arm off and marched off in a huff. He made a shrill whistle after the girl and pumped his hand up and down in a lewd gesture.

As the two men approached the hunt club's table, the thing about them that struck Gallatin the most was their smugness, accentuated by malicious sneers on their unshaven faces.

Spencer made introductions. "Zollie, Mee-lan, this here's Mr. Gallatin. Come to help equip the hunt club," he said.

None of the introductees offered a hand; as if by instinct, they distrusted each other. Gallatin glared.

"These boys are recent members. Just off the boat," Spencer said.

"From where?" Gallatin asked coolly, his eyes unwavering.

"Escaping bad times over there in Europe somewheres. But these boys are our EOD experts. They know mines, munitions, detonators, you name it. They may be new here, but they're more American than Dan Rather, Hillary, Ted Kennedy, the owner of the *Jew York Times* and ol' Romeo-boy Merriman all put together," Spencer declared.

"Last name?" Gallatin asked, a bit too insistently.

"Tito," the tall one replied with a smirk.

Spencer sensed the tension. "Let's go see whatcha got," he said, gesturing toward the exit.

Spencer instructed Jeffrey to ride in Gallatin's car as the latter followed Spencer's pick-up. The rest followed behind Gallatin. They drove five miles off into the hills and stopped on a gravel road in the middle of farm fields barely illuminated by a clear half-moon in a pitch-black sky. They all got out of their vehicles and crowded around Gallatin's car.

Gallatin opened the trunk, reached in and pulled out a foot-long, steel mag light. He shined it on an assortment of weapons which he unwrapped from blankets. There was an AR-15 assault rifle, an Uzi machine pistol, a 9mm Tec-9 semiautomatic pistol and two silencer-mounted .22 rifles -- all clandestinely borrowed from the Cleveland police

department's seized weapons cache, care of a very reluctant
Ray D'Angelo.

Milan Branko reached down and picked up the
assault rifle, along with a loaded clip from a box. He
expertly slammed the clip into the weapon, released the
safety, then unhesitatingly pointed it at Gallatin's face. The
others took a step backwards.

"Mee-lan, put the goddamn gun down!" Spencer
commanded.

He ignored Spencer, thrust the barrel an inch from
Gallatin's nose.

"He lies. He is American government agent," Milan
said.

"I told you to put the friggin' gun--" Spencer began.

"We kill him. Nobody will know. Bury body in
field. Deep," Milan said. Zlatko pulled his own nine-
millimeter from inside his leather jacket.

"They're nuts. Make them heel," Gallatin said.

"Maybe Milan's right," the perennially angry Dave
interjected. "This guy's setting us up. Nobody checked
him out. I say he's a Fed." Dave hawked and spat.

"He's got a point there, Jer'," Al said. The others
looked uncertain.

Seeing his authority eroding, Spencer changed tack.
"Okay mister. What is it? You a government agent, or
what?"

"Of course not!"

"You seem to know these fellers," he said nodding
at the Brankos.

"Never met them."

"You know something about them."

Gallatin clammed up.

Spencer placed his hand on the barrel of the AR-15, forcing Milan to lower it groundward. He then pulled out his own gun from a vest holster, cocked it and pressed it against Gallatin's temple.

"What is it? Speak," Spencer stated.

Spencer's unflinching coolness frightened Gallatin more than Milan's hotheadedness. The object of his coming here, after all, was not to receive a bullet in the brain and be buried in an anonymous, unmarked grave in a cornfield by a bunch of paranoid hicks straight out of central casting for *Deliverance.*

"I am *not* a government agent," Gallatin repeated. Raging anger consumed him as he realized he was face-to-face with the men who had almost killed his daughter. In an upward martial arts chop, he knocked the gun out of Spencer's hand, then lurched forward, ramming the end of the steel mag light into Milan's crotch, then up in an arc, crashing it against Zlatko's cheekbone.

Milan fell to the earth clutching his testicles in blinding pain. Zlatko plopped onto the hood of Spencer's pickup, desperately trying with both hands to hold back the blood now smearing the vehicle.

Jeffrey, Dave and Whore jumped Gallatin and wrestled him to the ground. Spencer snatched up his gun and thrust it flush between Gallatin's eyes.

"Man, you almost bought it. Who the fuck you think you're dealin' with?!" Spencer growled.

A moment passed as Gallatin fought to regain his breath. "I've got no quarrel with you!"

"Then what's your game, fella? You *are* ATF, aren't you? Or is it FBI? Or what? It'll all end right here and now. And nobody'll know." His finger twitched nervously on the trigger.

"Take out my wallet. I work for an insurance company. If you don't believe me, call them. *I have no quarrel with you.* I don't give a shit about your militia!"

"You got thirty seconds, friend. What's your game?" Spencer demanded.

The cold steel of the gun barrel pressed hard against Gallatin's forehead.

"Those two," Gallatin said, glowering at the suffering, barely conscious Brankos, now restrained by Hank and Al. "Those two may be responsible for murdering a married couple and seriously injuring two young girls, including my daughter."

Spencer's men all looked at him, their faces revealing that this was a whole different can of worms.

"If you're going to check anybody out, check your own members for chrissakes. Last thing you need in your organization is wanted felons. The law will come down on you like a ton of bricks. Ask them. Ask them about the firebombing in Cleveland." Gallatin jerked his head to nudge Spencer's gun away.

"That true?" Spencer asked.

Milan fidgeted. "Hah! Bullsheet!"

"Jer', I say we end this. Go back home," Jeffrey said. The others nodded in unison. "Don't need to get involved. Some kinda personal quarrel, sounds like to me. Leave 'em to each other."

"He's right. This ain't got nuthin' to do with our mission. No sir!" Al added.

Spencer retracted the gun from Gallatin's head, then directed it point-blank at Milan.

"Seize their weapons," he ordered. Spencer's men obliged. They then frisked the Brankos, finding another small pistol, three knives and brass knuckles.

"I suggest you boys get outta town. Fast. This fella knows something about you. Something tells me, whoever's lookin' for you two will be snooping around these parts. We want no part of it.

"And as for you, my friend, you seem like a good sort. Not a cop. But we got no bone to pick with you either." Spencer toyed with a toothpick between his teeth. "And we're not interested in no . . . illegal weapons. After all, we're just a huntin' club," he said lamely.

Spencer allowed Gallatin to pack up his arsenal, then held him behind for an hour to give the Brankos time to get away.

As Gallatin closed the car door and started the engine, Spencer said, "If I'm wrong and you are a government agent, tell President Merriman to leave us alone. That's all we ask."

Graham Merriman took a deep breath and relaxed in the jacuzzi. His cheeks were pink in a face Hollywood could have invented. He sipped a tall glass of V-8. He was renowned for his ability to devour gigabytes of information and then to use it skillfully and self-confidently in his speeches, press conferences and cabinet meetings. To gird himself for such high-pressured events, the President resorted to a good lay.

The door opened. Into the rec facility in the White House's basement walked Walter LaFontaine. The young aide, at Merriman's side since the first primary, was a specialist in getting what the President needed, on the campaign trail or off.

"Mr. President, all systems are go for the Cabinet meeting in ninety minutes time. I made sure that they were all briefed up on Bosnia. The press conference is also a go right after that. Here's some last-minute input -- intel reports, a note from Secretary McHenry, and, well, some other stuff you might want to glance at." LaFontaine's neat, perfect son-in-law good looks masked a wily political operative who had yet to abandon frat boy inclinations.

"A double-header. I hate these back-to-back events."

"We had no choice, Mr. President--"

"I know, I know. So, who is she?"

LaFontaine shifted his eyes and spoke sotto voce, the way he used to when he would recommend an easy lay to a college buddy.

"She's a fellow constituent, from Highland County."

Merriman scrunched his nose. "Highland County?! Doesn't that place have the highest incest rate in Virginia? I recall the women out there looking like the product of interspecies breeding."

"This one's different. She's a malungeon."

"Ahh. That could be different," Merriman said, relieved.

Malungeons inhabited rural pockets of the Appalachians. They had the blood of Africa, native America and of Europe in their veins.

LaFontaine looked at his watch. "I'll get her." He walked out.

Two minutes later, a nervous young woman entered the rec room. She held her hands before her at navel-level, her wide, dark eyes cast shyly downward. She looked at her naked president, then down again.

"You're from Highland County?" Merriman asked.

"Yessir," she answered softly.

"I just love the sweet air out there. Pine, oak, cedar, all mingling in those beautiful blue hills. So sweet. Come here, darling. Have you got a name?"

"Marielle." She approached, knelt down at the jacuzzi's edge.

Merriman put his hand behind her neck. He found the zipper and slowly pulled it down. The girl's simple, flowered cotton frock dropped with the ease of Highland honey in the summertime. She undid her bra. Merriman took her in with his eyes. She was tall, slim, with long ebony curls that ran down her back and teasingly touched supple breasts of honey-hued skin. He pulled her into the jacuzzi.

Marielle, all of 19, possessed skills in the art of lovemaking that most other women did not acquire in a lifetime -- that included the First Lady whose idea of good sex was body slamming. Marielle's full lips performed wonders in all the right places. Her silky brown skin against his pale torso added to Merriman's excitement. He adored dark-skinned women. And, for him, Marielle was truly exotic.

The splashing around in the basement jacuzzi that morning would have had the Secret Service barging in to check on the President's well-being were it not for the fact that the Chief Executive's protectors were accustomed to their boss's trysts.

President Merriman would feel like a new man in ninety minutes time. Ready to take on the world.

CHAPTER SEVEN

Lisa Valko didn't like the way the Deputy National Security Adviser stared at her legs. A man comfortable with power, who had risen fast by having his way most of the time, John Tulliver simply looked at what pleased him and took what he wanted. And despite the changes in the rules of the game, sex was still easily gotten. The art of the lover was little different from the art of statecraft: charm, persistence and power opened the door to a female's boudoir as easily as to a treaty signing room. With women, the new rules simply required more emphasis on the first two elements over the last. But power remained key. Without it, diplomacy was hollow, and a man could go a long time being celibate.

She shifted uneasily in her chair against the wall just ten feet left-rear of the President, who was seated at the center of the long, mahogany conference table. She uncrossed her legs and tried to concentrate on notetaking, then self-consciously pulled her navy blue shift as far to the knees as it would go. She forced a cough, glancing up ever so fleetingly to catch his unflinching eyes now focused higher, on her breasts. The slightest hint of a grin creased his thin lips. A shiver ran through her, goosebumps broke through her skin. To be admired by an attractive man could be flattering. This man, however, committed rape with his piercing eyes.

"This Administration will go down as the Peace Administration," Merriman said. "Nixon and Reagan used to talk about 'Peace through Strength.' That was the Cold War. Now it's strength through peace. "

The President's advisers nodded in unison, each writing it down in their notes. Walt LaFontaine sat directly behind the President with his arms crossed. He stifled a yawn.

"Now, we cannot let the Dayton Accord fray any further," Merriman stressed. He appeared to be in exceptionally good form. "Foreign Islamists are stirring up trouble there as well, provoking violence between Bosnian Muslims and the non-Muslim groups. I'm worried that with all this sniping going on over there, it'll come apart again. Next thing you know, they're at it again and Moscow and the Muslim world start getting antsy. It's foreign interference that always lands Europe into a major war. And then we get sucked in. We've got too much going on in Iraq and Afghanistan, not to mention Iran and North Korea to risk facing yet another blow-up, this time in the Balkans."

"A few indigenous troublemakers are also adding fuel to the fire, Mr. President," Tulliver intoned self-assuredly, not even feigning deference to his immediate boss, Merwyn Fennimore, the bookish National Security Adviser sitting on the President's left. "They're being removed from the scene. The three prime ministers assure us that they're reining the bad apples in, even eliminating from positions of authority the worst offenders. With these provocateurs out of the way, all parties can then concentrate their efforts at going after the alien Islamists."

Lisa took it all down. She felt a bit more at ease with Tulliver's attention diverted elsewhere. The Presidential Management Intern, in her third month at the National Security Council, felt like an awestruck little girl in these NSC meetings with the President. She did all she could to conceal it and to fit right in with the other aspiring young careerists who stood in the shadows of power, serving the power elite energetically if not selflessly.

"In the ten years since it was signed, the Dayton Agreement has achieved its goals despite almost collapsing the first year. The Bosnians have their own republic. Reconstruction and coalition strengthening are proceeding apace. The Serbs are in check. Our European allies are footing most of the bill. We cannot allow a few frustrated fanatics to knock over the applecart," Secretary of State Herbert McHenry stated in his flat Nebraska delivery.

During pauses, Lisa looked around to take in the trappings of authority: the fine, blue carpeting, heavy walnut paneling, stuffed leather conference chairs as soft as a baby's bottom, the elongated oak conference table, the gilt crest of the President of the United States mounted on the wall behind the Chief Executive himself. And the chief cabinet officers, whose faces one saw regularly in the papers, news programs and magazines, seated as a group in this august room. Sometimes, Lisa had to pinch herself. To go directly from grad school to the White House had been beyond her wildest imaginings as a poli-sci major at Cornell. And she was in her element. History in the making almost on a daily basis and she was there, Lisa

Valko, daughter of a coal miner and factory worker, from
Wheeling, West Virginia. She felt satisfied with herself.
But those eyes, those small, steel-gray, smug eyes were on
her again. As if an ice-chilled zephyr had coursed through
the room, she instinctively wrapped her left arm across her
bosom and resumed notetaking with the other. As she
tilted her head downward toward her notepad, her auburn
hair fell teasingly forward. Tulliver openly smiled. Oh,
why couldn't she have tied it back?

Fennimore, a painfully shy, tweedy professor from
the University of Chicago, began to squirm in his chair, an
indication that he was mustering the courage to speak. The
President focused on him.

"Well, Merwyn. Any views? How are we going to
make sure this thing sticks?" he asked in his patrician
Tidewater lilt.

Fennimore cleaned his dense, horn-rimmed glasses
and, moving only his rabbit-like eyes upward, said in a
voice akin to the sound of a wheezing carburetor, "It was
individuals who started this war. Milosevic. Karadzic.
Others. If the peace is destroyed, it will be by individuals."

"But all the leaders have been cooperating so far,"
Vice President Jay Ransom interjected. "And we managed
to evict the Iranians from the country." Seated on the
President's right, the ex-football athlete with the baritone
voice virtually hovered over Fennimore.

"Yes. But it's the men two, three rungs down the
ladder we have to worry about." Fennimore blew his nose
sloppily, emitting the sound of a baby trumpet. "Look at
Balkan history." With his hanky, Fennimore wiped
wayward mucous from his left cheek, pointlessly stared at
it for a moment, then shoved the mess into his pants pocket.
"Gavrilo Princip. All it took was one deranged Serbian

nationalist to touch off World War I. It underscores the fragility of state structures in the Balkans. All it takes is one man, a group of men, to set everything on its head."

Lisa greatly admired the nerdy, but brilliant National Security Adviser. A patient man, he typically let others say their piece before weighing in with an irrefutable summation of how things were and ought to be, drawing from a deep knowledge of history, political theory, even art and literature. She'd read all his works in college. He was a proponent of balance of power theory. Like Kissinger, he was keenly aware that a concert of the great powers was needed to keep the peace. Where he differed from Nixon's foreign policy guru, however, was in the need for idealism. A distinctly American trait in foreign affairs, idealism was alien to the cynical practitioners of the European school of diplomacy, who relied on sheer power, sleuth and cleverness to achieve national goals. Where Kissinger's idols were Metternich and Bismarck, Fennimore's were Jefferson, Franklin and Paine.

"Mr. President," Secretary of Defense Lloyd Beringer spoke up. "We're helping the Bosnians arm themselves and to receive training. Military Professional Resources, Inc. has done a marvelous job under U.S. government contract to beef up the Bosnian defense forces. And the covert programs are going smoothly. Turkey, Pakistan and Egypt have helped out enormously, as have the Saudis."

Gen. Mack Krautscher leaned forward, his bemedalled chest glistening from the light of the overhead chandeliers. "That's right, Mr. President. We're confident that the Bosnians can fight back should the Serbs ever get itchy for another scrap."

President Merriman caught special advisor Walter LaFontaine's eye. With a slight nod and sparkle in his eyes, Merriman telegraphed, "Good job Walt." He rubbed his face, stifled a yawn and forced himself to focus.

With both hands, Fennimore smoothed back the few graying strands of hair on his balding head, straightened his coke-bottle glasses on his nose and delivered the anticipated verbal coup de grace. "You miss the point. Don't you see? The more we do to ensure that they can fight well, the less motivation there will be for peace. They will dig in their heels."

There was a protracted silence in the room as each participant digested this particular insight.

"Will you have the Bosnians fold then, should the Serbs get aggressive again?" asked Vice President Ransom with a touch of incredulousness.

"No. I go back to individuals. Remove the troublemakers. Insist on it while holding out the threat of sanctions. This goes for all the parties. Croats, Serbs and Muslims."

"CHASM," Beringer said in a barely audible voice.

CIA Director Will Agropoulos cleared his throat loudly. "This really isn't the forum to get into details of various programs," he said pointedly.

"He's right," President Merriman said. "I'm off to Africa tomorrow. Herb, things still on track to polish off that peace treaty in Sudan?"

"Yes, Mr. President," the Secretary of State replied. "We've learned a lot from the Bosnia experience. All parties are ready to receive you and to sign." He shuffled frantically through a stack of papers with trembling hands. He had difficulty focusing. An aide approached from behind to assist.

Lisa felt sorry for the Secretary. A party stalwart who practiced major league law at one of the capital's most prestigious firms when not holding one senior position or another in government, the seventy-year old had gone through life-draining chemotherapy. Though the leukemia was in full remission, he wasn't the man he used to be. The scuttlebutt was that he would stay on until the next election, then retire.

Lisa discreetly observed Tulliver while Secretary McHenry fumbled with his briefing papers. The Deputy National Security Adviser eyed carefully every tremulous move, every twitch of the brows. He looked uncannily to Lisa the way her cat did before pouncing on an injured insect or baby mouse.

"I hate to sound overly political, but the NAACP is praising us to the rafters on this one. And Congress has no choice but to cough up the funding necessary for the aid package. Can't hurt when election time comes around again, eh gentlemen? . . . er, ladies and gentlemen?" Merriman said.

Little question marks and asterisks started gracing Lisa's notetaking. They were losing her at times, starting with Beringer's utterance which she could hardly hear. She nudged the Marine lieutenant colonel who sat adjacent to her against the wall. She pointed her pen at *Chasm* which she had scrawled in large letters and underlined twice. "What is it? Do you know?" she asked.

A flicker of recognition, followed by agitation crossed the rock-like face of the Marine officer. He thought quickly, then took her notepad in his hand and scratched out *Chasm* till it was completely blotched out. In its place he scribbled, *Kashmir* .

He leaned over and whispered, "Beringer was referring to past peace efforts in Kashmir. That's where Fennimore's ideas fall apart. Fulla shit." He winked at her.

"Oh," Lisa replied, nodding. It didn't quite make sense to her at first blush. She'd tuck it away in a mental shelf to be taken out later for fuller consideration.

She began to put the finishing touches on her notes when all in the room rose. She looked up. The President had adjourned the meeting and turned to leave the conference room with LaFontaine in tow. Clumsily, Lisa jumped to her feet too, her notepad and pen falling to the carpeted floor. So fast did she rise that she lost her balance, caught in time by the iron grip of the Marine officer. She quickly brushed wayward hairs back away from her eyes. Tulliver saw it all. He wore a bemused and inviting expression.

She bent to pick up her notepad and pen. On rising, a muscular forearm and large hand confronted her. "I'm Dan Haley," the Marine said, offering a handshake. A broad smile marked an open face framed by a quarter-inch jarhead haircut.

"Oh, Hi. Um, I'm Lisa. Lisa Valko." They shook hands. Though he pressed lightly, she felt the bones scrunch uncomfortably in her right hand.

"You're new, aren't you?" he asked.

"Three months. I'm a PMI. The first eight weeks, they had me doing research, gofering, learning the ropes. Now I'm notetaking and writing reports. I'm in the Democracy shop now. And you?"

"I'm special assistant in OPC," he said uninformatively.

"OPC?"

"Office of Policy Coordination."

"Uh huh."

"They got you working on Bosnia full time?" he pressed.

"Looks like it. What does OPC do?"

"We synthesize policy. Make sure nothing gets out of joint. That kind of thing."

An exclusive circle of attendees had formed in a far corner of the room. Beringer, Agropoulos, Fennimore and Tulliver were engaged in animated, yet hushed conversation. The CIA Director gestured to Haley that he should join. The "special assistant" mumbled something about seeing each other around and beat a direct path to the group.

The Secretary of State, fourth in line of succession to the President, stood alone, bowed, gathering his papers. In the peculiar prism of Washington politics, those sliding downside on the power curve received the kind of attention a floundering shipwreck victim gets when all seats in the life boats are taken.

"Sort of pathetic, isn't it?"

Lisa turned. A thirtyish fellow with a preppy air stood smiling at her. His cheery demeanor was accentuated by bright red suspenders and a large bowtie. The unstated message he sent in the starched, subtly pretentious corridors of power was of non-threatening non-conformity -- horn-rimmed glasses and short hair combed back notwithstanding.

"Buckwheat Thompson's my name." He offered his hand.

Lisa stifled a giggle. "Oh. Sorry." She recomposed herself. "Lisa Valko, PM--"

"PMI, Democracy and Humanitarian Affairs. I know. I always do my research. And don't apologize. I'm

used to it. Buckwheat isn't exactly your run-of-the-mill
name in these quarters. I ditched Munro Bathgate
Thompson III in college. The only place anyone will see it
is on my tombstone -- that is, unless I legally change it in
the interim."

Lisa took an instant liking to the man. He exuded
openness and warmth, not superiority and ambition, which
were as de rigeur in the upper reaches of government as
Brooks Brothers pin-striped suits and a bad back.

"Look at poor McHenry over there." He nodded in
the Secretary's direction. "Nobody wants to know him, not
even his own senior staff. Pity too. He knows a lot. Been
around a long time. He also knows where the skeletons are
buried, but he's too much of a gentleman to play hardball."

"Just because he was sick is no reason for people to
treat him with indifference," Lisa said.

"Look around you. What do you see?"

"I'm sorry. I don't get you."

"What do you see?"

Responding to Thompson's persistence, Lisa took a
careful look around the chamber still cluttered with
officials huddled in various power pow-wows, arms
crossed, nodding gravely, ensuring outsiders weren't
eavesdropping before driving home an important point.

"Well, I see an impressive conference room where
the President holds meetings--"

"Wrong." He was shaking his head in the manner
of a grade school teacher when a pupil makes an obviously
wild stab at answering a question for which he hadn't
prepared.

Lisa was now getting impatient with this character.
Maybe he wasn't as nice as he first appeared. She folded

her arms, arched her eyebrows and interjected, "Okay. I'm hallucinating. What am I missing, Professor Socrates?"

Thompson chuckled at her sassiness. He surveyed the room expansively, extending his arms outward. "This. Where we're standing. You and me. This is a fish tank and those are sharks. They circle around endlessly, constantly sniffing for blood. Once the sweet smell hits their vicious little snouts, they go in for the kill."

"Uh, sure. Right. I get your point." Lisa gathered her notetaking materials, stuck them in her purse. Time to get away from this clown. In a town dripping with cynicism, this guy appeared to be trying to corner the market.

"Wait." He softened up. His voice lost its edge. "Sorry if I come on a little strong."

"No sweat."

"But you're new here. I wouldn't want to see you get hurt." His eyes searched her face sympathetically.

This struck a chord. She looked directly at him. "Hurt? How do you mean?"

"Look over there. Look how he's eyeing McHenry from the corner of his eye."

"Tulliver."

"Right. He's bucking to replace McHenry. Doesn't give a crap about anybody else, least of all Fennimore. He sucks up to him on the job, but otherwise connives against him behind his back. He's either at your feet or at your throat."

"Or in my face."

"I beg your pardon?"

"Uh, never mind."

"Anyway, be careful. These people devour little PMI's like you as a pre-breakfast snack."

Lisa smiled again. Her big brother in Wheeling used to protect her in the same manner. Oh, how she missed Arn, ma and pa, her old friends.

"I can look after myself. Thanks. I didn't catch what you do around here."

"Yep. Right." Thompson fished around his pockets, pulled out a business card and presented it to her.

Buckwheat Thompson
Deputy Director, Office of Policy Coordination
National Security Council
The White House

"OPC," Lisa stated curiously.

"Right, OPC. You know it. How?"

"Well, I just met that Marine officer . . . Dan . . ." She visually searched the room, but the Marine lieutenant colonel had departed, along with the others he'd been conversing with.

"Haley."

"Right. Is he your boss?"

"Not in a million years." He caught himself. "Actually, yes."

"Should I drop by and talk to you guys? I mean, you work on Bosnia too, right?"

"We work on everything." He broke eye contact and looked at his watch. Suddenly, he seemed to be in a hurry. "Hey, how about lunch soon? I'll call." Thompson parted as abruptly as he had appeared.

Lisa shook her head briskly as if to clear clouds from her vision. Washington's full of strange characters, she pondered. Always best to be on one's toes. If for no other reason than to be ready for a host of personal idiosyncrasies.

Lisa returned to her windowless office space tucked away in a loft, which she shared with two other interns in the sprawling Victorian mansion adjacent to the White House known as the Old Executive Office Building -- OEOB for short. A message slip by her phone said, "Mr. Tulliver wishes to see you tomorrow at 4:00."

CHAPTER EIGHT

"Hi. I'm Molly Jacobs. This is my husband, Harlan." The sixtyish matron extended her hand. The Brankos remained silent.   Mrs. Jacobs pulled out one of those pre-computer era fat ledgers which nobody uses anymore. She licked her right thumb and began to flip through the oversized pages. "Let's see. We're fully booked through the fifteenth. When were you boys looking to stay with us?" One of those smiles that belongs to all good grandmothers blossomed across her beneficent face.

Seven guests were digging into homemade scones, butter and jam preserves on the wide old table in the dining room behind Mrs. Jacobs. Harlan poured coffee.

The aroma of freshly baked breads and just-brewed coffee perfumed the air. Overstuffed furniture in lived-in rooms, photos of children now fully grown, the trappings of comfortable middle class living defined sweet domesticity in early twenty-first century America.

Milan carefully cased the interior of the bed &
breakfast tucked on a quiet street in the leafy, upscale
Lakes District of Minneapolis.

"How many people can stay here?" he asked curtly.

"You mean guests? Why, we have five rooms. So
that means we can accommodate--"

"How many here now?" He jerked his chin in the
direction of the breakfast table.

Mrs. Jacobs looked perplexed. She cast an eye over
her shoulder. "Eight. Uh, eight boarders at the present
time." Harlan nodded assuringly.

Milan moved his lips as he silently counted seven at
the table: two elderly couples, another pair who were
middle-aged, and a portly traveling salesman.

Zlatko slowly made his way to the hallway door,
blocking any egress.

"Would you boys like a cup of coffee?" Harlan
asked, steaming pot in hand.

Milan looked at him with hard eyes, then returned
his gaze to the man's wife.

"Seven. Only seven." He jut his chin again toward
the table.

Mrs. Jacobs was getting nervous.

A huge old grandfather clock clanged eight bells.
The guests continued to attack the goodies.

"Oh! Caitlin. She's in the . . . the . . ." Harlan
nodded helpfully toward the restroom in the corner.

"Eight," Milan said. He moved toward the restroom
door.

Mrs. Jacobs's face betrayed her sense that
something wasn't right. These unshaven men with their
brusque foreign accents. Determined not to provoke them,
she glanced at the table.

"Oh, dear. Out of scones, are we? Well, I'll just fetch you all some more straight from the oven. Mrs. Jacobs proceeded toward the kitchen. Weighing more importantly on her mind than scones right now, however, was the phone. 911 flashed in her brain. Zlatko blocked her way. He smelled of stale sweat and liquor. His cold, flint-dark eyes challenged her.

She looked up at him, her face devoid now of gracious hospitality. "What is it you want?" she asked in a low voice.

The breakfasters halted their feasting in unison. Like deer sensing a predator, they instinctively froze. Slowly they put down their scones, butter knives, napkins and coffee cups and beheld the confrontation before them. Harlan, trembling, but still holding up the coffee pot, retreated backward into a corner.

"Eight!!" Milan bellowed as he yanked open the restroom door. The occupant screamed. She frantically tried to pull up her panties as she faced instant exposure.

Milan's hand enmeshed itself in the front of her blouse and yanked her off the toilet. A loud rip pierced the air. The girl screamed again, this time louder. "Stop!! Please, no!!!" Tears streamed down her terrified face.

The girl's father bolted up. Zlatko planted a 9mm Beretta squarely in the man's face.

His hand locked tighter into the blouse, Milan pulled the girl to him. "So, now we have eight!" he snickered. He held a long, narrow blade against her neck. "Do not move, beautiful. Do not move." With his other hand, Milan deftly removed the girl's panties and used them to bind her hands behind her back.

"For God's sake! Leave my girl alone. Take what you want. But please leave her alone!" the father pleaded.

Zlatko brought the Beretta crashing against the side of the man's face. Blood sprayed on the scones, he collapsed onto the floor. His wife screamed hysterically and bent down to attend her husband.

"Oh, my god! Oh, my god!" Mrs. Jacobs cried. The other guests sat back in their chairs with hands raised and wearing expressions of horror as they faced Zlatko's Beretta and the brute force of Milan.

Milan grabbed the table cloth and pulled hard, sending everything flying off the table. He threw the girl onto it stomach down, then trussed her legs like those of a pig in an abattoir. She cried uncontrollably, the tears soaking red curls hanging limply over the edge of the dining table.

"Okay. Money. All money on table. Now!" Zlatko yelled. The guests emptied their pockets and gently placed the cash on the table.

In a lightning motion, Milan slashed the arm of Harlan, a man on the cusp of seventy with a heart problem. Zlatko slapped Mrs. Jacobs with a devastating blow to her face as she instinctively moved to protect her husband.

"Money! Money you get from them!" Zlatko waved at the boarders. Where is? You keep where?!"

Mrs. Jacobs, her hand covering the reddening cheek, pointed meekly at a jar on a shelf. Zlatko darted over and pulled it off. He emptied the contents onto a sideboard. He looked incredulously at the multicolored checks and credit card slips that tumbled out. Only a few greenbacks poked through. He examined a fistful of the financial instruments as an ape does some object it cannot comprehend.

"Not money!!" he shouted. In a single motion of rage, Zlatko knocked the sideboard over. The antique crystal which graced its top crashed to bits on the floor.

The Croats pulled out rolls of packing tape and proceeded to methodically bind the legs and arms and cover the mouths of each of their victims. Their pitiful pleas went unheeded. The pure cruelty which emanated from these men was as deathly potent as any fissile material found in a warhead. The muffled wails of their helpless victims seemed only to goad them.

Zlatko frantically pocketed the small pile of cash on the table, then vaulted up the stairs to ransack the rooms in search of more.

Milan looked evilly at the bound and gagged B&B occupants. His eyes then fell onto the girl, still on her stomach weeping. He sidled up to her. He pressed the knife tip tight against her skin just below the left ear. "You move. You die. Understand?" The girl whimpered.

He ran his free hand under her skirt, on her buttocks, along her thighs. His skin was as coarse and scarred as hers was soft and smooth. The girl squealed when his hand pressed her pubic area.

"Yes. Beautiful. Very, very beautiful," Milan gushed. A lustful grin and trance-like expression locked on his face. He unbound her legs and spread them apart.

For the first time since he'd left Bosnia, Milan felt all-powerful. A rush of strength coursed through his being. Finally, again, he felt validated as a man. Totally free to prove his manhood, to vent an undefined, yet limitless, anger, to give meaning to forces in his nature which he did not fully comprehend. Yugoslavs could not constrain him. The United Nations could not constrain him. And, while his own leaders in connivance with NATO could sidetrack

him -- strip him of command, and exile him to America --
even the great and mighty United States could not constrain
him.

He tossed his head back and shut his eyes. In his
mind, Milan Branko was again free, to assert his power, to
prey on the weak. Like a beast in nature free to exist and
act as God had intended. The suffering and destruction he
inflicted, the gagged B&B patrons, the injured and terrified
owners, the damaged Victorian home, the sobbing girl
whom he was violating, were the natural outcome of his
unfettered freedom. In his ears and eyes, it was beauty, just
as he imagined a field of carnage was to a lion after a
successful hunt.

For the Branko boys, the ends were not as important
as the means. A few dollars, a ravaged woman, shed blood.
These actually meant little in and of themselves. The
means empowered them. And power meant everything.

Ray D'Angelo was right. In the five hours Gallatin
had spent already at the district office of the Immigration
and Customs Enforcement, there was only one thing he'd
observed that they were good at: honing their analness. At
least that's what Gallatin imagined after one unproductive
meeting after another with waffling functionaries so strung
up in rules, regulations and their own incompetence that it
was a wonder that anybody got into the country legally.

He sat restlessly along with about a hundred others
in a holding pen that somewhat resembled an airport
waiting lounge but with even less comfort and ambience.
Above a bank of interview windows was one of those

electronic number displays used by the deli sections at large supermarkets. Each supplicant clutched a flimsy scrap of paper with his or her number on it. Gallatin had waited three hours at this particular waystop in purgatory for the system to work its way through one-hundred fourteen poor souls. His deli ticket was one-hundred-fifteen.

Gallatin looked around. The faces were Asian, Hispanic, African, with a sprinkling of others, East Europeans, or Russians, he thought. Some had brought their kids, who raced up and down the rows of plastic chairs playing tag. The ones who could scrape the money together were accompanied by hired immigration attorneys, street lawyers with pinched faces and suits from J.C. Penney.

Just as Gallatin's bladder was reaching full-tank again, "115" flashed on the electronic counter. He gathered his stuff together and went briskly to the bank of windows. He shoved his paperwork through the slot.

After thirty seconds, the female face on the other side wordlessly slid an information notification back through. In red ink, she had asterisked the section on fees.

"You can't be serious. I just paid $75 to some guy downstairs to try to get the information I want," Gallatin, barely in control of himself, told the officious, middle-aged woman standing behind the security window.

"That was Admissions. This is Adjudications," she told him perfunctorily. "The only way we can begin a trace is for you to complete form OF-1546 and submit it with a check for $75."

"Look. I'm a professional investigator. I have this letter from the Cleveland police department attesting to my participation in their investigation of . . ."

"Next!" the woman shouted to the long, snaking line of hapless immigrants behind him, each with his or her own special request to an omnipotent but impersonal agency.

If it weren't for the security window, Gallatin would have made this unpleasant woman eat form OF-1546. A hefty security guard, arms folded, stood watch over the crowd from the back of the large room.

"Okay, okay." Gallatin took his checkbook out from his inside jacket pocket. He signed it and handed it over along with form OF-1546, duly completed.

The woman, affecting a well-honed expression of disinterested boredom, looked past him into space. She extended her right hand forward, palm upward and wiggled her fingers for more.

"What?"

"Well, information on applicants is protected under the Freedom of Information Act unless you have something official from a court or law enforcement organization stating that it's needed for an investigation."

Gallatin fumbled with the letter that D'Angelo had written on Cleveland police stationery authorizing Gallatin to request all the information ICE had on the Brankos.

Still focused on nothing in particular somewhere past the planet Neptune, the wretched woman tossed it back to him with no explanation.

"Now, what?"

"Need five copies. Notarized. Next!"

"Now, wait a goddamned minute!"

The security guard unfolded his arms and approached Gallatin. He placed one hand firmly on Gallatin's tricep, pointing to the door with the other. "Do what the lady asks, sir," he said unequivocally.

"How long will it take before I get a response?" Gallatin asked lastly.

"Six to twelve months," the female functionary replied dismissively as she took on her next victim, a petrified Salvadorean clutching a wad of documents.

"Jesus Christ!" Gallatin muttered dejectedly. At that point, he knew that he would need to go up the chain, to the source of the great American paper tributary: Washington, D.C.

The evening news snippet struck him like a curve-pitched hard ball to the head.

"Ten people perished in a spectacular house fire in Minneapolis early today in a crime scene law enforcement authorities describe as straight out of hell. The victims, an elderly couple who owned the B&B and eight guests, apparently had been tied up and tortured before the blaze, the result of arson, police say. The authorities are investigating," the male correspondent said.

The television screen lit up with scenes of the neat home engulfed in roaring orange and yellow flames, black smoke billowing to the sky. Fire trucks, police cars and ambulances surrounded it, their emergency lights flashing.

Gallatin bolted upright from his TV dinner. It sounded all too familiar. He threw some things in a suitcase, jumped in his car and headed to Minnesota.

The municipal police had set up barriers of black-and-white striped sawhorses draped in reflective tape around the B&B. Signs warned, "Off Limits Police Department." The scene reeked bitterly of incinerated wood and furnishings. Gallatin walked back and forth along the sidewalk, assessing the destruction, but also the barriers. A young couple with a baby carriage strolled by. Gallatin directed his eyes forward and walked past as any person out on an errand.

He about-faced at the corner and went back. Quickly, he looked around. No one. He sprang over the barrier and entered burnt shell of the house. Among the ashes and detritus of destruction were broken vases, chinaware, a smashed grandfather clock, crusted wires, glass shards and myriad signs of middle class life, now bent, broken and scattered.

The stairs were gone. Something shiny caught his eye. He bent down and picked it up. A girl's barrette, made of metal.

"Get out!"

Gallatin whirled around to find a cop, clearly on the cusp of retirement, staring angrily from where the front door used to be.

"Can't you read, pal?!" the cop demanded, pointing with his billy club.

Gallatin fumbled inside his jacket and pulled out his wallet. He opened it to reveal his work ID.

"I'm an investigator. Erie Mutual Insurance. I've been sent here to conduct the investigation for my company."

The cop took the ID and squinted at it at arm's length. He clearly needed reading glasses.

"Uh, huh. Well, you gotta go. Get authorization from police headquarters before you do anything. Those are orders."

Gallatin played dumb. "Uh, sure. Most of our cases are pretty straightforward, not involving crime. Guess this one's special, all right. Yeah, well, I'll go down there to--"

Another man walked in. He was of medium height, balding, nondescript, in a boxy rain coat. He stopped eight inches from Gallatin, keeping his hands in his coat pockets. "Who are you?" he asked.

Gallatin delivered the same lie he'd just given to the cop.

The man snatched the wallet away from the policeman and scrutinized it. He took out the ID and Gallatin's driver's license.

"I don't know who you really are or why you're really here, friend, but I aim to find out," the man said coolly.

"All right, so I made a mistake. I'll get right on over to--"

"Shut up. USAA has the fire policy on this place. Not Erie Mutual," the man interrupted.

Gallatin's blood boiled. "Who the hell are you, then?!" he blurted.

Just as coolly, the man reached in his jacket and pulled out a leather holder. He flipped it open. "Special Agent Jack Holt," it read underneath the glittering brass badge.

"Special agent of what agency?" Gallatin asked.

The man put his badge back in place. He gestured to the cop. The two men simultaneously grabbed Gallatin by each arm and began to forcefully evict him from the premises. Gallatin's first instinct was to resist, then thought the better of it and calmly allowed himself to be escorted away. At the barrier, Gallatin's controllers pushed him forward, causing Gallatin almost to lose his balance, and adding indignity.

Gallatin brushed himself off. "I want my documents back!" he shouted.

Special Agent Holt shouted back. "We'll mail them."

CHAPTER NINE

The First Lady liked to make love in the Lincoln Bedroom. The sacrilege of committing adulterous sex on the very bed in which the sixteenth President had slept intensified the excitement. Her orgasms came deeper and fuller in that room. There was a practical reason as well. The heavy oak bed, virtually anchored to the floor, neither moved nor creaked as she quickened her athletic grinds and thrusts in the heat of passion, thus, minimizing the risk of attracting the attention of some alert White House worker.

It was at this pre-orgasmic state that Tulliver braced himself, grabbing the mattress with both hands for all his life as the President's wife rode him as she would a bronco on her family's Oklahoma ranch. Manny Merriman was definitely a good fuck. At 40, the former Miss Kansas was in excellent shape. Physical fitness was her bag. She launched an array of fitness and sports programs aimed at America's youth. She ran in the Boston Marathon. Tennis finals and golf tournaments were held in her honor. A delegation of deaf girl soccer players had that morning presented her with a ball which was used in a match they had won over a hearing girl's team.

Yet Tulliver endured these rigorous trysts in the same manner he did aerial turbulence on one of his diplomatic travels. While the First Lady was attractive, Tulliver was into younger women, early-to-mid-20s being ideal. He recruited a bevy of such young women straight out of universities to work on his staff. His luck in bedding any number of them was surprisingly good. He was an old-fashioned lover, preferring to take his time, perform languorously and to be always in control. He liked being in control whether practicing politics or the art of love.

"Uhh. Uhhhh!" Mrs. Merriman groaned, a sure sign that the Big Event was nigh.

She tilted her face down to Tulliver's and bored in on him with her green eyes in a bobcat's frenzied gaze. Her shoulder-length brown hair fell wildly over her face, accentuating a savage beauty.

"You want it? Huh? You want it? . . . Tell me you want it. C'mon. Tell me!" she demanded teasingly of her prostrate sex-mate.

Tulliver always disliked this stage of the lovemaking. He didn't fancy himself an actor. And the New Hampshire-born Yankee never felt comfortable wearing his emotions on his sleeve, or, in this case, his bare wrist.

"Ah, yeah. I want it--ouch!" The First Lady's taut thighs griplocked Tulliver's groin, sending a spasm of pain right through to the top of his head. Before he knew it, he had come, though pain replaced any incipient pleasure in the act.

Manny Merriman scrunched her eyes shut, released a series of forced exhales, paused motionlessly atop the

Deputy National Security Adviser, then collapsed on his chest.

Relieved that the ordeal was over, Merriman glanced at the 19th-century brass clock on the dresser. "Christ!" he murmured.

Catching her breath, Mrs. Merriman turned her head and said in a breathy voice, "What, baby?"

"Uh. Nothing. I mean, I said 'Christ.' What an experience. It's amazing. I mean, you're amazing." Tulliver's clumsiness in intimate situations showed.

She snickered. "You're precious. Did I ever tell you that?" She rolled off him gently and snuggled against him.

Mrs. Merriman usually metamorphosed from sexual assailant to a whimpering little girl immediately after lovemaking.

Tulliver had appointments to keep. Sleeping with the First Lady, though as risky as smoking in a natural gas plant, definitely contributed to his fast rise in the Administration's hierarchy. But it wreaked havoc on his schedule.

"What do you think of me? Am I pretty?" Mrs. Merriman cooed in a little girl's whiny voice.

He winced slightly. Tulliver hated this part of their liaisons. "You are . . . you are special," he assured her as he slowly moved to leave the bed.

"How special?"

"Er. Um. Like no other woman I've ever known," he replied truthfully.

"You're a sweetie, Tully."

"Oh. Thanks." He looked again at the old clock. Another fifteen minutes had passed.

"You know, I told Graham that he'd be crazy not to make you National Security Adviser or Secretary of State once one of those old fartsies cashes in or quits." She played with his hair.

Suddenly, Tulliver had all the time in the world. He kissed her gently. "All I want is to be near you."

"Graham pays no attention to me any more. A woman needs confirmation, you know. My Daddy always made me feel confident and needed. And so did Graham till he got into politics. I need you, John."

And you need a good therapist, Tulliver thought to himself. "Don't worry. I'll be there," he said.

"You heard the President and Merwyn. Peacemaking is as important an element of the Administration's foreign policy as peacekeeping. Part of the formula for maintaining the peace is keeping the chief troublemakers out of the way," Tulliver told the interagency CHASM team. They met at the senior level once a month, more often if the need arose.

"The Bosnians arrested three more Serb officers yesterday. Belgrade is threatening to back out of the agreement, saying this is the last straw," the State Department's Goldman informed the group. "Add to that the fact that these particular characters are on The Hague Tribunal's list of wanted war criminals."

"Great. That's just great," Tulliver rejoined. "Guess who's going to have to untie this Gordian knot just when the President is off to Africa?"

They all looked at Tulliver expectantly. The deputy NSC chief was steadily building up his reputation as a Presidential envoy who could pull rabbits out of his hat. He had gone at it up till now with little public aplomb, so as not to upstage Fennimore, in Central America and South Asia. Behind the scenes, however, he had assiduously cultivated the media. As often as not he was the "official who declined to be identified" in front page articles and op-ed pieces covering the major foreign policy issues of the day. In the process he had laid a foundation of success upon which to now launch himself before the public eye as a diplomatic *Wunderkind*. As Secretary McHenry's physical and political health waned, Tulliver positioned himself nicely to succeed the elder statesman. All that remained to be done was to sway Merriman so that when it came time to name a successor, all eyes would turn to Tulliver, particularly those of the First Lady, Tulliver's not-so-secret protector. But first there was Fennimore. He would have to be stepped over initially.

As the Dayton peace accord steadily eroded over the months after its signing in 1996, the Administration had done everything possible to make it work. The CIA was tasked with being more aggressive in recruiting, bribing and threatening political leaders to cooperate. The key NATO allies either turned a blind eye or played their own games. All parties had too much at stake in the Balkans, or so they thought. From legitimate concerns over containing the conflict to winning elections at home, the European leaders were as eager as the Americans to keep a lid on the obstreperous inhabitants of the Balkans. A decade had now passed and there was no hope in sight of ending the multinational troop presence in the ex-Yugoslavia. CHASM, originally set up to remove a handful of troublemakers and intelligence assets from the scene, had been steadily expanded. Now war criminals by the dozens were being resettled. It was a cheap means to keep things on track -- for a while, at least. And it was Tulliver's brainchild.

"The President's Africa mission must be a success. The Sudanese and Darfurians must be persuaded to accept a cooling off period, to be followed by a Bosnian-style peace agreement. Otherwise, more bloodbath, a failed Presidential mission and grist for attacks against us in the next election," Tulliver declared.

"We're all set to fly the first batch of Sudanese here whenever we're given the go-ahead," Menard, from Defense, added.

Ferret cringed. He sat silently behind Goldman, taking notes. He didn't like Tulliver. With his British suits, fifty-dollar haircuts and studied air of being always in control, the number two foreign affairs official in the White House struck Ferret as a vain self-promoter who practiced foreign policy as if it were a board game.

"We've got communities in Florida, New York and the Gulf states ready to take them in," Goldman interjected. "Of course, the church groups and nongovernmental organizations have been told only that they'll be taking in war victims. The black congregations are strong on this resettlement, just as they were with the Haitians we brought in after we replaced Cedras with Aristide."

"State will do its usual effective job of indoctrinating the Africans into the ways of their new homeland? The last thing we need is for some of these characters to continue their deviant ways here," Tulliver admonished.

Goldman smiled reassuringly. Ferret loathed Goldman as much as he did Tulliver. Goldman was after that additional ambassadorship before retirement, and to get it he'd have to impress the White House crowd with his effectiveness as State's CHASM director.

"No problems thus far." He nodded at Ferret. "Our staff is very skilled in retreading such people."

Ferret stiffened as everyone directed their attention to him. Something deep inside him told him to use the occasion to get something off his chest.

"We have problems already," he blurted, to Goldman's astonishment.

"Two Croats. They've absconded and are committing ghastly crimes, including m--"

"We have two cousins who haven't shown up for work," Goldman interjected. "It's by no means certain that these two Croats have 'absconded.' We're checking into it. But not to worry." He again flashed an avuncular smile.

Ferret was not stupid. He knew a put-down when he heard one. But he had to let them all know.

"These men are . . . are . . . evil. They're killers. Nothing more. And they're here. In our country." The tone of his voice rose.

Tulliver spoke up. "Joe, if there's a problem, fix it. If you have CHASM protegés who've gone AWOL, well, track them down and read them the riot act."

"Like I said, we're looking into it." Goldman's jaw muscles tensed. Brief eye contact with Ferret sent the latter an Arctic blast of rebuke.

"We need to bring in some more assets whose positions have become untenable," the CIA rep, Sarah Bramley began. "Assets" is CIA jargon for foreign spies they've recruited.

Ferret saw right through the Agency. A cold war provision of law permitted the CIA to bring into the United States each year up to one-hundred of its foreign spies who had landed in dire trouble in their own countries. No visas, no immigration inspection. No questions asked. But one-hundred was a small number and Langley chafed under the limitation. Over the decades, CIA officials had tried every devious way imaginable to sneak scumbag "assets" into the country by whatever means. CHASM was to them a godsend.

Ferret stopped his notetaking, his eyes became transfixed a thousand miles away. His brain blocked out the voices. His eyes did not see the lush office surroundings of the White House's West Wing. Instead they saw brilliant, vibrant, contrasting colors running together in electric waves. He felt himself a figure in a van Gogh painting. A loud buzzing noise replaced the voices in the room. As the colors in Ferret's mind reached a hallucinogenic intensity, the buzz turned into distant shrieks and wails, the death screams of countless victims of all the holocausts. The result of the collective hypocrisy of those who turned a blind eye. He sensed that he was on a precipice, about to join the ranks of the victims. In doing so, he would be liberated from these callous people, who would turn killers loose in their own society for the sake of a paper agreement and their own ambitions. Ferret would finally be free. Free.

Lisa showed up at Tulliver's office five minutes early. She wore her hair pulled back into a bun and sported an ankle-length black skirt with a gray, Scottish-cut worsted suit jacket over a plain white blouse. She had no make-up on.

The secretary asked her to take a seat. Lisa sat primly erect with both hands poised on the knee of a crossed leg. Despite her efforts at nonchalance, she was anxious as revealed by a nervous bouncing of her leg and a forced scrutiny of humdrum office art. She shuffled through the requisite *New York Times, Washington Post* and predictable, out-of-date news magazines on the coffee table in front of her. Here was a *People* magazine featuring ex-con Martha Stewart, dated April 2005. Just like at the dentist's, she thought.

Tulliver's door swung open. A distinguished older man and a much younger one stepped out.

"Rest assured Senator, we'll keep Congress in the loop at every juncture," a grinning Tulliver schmoozed. "We're counting on the Hill to deliver. Peace is bipartisan." He slapped the old senator on the back and flashed his perfect pearly-whites again.

The old man stopped and wagged a finger in Tulliver's face. "You've got America acting like it should be acting," he drawled. "A superpower with principles. This is fine with the folks back home. *No more Iraqs! The people just won't support any more of our boys and gals getting shot and blown up.*"

Tulliver nodded agreement, then caught sight of Lisa. His eyes lingered a moment, as if to say, *Ah, yes. Her. Get rid of this old fart, and on to more pleasant things.*

Lisa kept a stonily dour expression. But her wide, childlike eyes gave away her trepidation.

The top half of Tulliver's body was out in the hallway waving cheerfully to the departing legislator, though his feet remained anchored in his office. As his guests departed the West Wing office suite, Tulliver swung around with his hands clasped, still smiling.

"Hi! John Tulliver." He offered his right hand and motioned with his left for her to enter his office. He clenched her hand a second or two longer than protocol required.

As was the case with all offices in the White House proper, his was cream-white, accented by a presidential-blue carpet and Federalist flourishes in the form of carved doors, wide, paned windows and a piece or two of pineapple-crested, 18th-century Goddard furniture. Otherwise, it displayed the usual trappings of the Washington power set: the obligatory ego wall of Tulliver in the company of various kings, prime ministers, saints and satraps; bureaucratic awards and diplomas from august institutions of higher learning, most of whose grads had surnames that did not end in a vowel. On the ponderous Pennsylvania oak desk, a framed photo featured the smiling visage of a generic, middle-aged WASP wife; another of two female teenaged trophy children.

He gestured for her to have a seat on the standard GSA-issued cloth couch. He plumped himself down in one of those fat, dark leather chairs one normally associates with old money.

His eyes quickly assayed the young woman before him. Lisa wasn't sure but she thought she detected the slightest hint of disappointment on his face after taking in her well-wrapped form.

"Lisa. First, welcome to the NSC. The Democracy shop is a perfect fit." He shifted in his chair. "I make it a

point to meet all staff after they've settled in. And, so . . .
now we meet." His voice changed from chirpily official to
warmly intimate with the last three words.

"It's a dream job." She smiled uneasily, her eyes
moved nervously side-to-side. *Stay cool, Lisa. Stay cool!*

"Tell me a little about yourself."

"Not a lot really. I'm from Wheeling, West
Virginia, up in the needle point part of the state. Parents
are working folks. I went to Cornell on a scholarship."

Tulliver nodded deeply, indicating that he was
impressed.

"Otherwise, it would've been WVU -- West
Virginia University for me." She gave a forced laugh
which she quickly stifled. "Ahem. I majored in political
science. Maybe I'll go back. To law school, that is."

"How is it that a bright-eyed, bushy-tailed girl from
the Mountain State leaves kith and kin, to go off to college
out of state and end up here, at the White House?" he
probed.

"To get out," Lisa answered without hesitation. She
paused, took a deep breath. "I mean, I had to go places, see
things, that is . . ."

"I understand," Tulliver said with empathy. He
leaned toward her and inched his chair forward. She could
feel his breath on her cheek. He placed one hand on the
armrest of her chair. Lisa became rigid. Tulliver's gray
eyes lingered on her face, then worked themselves, almost
caressingly, down to her neck, her breasts, waist, legs, then
up again.

"Lisa," he breathed, as if he were about to divulge
the greatest secret of the government. "I look at myself as a
mentor to young people on the staff. At the same time, I'm
very demanding. I will call on you to produce and I expect

you to be responsive, to give as good as you get. And I
want you feel free to consult me. That door is always
open."

Lisa didn't need this. She was going out of her way
to keep men out of her life for the time being. And she
certainly wasn't attracted to this smarmy, middle-aged
egomaniac. She'd been getting calls from Craig who had
joined the Yuppie Army at Citicorp in New York. He
spoke sweetly about wanting to get together. She put him
off. Too many cobwebs of confusion lingered in her heart.

"Thanks. You see much of your wife and kids in
this job?" She glanced at the portraits on the desk.

Tulliver looked deflated, as if he'd just been told,
"root canal."

"Ah . . . Not as much as I wish." He leaned back.
He studied her for a moment, the silent scrutiny making her
even more ill at ease. "Part of the job entails travel. Do
you like to travel? I assume that you do. Otherwise, you'd
be fat, dumb and pregnant in Wheeling." He chuckled at
his lame humor.

"I never had enough money to go abroad. I'd love
to."

He'd bagged his quarry. "I travel to Europe
regularly, other places less frequently. I'll be asking you to
accompany me on occasion as my staff aide." He stated
this with measured authority, a kind of Ivy League
command.

"Oh. Great. Sure," Lisa replied uncertainly.

The door opened. It was Lt. Col. Haley.

"Lisa, this is Dan Haley." Tulliver made some
distance between himself and Lisa.

"We've met," the Marine said jovially. He took a
seat next to Lisa.

"Lisa, I want you to work with Dan here on a special project."

The Marine looked warmly at the PMI. He held a number of folders in his arm.

"You know that we've been catching some flak over our involvement in peacekeeping abroad. Some people on the Hill and in the media have attacked us for going too easy on the malefactors as we conclude one peace settlement after another. They complain that we set up these war crimes tribunals, but then don't go after the bad guys because we allegedly don't want to rock the boat. The less charitable among them charge the President with using foreign policy to make himself look good for the next election. And they charge Merwyn Fennimore and me of pursuing diplomatic successes to burnish our own image. It's all hogwash, of course. But we need to respond. And that's where you come in."

Haley removed some papers from a folder.

"The Administration needs to get its message across more effectively. Better PR. Dan, here, is working with the President's speech writers, the press spokesman and the other agencies to make sure that message gets delivered. I want you to work with him and the other players to draw up key points for that message. Let the world know how vigorously we're pursuing justice as well as peace. Are you up to the job?"

Lisa was flattered. It was a lot of responsibility for someone with her limited experience. But she was confident she could do it well. She would put everything into it. And maybe do some good in the process.

"I am," she replied.

"Good, go at it."

As Lisa was half way out the door, Tulliver added, "And, don't forget. The door is always open."

CHAPTER TEN

Gallatin had been to Washington only twice before.
Once as a kid with his family on vacation. The last time
ten years previous for a convention of insurance
investigators. Even with this limited exposure, the place
had struck him as unreal. A city where people park
themselves for a while, then move on, whether as tourists,
bureaucrats or politicians. Not a real place, like Cleveland,
or Baltimore, or any city where things are produced and
people finish their lives in the same neighborhood in which
they grew up. The great monuments, the histrionics of
national politics, the careful planning had Washington
having more in common with Disney World than with any
city in the real world.

The nine-hour drive from Cleveland was good for
him, enabled him to sort his thoughts, make him relax. He
had always liked long road trips for that reason. They were
therapeutic. Not long after Celeste died, he had placed
Lauren with her aunt and uncle, jumped in his '69 Mustang
convertible and drove west. The first thousand miles was

of gently rolling plains, like a placid sea that beckoned and swathed. It was an endless horizon marked by broad fields of ripening crops, proudly erect silos and sturdy barns and farmsteads. This limitless expanse, which rushed at him through the windshield, had an alluring, almost hypnotic effect. The flatness of the land helped steady and pacify his soul. It carried him into the science fiction landscape of the Badlands whose towering, otherworldly rock formations lifted his mind further away from his pain. The abrupt majesty of the Grand Tetons confronted him with unassailable beauty to which he surrendered his growing doubt as to why he, or any of us, was here.

Finally, as he stood on the dizzying palisades of Oregon's coast, Gallatin found resolution, or at least a culminating comprehension as to why we live and why we die. Each crash of each wave on the ageless boulders below was an utterly unique event with its own shape and form, making its own impact on the land, some greater than others. But all, cumulatively, over the ages, lent shape to the earth, just as each life, great or humble, helped shape humanity. Celeste not only had brightened his life with her existence; she had also lent her beauty to the world, making it a better place. Gallatin could see this clearly now. His bitterness and regrets were, from that point onward, tempered by newly found serenity – Celeste's presence within him till the day he died.

The low, craggy, brooding Shenendoahs gave Gallatin a mildly unpleasant feeling. As he traversed West Virginia's hulking heartland of bleak forests and impoverished hamlets, he imagined trolls lurking behind trees and in ditches warning him to neither stop nor to proceed, Go back. Go back, they called out in muffled yelps.

His mind shook off the trolls as the undulating West Virginia landscape gave way to the lowlands of northern Virginia with its colonial towns and surfeit of memorials to Civil War bloodletting. As he entered the Washington, D.C. suburbs, Lauren preoccupied his thoughts. It was for Lauren, after all, that he was doing this.

He had exactly one week to poke around the vast federal bureaucracy for information on the Brankos. That's all the leave his employer would give him. He rubbed his forehead with one hand as he contemplated the daunting task ahead of him. To start from scratch in developing leads in a strange city with so little time . . . He concluded that he must be nuts.

Gallatin checked into a reasonably priced boarding house on Capitol Hill. His body, weary from the long journey, told him to sack out, relax. But his heart told him not to waste a minute. So, he used the first weekend in the nation's capital to devise a plan of action and to familiarize himself with the city's layout.

Early Monday rush hour traffic awoke Gallatin before his alarm went off. In the dream he had been having up till then, he was back home, fixing breakfast for Lauren and . . . Celeste. He sat up in the small bed, rubbed his face with both palms and shook his head in an effort to dispel the vestiges of the dream scene. He felt like having a drink. But, no. He had a task to accomplish. A task that would salvage his daughter from her psychological isolation cell. He realized that the odds were about as long as they could be. But what choice did he have? He was convinced that the Branko cousins were responsible for the firebombing that killed Adnan and Leah Suleijmanovic and maimed their sole remaining child. They therefore must be caught and punished.

His first stop was the office of the Honorable Ernest T. Calloway, Representative of the tenth district of Ohio. The broad, high-ceilinged corridors of the grandiose Rayburn Building bustled with young aides, attaché-toting lobbyists, rubbernecking tourists, shapely young secretaries and the occasional distinguished-looking legislator. The latter were usually a dead giveaway. They had an air of patrician command over their fellow human beings, which was assisted by the constant numbers of those in the other categories who hovered around them like pilot fish, seeking favors, decisions or simply attention. As he trod down the marbled halls, Gallatin chuckled to himself. Washington: Land of the Serious Suck-up, he thought.

"Hi. I'm Mike Gallatin." He stood before a pleasant-faced receptionist, of the young, shapely variety. "I was wondering if I could have a few minutes time with your chief of staff concerning an investigation I'm carrying out." He produced his business card.

The receptionist grinned broadly, welcomed him to the office of Representative Calloway and asked him to have a seat in one of the studded leather chairs near the doorway. A fat man in a stretched, gray suit sat in the next chair. He too was smiling. Plastered on his leather portfolio bag was a bumper sticker which declared: "Stay Healthy: Eat More Pork. *National Association of Hog Raisers*."

"Hiya," he said, nodding at Gallatin. "Crazy town, isn't it?"

"So they say. Just got in myself."

"You a constituent?"

"Yeah."

"Not me. I'm from Iowa, but been living here for the past fifteen years."

"What brought you here?"

"Pigs."

"Oh. I see." He really didn't see.

"You here to see the Congressman?" the fat man asked. He looked Gallatin up and down, as if making an expert estimate of a hog's weight.

"Nope. Just here to see a staffer about something."

"Staffers. Yeah, well. They hold the Congressman's bag and carry his water sometimes all right." The man snorted loudly to clear out blocked sinuses. "Let me offer you some advice from an insider." The chair creaked as he leaned over and planted his huge head just inches from Gallatin's left ear. He half covered the side of his mouth with one hand to ensure confidentiality. "Staffers are the mannequins in the store front window. They hire these kids from good schools, pay 'em peanuts and have 'em sit here and look real good. They'll smile atcha. They'll talk real fine and make yah feel good to be within glint distance of the old man's halo. Especially the girls. Why, your mind gets to racin' with so many thoughts of pussy, you forget why you came here in the first place." He laughed wheezily at his own wisecrack.

"So, it's the 'old man' or nothing. Is that what you're saying?"

The fat man winked and nodded solemnly. "For a constituent, you're not so dumb, see?" He wheezed again, then snorted. Finally, he pulled out a red bandanna that served as a handkerchief and blew his nose, sounding to all the world like a porpoise with double pneumonia.

The fat man reached into a side jacket pocket and pulled out a card. "Muhlhauser's my name. Jack Muhlhauser. National Association of Hog Raisers. Glad to meetcha." He extended a fleshy right hand. "Pork's big on the Hill. You look like a smart fella. You ever want some part-time work, give me a call. We're always lookin' for new shock troops to lobby for pork."

"Mr. Gallatin?" A clean-cut male with horn-rimmed glasses, red suspenders and a starched white shirt appeared. "I'm Kevin Crandler. I'm a legislative aide for the Congressman," he said cheerily.

Gallatin rose and shook the young man's hand. He looked down at the pork lobbyist. "See you around."

"Hey, and don't forget what I said about the big 'P',"
he said under his breath, cupping his mouth with one hand.

Crandler brought Gallatin into a room with ornate wall molding which had been turned into a bull pen of improvised modular work spaces crammed with aides, computer equipment, filing cabinets and banks of beeping telephones and fax machines.

"So glad you could drop by," Crandler chirped with a plastic smile. "Unfortunately, the Congressman will be occupied on the floor all day. But I'll be glad to help you. By the way, he'll be in Cleveland on Memorial Day, if you'd like to meet him then."

"Uh, right. But the reason I'm here is that I'm investigating--"

"Oh. This is Mary Chrisabelli." Another attractive young woman appeared, also smiling broadly. They shook hands. "Mary's helping out on special projects." The phone beeped. Crandler took it and immediately got into a involved conversation about 'conference discussions on the Riverine Commerce Bill.'

"It looks like Kevin will be tied up for a while. How can I help you?" Ms. Chrisabelli said with affected sincerity as she led Gallatin to a nook near the supply cabinet. She commandeered two cannistered, secretarial swivel chairs.

Ms. Chrisabelli, at most one score and one year, had a model's face, straight dark hair which ended just above her ample breasts, and filled a black skirt with contours Michelangelo could have sculpted. Gallatin found his mind wandering, just as the pig man had warned.

"Uh. Uh. Yes. I'm . . . I'm carrying out an investigation. I could use some pointers on how to get started with the government agencies."

The girl put just a little too much effort in expressing sincere interest in what Gallatin was saying. All of these smiling, 'I'm here to help you' people reminded Gallatin of first class flight attendants or theme park guides. They weren't there so much to help you as to humor you and send you on your way.

Gallatin explained that his insurance company had sent him to Washington to dig into the case of arson suspects, two recent immigrants from Croatia named Branko. He felt less guilty lying to people who looked and talked like they had just stepped out of a *Pepsodent* commercial.

"That's very interesting," Ms. Chrisabelli said in a tone of voice one would use if told that Michael Jackson really was interested in grown-up women. "You know, I'll call ICE -- United States Immigration and Customs Enforcement? -- and tell them you're coming. They'll be prepared to answer your--"

"My God! No! If I can make a suggestion, Congressman Calloway should sponsor a bill to have the entire ICE gathered up and thrown into a nuclear waste dump in Nevada. Let me explain. There may be no records on the Brankos."

"Ah yes. I see. Illegal aliens. I'll inform the Border Patrol that you want to speak to them." Ms. Chrisabelli picked up a phone and was about to punch in the number.

Gallatin blocked her hand. "Thanks. But that's not necessary. You see, I'm not sure these guys are illegals exactly, but they probably don't have visas. They seem to be criminals who—"

"The State Department! I'll find the name of someone you can contact—"

Gallatin was at the end of his rope. He shook his head in frustration. "You people just don't get it, do you? I'm trying to track down two criminals in this country under mysterious circumstances and you're going to tell such-and-such an agency that I'm coming." He stated the latter half of the sentence in a mocking tone. "I don't mean to seem rude, Miss, but why do you keep on saying that you'll call somebody to tell them I'm coming? I can do that myself. Anybody can."

Ms. Chrisabelli looked a little embarrassed. "It's what they tell us to say to constituents," she confided shyly.

"Who?"

"The staffers here."

"You're a staffer."

"Uh, well. Not quite."

Gallatin looked at her sporting a question mark on his face.

"I'm an . . . intern. Poli-sci major at AU. I work here in my spare time. Gives me work experience and doesn't look too bad on the old resume." She shrugged. "I answer routine correspondence, phone calls, stuff like that."

Gallatin smiled benignly. "And I'm sure you do a fine job. Thanks for taking the time." He got up.

"If there is anything I can do -- really -- please let me know," she said, dropping the flight attendant demeanor.

"I'll keep it in mind, sweetie." Gallatin winked at her as he walked out.

The Metro ride from Capitol Hill to Foggy Bottom is a mere fifteen minutes, though the political cultural gap is infinitely greater. The State Department's chief political players -- the Secretary, his immediate deputies and the regional bureaus -- fancy themselves Congress's match on foreign policy issues. Truth be told, however, except for the rare President with enough balls to play serious chicken with the Kings of the Hill -- Ronald Reagan, for example -- State gets rolled every time. Too many eggheads, not enough chutzpah. In an I Can't Believe It's Not Testosterone bureaucratic culture, bullshit talks and power walks. On the Hill, power is everything.

The good ladies in the Office of Refugee Affairs couldn't care less about jockeying among self-styled power players. Situated cozily away from the mainstream foreign policy deliberations in an annex building, they devoted themselves diligently toward the protection, human rights, care and resettlement of hundreds of thousands of refugees from Afghanistan to Bosnia to Somalia to Cuba. Not unaware of the hot and heavy political foreign policy issues of the moment, their bag was maternal health, childhood disease prevention and family planning. Millions of escapees from totalitarianism, ethnic strife and starvation owed their lives to the highly effective female functionaries of the Office of Refugee Affairs.

Gallatin was steered their way by the information desk. In contrast to the hollow PR schtick in Congressional offices, these women really cared and wanted to help, even a citizen who just walked in off the street. The Office Director, Elizabeth Fitzhugh, personally attended to the visitor from Ohio.

She listened carefully to Gallatin's request and asked a subordinate to phone Catholic World Service's main office in Boston to have them check their computer listings for the name Branko. Fifteen minutes later, they had the answer: nothing.

"It's not significant," she said. "They may have come into the country with immigrant visas, in which case we wouldn't be involved. Or they may have changed their names to aliases, or they violated tourist visas. Heck, they may even be illegal aliens, in which case it's unlikely anybody has a record on them. We have whole shiploads of Chinese trying to crash the gates and, as you know, our southern border is a sieve. Two guys from Croatia could slip in with the flood and never be detected."

"But let's say that they did come here under Uncle Sam's auspices under their real names. Would you still not have information about it?"

Fitzhugh and her deputy looked at each other, then back at Gallatin. "No," Fitzhugh answered unequivocally. And no Serbs, Croats or Bosnians would be resettled in Cleveland through our refugee program without us and CWS's knowledge. None."

Gallatin let out a deep breath. "I guess I've hit a brick wall then? Any other possibilities? FBI? CIA?"

Fitzhugh pondered a moment, shaking her head. "I'll tell you what I'll do. I'll put a message out on the classified email along with your phone number and address."

Gallatin scribbled his temporary D.C. and Cleveland home phone numbers on his business card.

A bulb went on inside Fitzhugh's head. "There's one other thing we can do. Not likely to show anything, but, what the hell?"

Gallatin shed his dejected grimace for an expression of renewed hope.

"The AVLOS."

"The what?"

"The Automated Visa Lookout System. Our visa blacklist. Any alien who's ineligible for a U.S. visa -- anything from failing to meet the criteria for a tourist visa to murder. They get put into the system so that we'll know to turn them down if they apply for a visa anywhere in the world." She swung around to her computer terminal and banged a bunch of keys. A blue field appeared. In big yellow letters, "AVLOS" popped onto the screen.

"Let's see. Branko." She typed the name. The screen changed colors. Instantly a list of names and other data flashed. She turned to Gallatin with a smile on her face. "Bingo!" She invited him to look at the screen.

"There they are. Milan and Zlatko?"

"Yes."

"*Voila.* They were entered into the system in 1998. By our embassy in Zagreb." She scrunched her eyes. "That's funny." She turned to him with a puzzled look.

"What is it?"

"No reason is given for their entry. It just says, "Code 34." She grabbed the phone and dialed. A friend in the visa office at the other end explained what it meant. She hung up and turned back to Gallatin with a pout on her face.

"And?" Gallatin said eagerly.

"And . . . it's classified. Compartmented. Even I don't have access."

Gallatin melted in his chair, covered his face with both hands. "Jesus. I'll never get to the bottom of this."

Fitzhugh was struck by the intensity of his lament. "You're really emotionally involved in this case, aren't you? It must be an important one for your company. What did these guys burn down anyway? The state capitol?"

Gallatin looked at her with an air of resignation. He spotted a portrait on her desk. It was of two adolescents, a boy and a girl. "Those your kids?"

Fitzhugh eyed them proudly. "You bet. Justin and Hannah. They're what keep me going."

"I have a little girl. She's in the hospital. And the Brankos may be responsible for putting her there."

Fitzhugh turned dead serious. "Mr. Gallatin, you needn't tell me more." She quickly jotted on a pad. "Here, call this person. I don't know many people at the White House, but this one helps us out on refugee policy. Very helpful. Say that I sent you. And good luck."

Peace Maintenance: Keeping America Safe in the New Millennium. Lisa put the final touches on her draft op-ed piece. As her new duties to "get the word out" on the Merriman Administration's foreign policy successes, Lisa ghost-wrote articles on behalf of senior officials, drafted speeches and prepared talking points for the President's use in appearances before the press. For her efforts, she had won a career position and renewed recognition from the other NSC staffers. It was all going so well that she refused to allow herself to wallow in self-congratulation. It was just all too good to be true. All it would take would be one screw-up to send her crashing back down into Wheeling-style obscurity. She couldn't let up. The long hours and constant pressure in the White House were taking their toll. The supple contours of a figure with all the right proportions became a mite more linear with the loss of ten pounds. "Mirror, mirror on the wall. Who's the palest, bedraggledest of them all?" she recited plaintively in front of her bathroom medicine cabinet one recent, predawn morning. And the fact that she hadn't been on a real date since she broke up with Craig before leaving West Virginia didn't escape her either.

No longer an intern, but a full staffer, she now had her own, albeit small office, and supervised a secretary and two new interns. She was given a parking place between the OEOB and West Wing -- in the finely tuned Washington pecking order, a spoils equivalent to an honorary knighthood.

Col. Haley kept her busy with new projects, mostly of the PR variety. The more she produced, the more he gave her, it seemed. In a rare moment of reflection, she contemplated whether it was a way Marines tested others' mettle. Intentional or not, she was determined to show that particular Marine and her other superiors that she could keep up with the best of them.

Besides her looks, the punishing workload took a toll on her temper as well. She had inherited her Slovak grandfather's hotheadedness. A diet of coffee, cokes and cafeteria food didn't help matters.

When she got a call from Michael Gallatin, she was finalizing two press guidances, reviewing suggestions for Presidential foreign policy speeches, browbeating four federal agencies to reach consensus on aid for Bosnia and starting to get serious about making an appointment with her hairdresser. She just didn't have the time to deal with John Q. Citizen at this juncture in her busy life.

"Uh, you're investigating . . . some . . . immigrants?" She had one eye on CNN, the other on short-fuse briefing papers, while trying to finish the chicken sandwich she'd picked up at the lunch room three hours earlier. "I see, um . . . why don't I give you a number at Homeland Security you can call--"

"No!!"

His loud, sharp negative gave her a start.

"I mean, I've been there. Look Miss. I just need someone to help me on one small point. That's all. It shouldn't take much time at all."

"But, I really don't deal--"

His mind racing, Gallatin blurted, "Ms. Fitz--, Liz Fitzhugh at State told me to call you. She said you'd help me." He held his breath.

Lisa called Liz Fitzhugh up on her mental screen. Competent. Reliable. Friendly. She had delivered promptly on a couple of refugee-related requests Lisa posed to her on short notice. It had made Lisa look good to her bosses. And Fitzhugh took a motherly interest in the younger woman, having invited her to join the Washington Women's Forum. She cleared Gallatin into OEOB.

The lumbering Midwesterner didn't make a great first impression. Terribly polite and self-effacing, he reminded her of men back home. Real gentlemen, but b-o-r-i-n-g. Slow on the uptake in a city where everybody fancied himself cleverer than the next person. A Gary Cooper character in a Dirty Harry set. And she just didn't have time for slow yokels from the hinterland.

She continued to munch on her sandwich as she motioned him to have a seat across the desk. She sipped cold, black coffee from a stained mug.

"Hi. So you have a problem and Liz couldn't help?" she said, getting immediately to the point.

"My little girl was almost killed by people who shouldn't have been allowed to enter this country. She's in a near-vegetative state. To save her, I must find the culprits."

Gallatin was equally to the point. The Wheeling woman in Lisa sensed that this man didn't like East Coast, big city people. But first impressions could be deceiving, she told herself. Perhaps the Buckeye visitor was quicker than she thought. He had a direct gaze, held his 6'2" frame erect and, though courteous, came off as a no-nonsense man who didn't give up. Furthermore, his synopsized story about his little girl and his mission penetrated her emotional armor. Lisa Valko the High Flyer momentarily became Lisa the empathetic woman.

"How old is she?" Lisa asked, her face a picture of concern.

"Thirteen. Just turned thirteen. Miss Valko, I've been to Homeland Security, to my congressman, to the State Department, the Ohio state police, Catholic World Services. My employer is ready to fire me. I need someone to get one fact, and quickly." He leaned forward, placing one elbow on her desk. He proceeded to relate what he had gleaned about the Branko boys, including his close encounter with them and the Cuyahoga Militia, and the Brankos' having been blacklisted for a U.S. visa. "Can you help me?"

"Oh." She leaned back. His intense blue eyes directed themselves at her like a lighthouse beacon. The handsome face, however, took the sharp edges off that intensity. She rang up Buckwheat Thompson and explained Gallatin's search. In a minute, Thompson appeared.

Though amiable, there was an edge to his voice and a tautness in his smile. Thompson grilled the Ohioan. Had he met the Brankos? Did he know where they were now? Did he know anyone who'd had contact with them? What would he do if he found them? How could he be sure that they had attacked the Suleijmanovics?

"Then you know of them?" Gallatin asked.

"Well, no. Never heard of them. But . . . we want to be aware whenever any of the political refugees we bring into the country commit serious crimes. Bad PR. We may need to adjust policy. The NSC aide gesticulated nervously, his eyes were wide.

Gallatin crossed his arms and looked at Thompson coldly. There was an awkward silence.

Lisa sensed his skepticism. "So, er, can the White House ask for the low-down on those guys?" she asked.

"No." Thompson's reply was a little too quick and final. "I mean, it's a State Department internal thing. Probably nothing behind it. My advice, Mr. Gallatin: go home. Take care of your girl. You're barking up trees -- the wrong trees."

"Thanks but no thanks." Gallatin got up to leave.

"But if you do turn up anything, give me a call."
Thompson proffered one of his cards. "I'd be glad to . . . to
be of help . . . if I can." He left Lisa's office.

Gallatin reached for the door. "Thanks for trying,
Miss Valko." He nodded a polite farewell.

"Wait!" Lisa said a bit too eagerly. She felt for this
man, a strong man, but also vulnerable. She contrasted his
devotion to his daughter with the workaholics of the
nation's capital, the bureaucrats, politicians and attorneys
who virtually abandoned their families in their
singleminded quest to reach the top. Had she been so
removed from her roots that she had forgotten what real
people were like?

She scribbled something on a yellow message slip.
"Here. This man sits in on our meetings on Bosnia and
other hot topics. I can't say that I really know him. But,
give him a call. He may be able to help you."

Gallatin took the piece of paper. *Win Ferret,
Refugee Admissions, State Dept.*, it read.

"You may think I'm nuts, Miss Val--"

"Call me Lisa."

"Lisa. Everybody else does. But it's my little girl.
I have to start somewhere." His eyes welled up.

For that brief moment Lisa felt very human, very
womanly. The press guidances, briefing papers, phone
calls dwarfed in significance in that moment. She couldn't
put her finger on it, but she wanted to help this man. She
scribbled another note and handed it to him, her eyes fixed
on his face. "I'm only a workabee, but if I can help, call."

For the first time since he arrived in Washington,
Gallatin had connected with somebody.

Tulliver had a splitting headache. Big policy disconnects, he could handle. Iraq going down the tubes? Political meltdown in Saudi Arabia? Assassination of an allied leader? He knew exactly how to manage such crises. Alert Fennimore, the President, cabinet heads. Call meetings. Consult allies and Congress.

It was the blips on the screen, the stones in the shoe that threw him off, ate up valuable time, detracted from the Big Picture.

"What?!" Tulliver demanded impatiently of Haley. He gulped down a tall glass of fizzing bromo.

"CHASM. We've got a problem."

"Then fix it, goddamn it." Tulliver warily eyed a six-inch stack of memos he had yet to read in advance of a briefing of the Senate Foreign Relations Committee only two hours hence.

"It's not that easy. Two Croats, named Branko, have hit the road. They're out of control. On a killing spree." He related what he knew of the Minneapolis B&B massacre as well as of the Suleijmanovic killings.

"Can't you bring them back in? What do we pay those frigging CHASM coordinators for anyhow?"

"This one's an old guy, Glassman. Out in Cleveland. He's the dean of the coordinators, the most senior and very effective. But he's given up on these two. Says we're letting in too many psychotics. He's threatening to quit the program."

Tulliver let out a long breath. He was ready to seek a solution but even more eager just to get rid of the problem. "These guys are on the lam and dangerous?"

"Yes. If they're not stopped, they'll be caught and the cover will be blown. CHASM will be front page news."

"Okay, okay." Tulliver rubbed the bridge of his nose.

"There's more," Haley said.

"I feared there would be," Tulliver growled. His headache felt like ground zero at the Nevada nuclear testing range on a busy day.

"A guy by the name of Gallatin, Michael Gallatin, has been snooping around the edges. Our agent controlling the investigation in Minneapolis found him poking around the place the Brankos destroyed. And now he's here in Washington. Called on Lisa Valko. Buckwheat met him. Sent up this memo." Haley handed Tulliver the memo, plus a file on Gallatin, complete with a glossy eight-by-ten photo.

Tulliver flipped through it and skimmed the memo. Watch him. Keep the fucker out. And that goes for any other asshole samaritans out there. This is too important, too much at stake. And I don't need to remind you that your career, as well as mine, is riding on keeping things under control. Got it?"

"Loud and clear," Haley answered. "And the Brankos?" he added.

Tulliver took a deep breath. "Recall them, for crying out loud. Just do it!"

CHAPTER ELEVEN

Two bullets in the brain. One through the temple to destroy the "thinking" part of the organ; the other in the lower rear portion to eliminate motor abilities. Even if the Brankos' hearts and lungs continued miraculously to function, they would become mere human vegetables taking up space in some publicly funded asylum at great cost to the taxpayers. No, Horst Fechtmann would see to it that the taxpayers would foot the bill for a quick autopsy and pauper's burial only. And a short-lived homicide investigation that would go nowhere.

It would be the easiest fifty grand he had ever made, Fechtmann thought as he surveilled the drunken Croatians swaying through the parking lot of the *Sundance Motel,* each propped up on the shoulder of a whore. Fechtmann's major concern was that their loud singing and cursing would attract undue attention. In "wet affairs," the first lesson was that stealth was everything. *Stille gleicht Tod* -- silence equals death -- the Stasi had instructed its agents.

Go in quick and clean. Drop your targets in minimal time. Slither away leaving no trace.

Harrison Avenue, a commercial strip which traversed Butte, included the kind of generic suburbia that blighted America's towns and cities everywhere. *McDonalds-KFC-Dunkin' Donuts-Mattressland-Speedy Oil Change.* Perfect cover for a killer. Anonymity. No mutually reliant neighbors to keep an eye on things for the commonweal. Stepping out of the American century, economic conglomeratization and fear of one another have yielded sterile commercial wastelands that, paradoxically, have become the natural stalking grounds of urban predators, be they convenience store marauders, serial killers, or ex-East German hitmen for hire.

Fechtmann remained in the driver's seat of his rented Malibu, parked in the rear of the motel parking lot near the dumpsters, until the Brankos and their dates had turned the corner to the stairway of the cinderblock structure. The poorly lit parking lot was devoid of people. The rush of traffic on Harrison fronting the motel made highly unlikely any driver ID'ing any individual, much less one lurking in the dark shadows behind the *Sundance.*

Fechtmann glanced briefly at his reflection in the rearview mirror. The zinc eyes looking back at him told him it was just another mission, albeit not in the service of the state. After the Wall came down, Fechtmann became an instant capitalist. Have gun. Will travel. For the right price, eliminate an opponent through the services of a tried and true professional. His ear-length blonde strands were becoming increasingly gray. He pushed them back with his fingers. After he had built up a retirement cache that would guarantee him a comfortable life for the next thirty-to-forty years of his life, Fechtmann would quit, perhaps open a cozy restaurant in the Florida Keys, live the life of the immigrant who'd cashed in on the American Dream. After all, there was no Stasi pension in the offing. No secret police 401(k) to draw from.

He pulled the 7.62mm silent pistol from its shoulder holster inside his black bomber jacket and deftly released the safety catch on its side. The Russian-made weapon was his favorite for such operations. Holding six rounds and weighing a mere 700 grams, the only sound it generated was a pop like that of an air gun, trapping the noise and smoke inside the cartridge case. Yet a round could penetrate a quarter-inch of steel at twenty-five meters. Devilishly lethal, yet quiet. *Stille gleicht Tod.*

Like a specter riding a graveyard breeze, Fechtmann whisked across the parking lot and reached the bottom of the stairway just as his targets had reached the top. From the squeals of alcohol-induced laughter and foul language, Fechtmann discerned that the foursome lingered before the hotel room doors, the men no doubt fumbling for their keys. The boisterous voices became muffled with the slamming of the doors.

At the academy, new agents had drummed into their heads the so-called Three G's: *Geduld, Geheim, Geschwind.* Patience, Secrecy, Swiftness. Fechtmann would lie in wait, like a black puma eyeing its prey, waiting for the right moment to strike with lightning lethality. He slowly ascended the stairs, every sense alert to every sound, every movement, every smell. At the third level, he paused. It was 2:00 am. No guests stirred. The whoosh of vehicles coursing up and down the interstate provided the only sounds. Three doors before reaching rooms 307 and 308, the Brankos' rooms, he stopped. Carefully, he reached up and loosened the bulb in a broken corridor sconce, safeguarding his presence in the resultant darkness. He stood in the shadows. When the moans and groans had subsided, he would be ready.

An hour later, the first whore exited 307, followed within minutes by the second from 308. Fechtmann receded into the vending machine room. The women beat a hasty path to their car, started the engine, and sped away. He would wait another twenty minutes.

The cheap aluminum doorknobs with their wobbly locks shimmied open easily with basic lock picks. First, room 308. Fechtmann slipped quickly into the room. His eyes already accustomed to the dark, Fechtmann saw Zlatko sprawled out on the sagging bed, lost to the world in a deep slumber, punctuated by loud snoring.

Fechtmann approached slowly. He hovered over Zlatko like a vengeful god. In a deliberate, measured motion, he brought his weapon down, positioned it a hairbreadth from Zlatko's left temple. In his mind, he repeated, *Geduld, Geheim, Geschwind.* A countdown to mortality. Just as he finished the final syllable, Stasi major Fechtmann pulled the double action trigger and winced. *Pop.* The pillow was instantly covered in blood and gray matter. Zlatko's face remained that of a sleeping man. With his left hand, Fechtmann carefully turned the dead Croatian's head. Just above the top cervical vertebra, he fired again, tearing apart the cerebellum.

Methodically, with the stealth and swiftness of a leopard, he repeated the procedure in room 307, ending almost peacefully the life of the horrid man who had wreaked so much havoc on his fellow human beings.

Within ninety seconds, the German was back in his automobile and pulled out into the great anonymity of Interstate Route 15.

Stille gleicht Tod.

The call came at 9:00 that same morning. "Mr. Ferret, two Croatian refugees were murdered in Montana several hours ago. I thought the State Department might want to know." Glassman then hung up abruptly before Ferret could react. Ferret called back immediately and demanded a full read-out. Reluctantly, the old man related the Brankos' rampage of terror. "These people you are bringing in. Not like us pioneers. We built your space program, gave you priceless intelligence to use against Moscow in the Cold War. We were cultured. Mr. Ferret, I wish to finally retire, spend more time with my grandchildren. Goodbye."

"Holy Jesus," Ferret murmured while seated at his desk in the sterile, sunless office. He shut his eyes and massaged his forehead with his fingertips.

Gerrie, the receptionist, poked her head into Ferret's cubicle. "Ambassador Goldman wants to see you," she said, smiling.

White light, not from the overhead fluorescent lamps, but from within him, suffused Ferret's inner core. Unlike his previous episodes of rage, frustration, repulsion with his work, however, this particular sensation did not induce pain as manifested in the skull-crushing headaches he'd been experiencing. This time, he actually felt a sense of peace as his being was bathed in this strange, warm, white light.

He ambled slowly, as if without purpose, to Goldman's office.

Brenda Hitz was not having a good week. It had suddenly dawned on her that, at 45, she was unlikely ever to find the right man and lowered her unfocused gaze onto a stack of unread cables.

Goldman remained seated at his desk as Ferret entered the large, but spare office. He attempted a fleeting smile and, after a perfunctory greeting, got up and sat opposite Ferret, who hugged one end of the large leather sofa, as if it were a life preserver in a turbulent sea.

"These two Croats," Goldman began. "Seems they got themselves into some real trouble."

Ferret looked at him incredulously. "That's a true understatement if I ever heard one. They went on a rampage across the Midwest that would make Attila the Hun proud. In Minneapolis they robbed, tortured, raped and slayed eight vacationers and the grandparent owners of a B&B. They then burned the place to the ground. After that, they went on a robbing binge, knocking over a bunch of convenience stores in South Dakota and Montana. They stole cars, carried out drive-by shootings and beat elderly strollers senseless just for kicks. 'Some real trouble' for the Brankos is like saying Hitler inconvenienced Europe." His voice was shaky, his eyes bulged. He stood up and pointed a finger accusingly at Goldman.

"You are responsible for bringing them here. *You* and all those other asses who care only about your own careers. And now it's too late. It's only a matter of time before the public gets wind of this dirty little trick that their ingenious leaders have sprung on them."

Goldman jumped out of his chair like a cat on a hot stove.

"Sit down, mister! Who the hell do you think you are talking to me like that?! I said, *sit down!*"

The barrage knocked the emotional wind out of
Ferret. He dropped back onto the sofa.

Goldman stood over Ferret, as if he would pounce
on him at the slightest move.

"What do you think of JFK?"

Ferret hesitated, was caught off guard. "I don't get
what you mean--"

"I said, what do you think of John Kennedy?"

"The President with the most brains and style in half
a century."

"Of course, you recall his inaugural address. 'We
shall pay any price, bear any burden, meet any hardship,
support any friend, oppose any foe to assure the survival
and success of liberty.'"

Ferret nodded.

"Freedom doesn't come cheap. This country has
sacrificed over half a million American lives in all battles
since the Revolution. But fighting wars is only part of the
cost for safeguarding freedom. Sometimes, we have to
short ourselves on our moral commitments in order to
ensure that our *Pax Americana* holds firm, that our national
security is not threatened.

"This entails compromises, not only with others, but
within our national soul. Our alliance with 'Uncle Joe'
Stalin. The Manhattan Project. The Fabio Program to save
Europe from itself. Operation Paperclip. Nixon cozying
up to Mao. Propping up Diem and those other colonial
squirts in Vietnam. Training death squads in Central
America, the Tigers in Haiti. Overthrowing Allende.
Covert support to anticommunist political parties from
Canberra to Calabria. Using *robust* measures to get vital
information from Islamist terrorists at GTMO." With each
example, Goldman's voice climbed to a crescendo.

"The Phoenix Program. Iran-Contra--" Ferret interjected.

"Enough!!" Goldman shouted.

The office door swung open. It was Brenda Hitz. Behind her office workers who had heard the shouting appeared cowed, though alert; disconcerted about the commotion from their boss's office, yet with their ears pricked up, eager to catch a word here and there.

Seeing that no blood had been spilled, she said sheepishly, "I was wondering if . . . I mean, if something was the matter . . ."

Goldman collected himself. He took a deep breath, straightened his tie. He put on a stiff smile.

"Everything's fine. We're discussing . . . Uh. Just having a lively debate."

Ferret, wearing a dour look, stared unblinkingly into space.

Hitz excused herself and shut the door.

Goldman paced back and forth. "When were you promoted last?" he asked.

"Seven years ago."

"Hmm. You need a promotion. Otherwise, you're out the door in a year or two. Am I right?"

Ferret remained silent.

"That's why you took this job. Nothing like getting two cracks at promotion, eh? They give us that because of the unorthodox nature of this program. Not exactly your standard, Foreign Service write-a-cable, attend-a-meeting, gaze-at-your-navel, go-home-to-the-wife-and-kids type of assignment, is it?"

Maintaining a stoic composure, Ferret looked away.

"You need the career. You need the promotion. Because, otherwise, you're out in the street with a mortgage, two car payments, a wife, a mother, and three kids who one day will want to follow in their daddy's footsteps to Yale. And your puny little government pension."

"It's not just that--"

"Of course, it's not just that! You're where the action is! At the vortex of history! Chance to have an impact, be noticed! That's what every one of us has strived for since we took the oath as junior officers. Why be selling widgets when you can be remaking the map of Europe?"

Goldman sat down and put on the best sympathetic face he could muster, the kind of face Ambassador Goldman would don when he had to inform an African dictator that the United States was terminating all aid to his country because Washington didn't approve of disemboweling schoolchildren of an enemy tribe.

"Win. You're under stress. I can appreciate that. Especially when two bad apples turn up among our protection cases. But, we didn't keep out Al Capone or Sheikh Abdel Rahman or Mohammad Atta either. The bottom line is this: we've got Americans in uniform over in Bosnia. We lose one occasionally to a mine, a traffic accident, we can tolerate that. But the day we start losing a whole bunch to sniper fire or mortar rounds from fanatics like the Brankos, next thing you know, the *New York Times* is screaming for us to quit, get out. The pressure builds on Congress, then the White House. Our whole peace effort, which we brokered, goes down the toilet. We've only seen a preview of the kind of bloodshed that'll occur if this whole thing falls apart."

"You missed one point."

"What's that?" Goldman asked skeptically.

"The Merriman Administration goes down the same toilet. And everybody who ever had anything to do with this program is finished."

Goldman let out a long, deep breath, his patience having run out. He placed a hand on Ferret's shoulder.

"Win. Do your job. Please. Think about what I said. Go home to your wonderful family. Then take it easy. Go with the wife and kids to the mountains or the beach, away from D.C. I'll approve the leave."

Ferret rubbed both temples and stared wide-eyed. "My family."

"Right. This career may end, but they're with you forever."

Goldman opened the door. Ferret shuffled out and returned to his cubicle.

Ferret sat at his desk, replaying over and over in his mind his encounter with Goldman. Memos, cables and notices piled up unread in his in-box. Unread emails likewise stacked up like slices of bacon one atop the other in his computer screen.

Gallatin's call broke him out of his introspective trance. He asked to see Ferret immediately, upon the advice of NSC staffer Lisa Valko. Ferret tried to brush him off. Gallatin should see people in the Office of Refugee Affairs, he said. Gallatin said that he had. Homeland Security? Hopeless, per Gallatin. The visitor pressed until an exasperated Ferret had no choice but to agree to see him.

Ferret cleared Gallatin into Main State, receiving him outside the ultra-secure CHASM suite of offices in a small conference room used for meeting persons not briefed into the program.

"Mr. Gallatin, let me first explain to you that I don't really track refugee cases . . . individually, I mean. That is, our job basically is to ensure interagency policy coordination--"

"I thought the NSC did that."

"Well, yes. They do. On the macro level, that is. We focus on the more detailed aspects . . . budget, resources--"

"Funny. Mrs. Fitzhugh at the Office of Refugee Affairs told me that's what they do."

"Right," Ferret answered with a delay. "You see, in the broader parameters--"

"You *are* the Office of Special Admissions, aren't you?"

Ferret did not maintain eye contact. He constantly rubbed his hands together, fidgeted and was jumpy. He had the look of a man who had done something wrong, planned to do something wrong, or both.

"Mrs. Fitzhugh has never heard of you. Why's that?"

Ferret stared dumbfoundedly at Gallatin. The latter got to the point.

"Look. I want information on two refugees from Croatia. Zlatko and Milan Branko. They murdered an immigrant couple, almost killed my daughter, and came this close to blowing my head off. The police need information so that they can be arrested and punished. Now what's so difficult about that?"

Ferret's jaw was slack. He was cornered. No amount of mealy-mouthed doubletalk would get this man off his back. And he couldn't just kick him out lest he raise Gallatin's suspicions further.

The ballet of savagery pranced wickedly back into his psyche. He wanted this man, this tormenter, dead. There was simply no more room in his life for any more pressures. He glared at Gallatin, his eyes possessed a preternatural power. Ferret knew it, could feel it. He said nothing, didn't flinch, didn't blink. With all his power, he willed the other man dead. Star beams shot from his irises and penetrated his adversary's brain. Gallatin's head expanded, contorted, flushed to a scarlet hue. His mouth gaped from the pain, but no screams emanated. Then, like a balloon filled with water beyond the stretching point, Gallatin's head exploded. The ballet of savagery was overwhelmed by red. Blinding crimson, hot and empowering.

"Mr. Ferret! I said, Ferret!! You okay?"

Ferret blinked. There was Gallatin, each hand bracing Ferret's shoulders, shaking him vigorously. "Are you epileptic, Ferret? Diabetic? Shall I get a doctor?"

Ferret's body was as rigid as an ice sculpture. His widened eyes had locked onto Gallatin's face, then rolled back into his head, exposing only white. Sweat poured from his forehead, off his nose.

"Ferret! I'm going to get help."

"No!" Ferret came to, his right hand locked onto Gallatin's arm in a dead man's grip. "Don't go!" he gasped.

Gallatin tried to maintain control, but was terrified. Ferret was obviously ill, physically or mentally, but certainly he was not a well man. Ferret's iron grasp hurt the ex-athlete. He couldn't shake loose.

"Gallatin. Listen to me. I'm fine." Ferret let out a long, deep breath. He released Gallatin, then straightened

up, cranked his neck, and composed himself. He patted his
forehead with his handkerchief and ran his fingers through
his hair. "It's just that . . . I've been under a lot of strain
lately. At home. And here."

Gallatin sat back down cautiously. "You want to
talk about it?" he asked.

"No. I mean, yes. I mean I can't. I--"

"Take it easy. Let's take it one step at a time. Are
you in trouble?"

Ferret pondered a moment. "No, and yes. I have
seen things, activities, which are unbelievable. If people
knew . . ."

"Concerning what exactly?" Gallatin kept his tone
of voice low and even.

Ferret looked at Gallatin with a start, as though he
had just been rudely awakened from a deep sleep.

"It's secret. Top secret. Compartmented. National
security. I cannot divulge it. You understand, don't you?"
He almost pleaded for understanding.

"Okay, okay," Gallatin replied carefully. He smiled
sympathetically. "Ferret. Let me ask you this. Whatever
you're involved with -- these things you say you know --
are people, innocent people, being hurt?"

Ferret's wide, intense eyes penetrated Gallatin's
face. He blinked as he finished processing a thought.

"Mr. Gallatin--"

"Mike."

"Remember when you were a kid and you learned
some secret about another kid? Maybe he stole, or cheated
on a test. But you were afraid to tell anybody? Either
because the other kid would beat you up, or people might
suspect you were the guilty party but were trying to pin the
blame on another?"

"Yeah. Sure. Or when you were the guilty party, but were afraid to fess up even though you were guilt-ridden."

"You do understand!" Ferret appeared greatly relieved.

"Which are you, Ferret?" Gallatin asked carefully.

Ferret withdrew as if flames had suddenly burst before him. He placed both hands over his heart. "I am both, Mike. I am both. And I can't stand it."

"So tell me! What exactly is it? It's something the government is doing, isn't it? Is it something illegal?"

Ferret placed his face inches from Gallatin's. The latter could feel Ferret's labored breathing. "CHASM," he whispered barely audibly in Gallatin's ear.

Gallatin looked at Ferret with a confused expression. He shook his head. "I'm sorry, what--"

"I'm falling into a chasm, Mike. One with no bottom. Where evil overcomes us and we become the evil. Pure hell." He sported an eerie smile, a crown on his cryptic thought.

Gallatin looked at Ferret with worry and confusion. "Ferret. What about the Branko boys?"

"They're taken care of. Out of the way," Ferret responded matter-of-factly.

Gallatin paused to process Ferret's answer.

"What do you mean, Ferret? Are they caught? In jail?"

"No. Worse. Much worse."

"And?"

"Listen to me Mike. You're best going back home. Stay out of this. Nothing to do with you--"

"Bullshit! They almost killed my kid! Don't tell me to stay out of it, goddammit!"

"Yes. Your daughter." Ferret paused to reflect. He twirled a pencil against his lips. "May I ask a very personal question, Mike?"

"Shoot." The eerie expression on Ferret's face continued to trouble Gallatin.

"When you lost your wife. How did you feel?"

Gallatin stiffened. "It was the end of the world. Why?" he asked suspiciously.

"Um. Don't get me wrong. But I'm curious. Privately. That is, deep down inside, in your male's rough soul. Did you not feel . . . sense just a twinge . . . free?"

Gallatin shook his head in astonishment. "You really are one sick fuck, aren't you?"

Ferret drew his head upward, as though he had gotten a strong whiff of something putrid. He looked condescendingly down on Gallatin, but said nothing.

"I'm sorry. Look, can I return to my original point for being here? Can you tell me *anything* about the Brankos? Anything at all?"

"Only that they're no longer a problem. It was a . . . a mistake."

"What was a mistake?"

"They got through, but shouldn't have. Mike, go home. Stay out of this. You're a good guy. It's too late for me. But not for you. If you dig too deep, you'll get hurt. Seriously hurt."

Ferret rose and extended his right hand, signifying that the encounter had ended.

Gallatin took his hand. "I want to talk with you again. I'll call."

"I may not be here, Mike." He showed Gallatin out the door, then about-faced and disappeared behind the lock-festooned, steel door of the Office of Special Admissions.

CHAPTER TWELVE

Ferret liked dropping in on the Yale Club, though work and family obligations prevented him from frequenting the place as often as he would like. As with the surrounding Tudor homes on Washington's Cathedral Ave., the Yale Club telegraphed understated, moderate wealth; a neighborhood populated with gentle but ambitious white professionals who favored Volvos and tony private schools for their children. Like Ferret, they were liberal, yet protective of their own interests.

Ferret had begun his day in what had become for him a rare mood: positive, eager, something to look forward to. As he drove to work with the windows of his minivan open to take in the sweet air of a young summer, he rehearsed the address he would give that evening before his fellow alumni -- "Refuge in a Dangerous World: U.S. Obligations Toward Justice and Humanitarianism in the Post Cold War Era." He did mental editing, verbal polishing, rhetorical restructuring. And he did not forget humor. An anecdote or two to loosen 'em up; witty observations on life post-Yale; the ironic turn of phrase. These were the speechmaker's tools. In fifteen years as a public servant, he had them down pat.

At the office, he rushed through his work mechanically. He wrote his reports, made phone calls, attended meetings. But he was on automatic pilot. He did the right things, but his mind was elsewhere. Even Goldman was struck by his subordinate's relative cheerfulness. He took care not to push Ferret lest the spell break and his obstreperous employee return to his usual cranky self.

At 5:30 sharp, Ferret was out the door. He jumped into the driver's seat of his van as does a fighter pilot in his cockpit when on an urgent mission. His enthusiasm to leave his present reality for a previous one was such that he squealed his tires on departing the basement parking garage.

Ferret remained on automatic pilot as he negotiated the serpentine rush-hour traffic along Massachusetts Avenue's Embassy Row, across Wisconsin and left onto Cathedral Avenue. The newly leafed oaks and maples swathed inhabitants and passersby alike in a protective, cool shade. A tingling sensation ran up Ferret's back. He shook his shoulders in reaction. *Like a damn kid*, he scolded himself. A broad smile blossomed effortlessly across his face.

His four years at Yale were his best. Absolutely the best in his life. Memories of pals, all-night bull sessions, brilliant professors, gentle New England autumns, girls flashed across his mental screen. Sweet days.

He had met Lynette there. It was at a joint Yale-University of Connecticut classical music concert. She played Liszt. His smile evaporated. The present tugged at

him. He wished to linger in the past. Ferret shook his head
to shed the encroaching present as he would shake water
from his hair.

He arrived at the club twenty minutes early. People
-- mostly men, one-hundred percent white -- of all ages
milled around, sipping sherry, catching up on old times
with former classmates. As Ferret debarked from the van,
several immediately enveloped him to welcome him and to
shake his hand. Like a white light from heaven, he thought.
An encompassing warmth. Eternal. Or so Ferret wished.

The time for his address had come and he was led to
a podium in a large room filled with folding chairs, nearly
all occupied by alumni. Ferret was not nervous. On the
contrary, the juices flowed. He softened 'em up with a
couple of quips about what it was to be a Yalee in the late
twentieth century. He was repaid with ample chuckles. He
launched into his topic confidently, being sure to make eye
contact with his listeners. As he made key points,
contemplative faces nodded in comprehension, perhaps
even agreement.

"The foreign policy of a democracy worthy of the
name cannot be humanitarian if it is not also just . . ." He
carefully modulated his voice in the fashion of his hero,
John F. Kennedy. He had meaning. Being here among his
own, imparting his knowledge and his philosophy,
validated him as a thinking man, a man with a deep
conscience. The hypocrisy and lies of his work world
were, for these moments, banished from his mind.

"Too often, diplomatic theorists act in a vacuum,
and do not consider the common men and women and
children whose lives are ultimately affected by their
policies. Too often this ivory tower theorizing results in
refugees fleeing certain death, wholesale slaughter,

aggression and warfare . . ." As he drove home each point,
his pace quickened, he tapped the podium in emphasis. He
felt good; he felt strong. He felt righteous.

They applauded heartily. The activities director
praised Ferret for his thought-provoking insights, and then
invited questions. Ferret, standing back, patted his
forehead with his handkerchief. So intent had he become
that he had perspired rather profusely.

A short, dark lawyer in a pin-striped suit and horn-
rimmed glasses shot up with his hand raised.

"Does your position hold up against what's
happened in the ex-Yugoslavia? I mean, wasn't the
Bosnian tragedy, in part, due to Western governments
acting too late and, only then, with flawed policies?" he
asked in a nasally voice.

An invisible force tugged at Ferret. It dragged him
back to the present. He rubbed his left temple to ward off a
brewing headache.

"That's a good question. If you look at what's
transpired in the Balkans since 1991, you'll see that no
outsiders were in a position to really change anything."
Ferret went on to recite the U.S. government official line.
He looked up to maintain that all-important eye contact, so
key to a speaker's credibility. The faces staring back at him
were no longer contemplative. They were empty, lifeless.
Ferret lowered his gaze, blinked hard, then looked up again.
The faces hadn't changed. He could see them in more
detail. Still, blanched, rigid. The unblinking mass of eyes
were sunken and dark, reflections of death.

The self-confidence drained from Ferret as the
blood had from the conclave of seated corpses which now
faced him. He stuttered. His eyes were locked onto them
in a kind of hypnotic horror. As he fought to maintain his

composure, Ferret could see more closely his sepulchral audience. Most wore tattered garments of non-American design. Some were in filthy, bloodied army uniforms. Females' cold bosoms peeked through blouses that had been ripped open.

"Mr. Ferret. Mr. Ferret." A warm hand placed itself gently on Ferret's shoulder. The host's concerned face was directed at him. The Yalees fidgeted in their chairs. Ferret felt like he had just awoken from a bad dream. He forced a smile and looked expectantly back at the host.

"Mr. Ferret, the lady in the third row has a question."

"Of course." Ferret sucked in his breath. He retained a nervous grin. "Sure, go ahead," he said with shaky cheeriness.

A thirtyish woman in a dark power suit and with perfectly coiffed blonde hair tied back with a velvet ribbon stood up. She prefaced her question with a lengthy exposition on recent Balkan history indicating that she'd done her homework before coming. Another attorney.

". . . and so, my question is, why is it that only a handful of suspected war criminals have been taken to The Hague for trial? The President stated that 'We won't let war criminals walk.' Yet, they seem to be not only walking, but driving, swimming and skiing. What gives? Is the Administration leveling with us?"

Ferret stood motionless, appearing to be lost in thought. The force of the present tugged at him again. He rubbed his face with both palms. As his eyes reopened, they were back again. Victims of the Omarska concentration camp, the slain from the Srebenica death march, the massacred from Vukovar hospital. The violated women, the murdered children. They were all there.

Muslim, Croats, Serbs. Off in a corner were the kindly grandparents and the guests of the St. Paul B&B eradicated by the Branko boys. All victims of a sham foreign policy. And Ferret was its midwife. Dozens of hollow eyes riveted upon him, their vacant gazes demanding answers.

"Excuse me. I'm not feeling . . . well." Ferret mopped his brow again with his hanky and stormed out. Outside, he leaned against the stucco wall of the club house and cried.

"Ambassador Goldman would like to see you," Brenda Hitz informed Ferret as he dragged himself into the office forty-five minutes late. He made no acknowledgement as he lumbered past her toward his office cubicle.

"Uh, as in now. He needs to see you urgently . . ."

Ferret gently shut the door behind him, still paying no mind to the boss's secretary. Hitz looked down at her folded hands and shook her head in incomprehension.

Ferret sat himself down behind his desk and proceeded to stare into space.

The phone rang. And rang again. And continued to ring. Ferret sat still, and gazed onto some distant, unattainable horizon that only he could see.

The door opened. "Uh, good morning, Win," Goldman said softly. He eased his back against the wall and folded his arms across his chest. He studied Ferret for a moment. "Weather's getting better by the day. Don't you think?"

Ferret stared at the floor, his face devoid of emotion.

"Now's the time to begin making vacation plans. You and your family make any plans yet, Win?"

Ferret shook his head ever so slowly.

"Well, I know you will," Goldman added dismissively. "In the meantime, the work continues to pile up. Got another load coming in next Friday. Short notice, but there's urgency attached to it. White House wants this batch processed quickly . . ."

Ferret finally made eye contact.

"A dozen Serbs. They're arriving at some isolated Air Force base out in the back of beyond in North Dakota, or some such place. The White House is taking greater care that the program not get leaked or otherwise exposed. Call JCS to coordinate travel. Plan on spending a week-to-ten days . . ."

Goldman's voice faded out of Ferret's mind. He focused intently on the ambassador's face. He despised the man. He despised all of the so-called policy-makers who made him commit evil things for their own puffed-up egos. He -- all of CHASM's actors -- had become the evil. He knew now the task that lay before him: to eradicate it and to set himself free.

"Good evenin', Mr. Ferret," Gerrie, the receptionist, bade a totally unresponsive Ferret as he strode past her on his way out of the office at 5:30 sharp.

Ferret eased himself into the family van in the Department's parking garage – this time devoid of the enthusiasm he'd had as he launched himself for the Yale Club. He switched on the radio to WTOP, the all-news station. He listened as one correspondent after another reported on some crisis or political event and then signed off in their each unique manner. "And that's it from Win Ferret in Tel Aviv," he muttered to himself. As he wended his way through crowded District streets during a gray drizzle, he kept signing off. The methodical flip-flop of the windshield wipers provided metronome-like timing. *Flip.* "This is *Win* Ferret reporting from Baghdad." *Flop.* "And so it goes. Win *Ferret (dramatic pause)* . . . from Moscow."

Just under a half-hour later, he pulled into Montgomery Mall, a mile outside the Beltway, minutes from home. A grossly fat mother and her brood of four hyperactive children blocked the main entrance to Sears as she sought vainly to negotiate an overloaded cart of purchases toward the parking area while simultaneously trying to keep her kids under control.

Ferret tried to maneuver around her. A chubby son was yowling that he wanted mommy to buy him a toy. A three-year old dropped her near-liquid ice cream cone on Ferret's left shoe. "Justin! Justin! Get out of the man's way! Justin!!" the mother screeched in a porcine voice.

A flash bulb burst in Ferret's head. It was the same sudden white light he had been experiencing at increasingly frequent intervals. Perspiration beaded on his forehead. A primal force within seized him. His face contorted. Wolf-like, he glared at the boy. Ready to pounce.

Mommy, ever alert to strangers as potential threats to her offspring, immediately caught the wild expression on Ferret's face. With a broad sweep of a flabby arm, she

herded kids, merchandise and her own corpulent frame out
the door.

The obstacle to his immediate goal now removed,
Ferret briefly closed his eyes, took a deep breath, then
entered the department store. He knew exactly where he
wanted to go. First, the lawn care section. Without
hesitation, he pulled out a two-and-one-half gallon gas can.
He next made a bee-line toward the home repair
department. He was faced with a plethora of choices. So
many kinds of hammers. He pursed his lips, studying the
array of hardware carefully. He picked out a carpenter's
ballpeen hammer. He test-swung it into his left hand. Too
light. Ferret scrutinized a mallet. Hmmm. No. Too soft
and broad. His eyes rested on a line-up of seven mini-maul
sledges, ranging from two pounds to ten pounds. Heavier
than that, they turned into regular sledge hammers. He
rubbed his chin and pulled out the five-pounder. A bit too
hefty, he thought as he assessed its weight, shifting it in his
right hand. Ah, but the three-pounder was perfect. He
would take it. He paid with his Sears card.

At the Texaco station just off Democracy
Boulevard, Ferret filled the van's tank as well as the gas
can.

"Win Ferret here. Signing off!" A self-contented
grin sprouted across his face.

As he did every day after returning from work,
Ferret pulled the van up the steep driveway to his split-level
-- cozily concealed on a tree-enshrouded ridge. It was the

serenity and relative seclusion of this house nestled in the bucolic suburban neighborhood of Carderock Springs that had caught his fancy five years previous when he and Lynette were house-hunting.

Cloris Ferret stood on the front steps. She merely watched as she wiped her hands on her apron. Ferret waved. She responded with a slight smile.

In the garage, Ferret quickly got out of the vehicle and opened the back. He checked the gas can to make sure it was sealed tight, then carefully stowed it under a blanket the family used for picnics. His eyes darted around the garage until they fell on the next item he had in mind, a long-handled shovel. This he placed neatly in the rear of the van, off to a side. Finally, he took the boys' camping tarp, unfolded it and spread it on the floor, covering all the other items.

The Golden Retriever, Leo, galloped in and jumped up to Ferret.

"Nice boy. Good doggie, Leo," Ferret said, petting the animal to calm it down. He looked around again till he caught sight of a kid's jump rope. He took it off the wall, tested its strength, then tied a large knot in the middle and set it on the floor near the door to the kitchen.

Ferret slipped the mini-sledge in his brief case and snapped it shut. He checked himself in the van's outside rear-view mirror. He combed his hair, took a deep breath, shut his eyes, counted silently to ten. Assured that he looked no different from any other day of having just returned from the office, Ferret, checking once more that he had arranged everything as he had planned, entered gingerly into the kitchen.

Lynette was wrestling with the Cuisinart. Chopped carrots were spewn all over the counter.

Ferret kissed his wife on the cheek. "Hiya sweetie."

She closed her eyes and smiled. "Hi honey. This darn machine confounds me. Can you figure out what I'm doing wrong? You're late. Held up in traffic?"

Ferret placed the lid on the Cuisinart and turned it sharply until it snapped. "That's the trick. Strength and force. Works every time. Yup. Ran into a traffic jam on River Road. Car broke down. Right in the middle of the lane."

Cloris appeared.

"Hello mother."

"Win."

They did not kiss.

"How was work?"

"Same old, same old."

"Brandon and Win, Jr. each has a soccer match tomorrow evening . . ."

He cut her short. "*Yes*, mother. We'll see."

"They're your sons, Win. It's important."

"We'll *see!*" he shot back.

Lynette placed herself between mother and son. "Of course, we will," she said cheerily. "Let's all sit down and eat. It's Mexican night. C'mon everybody! Boys! Get down here. Dinner's on."

Three bumptious boys flew, slid and tumbled to the dinner table from upstairs.

"I'm starvin'," declared Win, Jr., the fourteen-year old, in his still-changing voice.

"I could eat a house!" added Jeremy, the kindergartner.

"It's horse, dumbass. You can't eat a house. Geez, how stupid can yah get?" corrected the all-knowing Brandon, a week shy of his eleventh birthday.

"Hush," rejoined Lynette sharply. "Who wants to say grace?"

"It's Daddy's turn," Brandon reminded everyone.

All joined hands as Ferret thanked the Lord for "these bountiful gifts" of tacos, burritos, salsa and guacamole dip.

They dug in.

"Pop, you comin' to the games tomorrow?" Win, Jr. asked.

"We'll see how things go," Ferret answered softly.

"If Dad's feeling well," Lynette added.

Cloris stared at her son worriedly. Ferret made sure he made no eye contact.

"Gee, we sure hope you can go, Dad," Win, Jr. implored.

"Well, I thought we'd all take a little trip," Ferret said. A quizzical look marked each family member's face.

"A trip, dear?" Lynette asked.

"To North Carolina. Back to the woods where we always go camping," Ferret continued.

His brood exchanged furtive glances indicating confusion and concern.

"We will return to Tyrrell County -- this summer. July perhaps," Lynette, ever the diplomat as well as the diplomat's wife, said without missing a beat.

Thereafter there was little in the way of dinner conversation. The main sound was that of Leo slurping down doggy chow from a large plastic bowl.

The usual family routine followed dinner. Ferret watched the news. Lynette went off to play a set of tennis with a girlfriend. Cloris sat on the rear deck reading Updike. The boys went off to play with friends.

By 9:00, all were back in their cozy suburban nest. The boys retired one-by-one. The three adults sat watching a PBS special on the art of ancient Rome. A light snore emitted from Ferret's mother as she nodded off on the love seat. Lynette, a budding artist herself, was engrossed with the TV program. Leo sat contentedly at Ferret's feet.

Ferret looked conspicuously at his watch. "It's getting to be that time. I'll take Leo to the garage." He got up from his barcalounger, stretched, then called for Leo to follow him to the garage.

In the garage, the frisky canine jumped playfully around its master. "Come Leo. Here boy. Come on!" Ferret sang out. He grabbed a doggy biscuit from a bag on a shelf with one hand and the kiddie's jump rope from the floor with the other. The dog stood with his paws up against Ferret's chest, his tongue hung out one side as he let out muffled "woofs" in anticipation of receiving the treat.

"Atta boy, Leo. Atta boy," Ferret said reassuringly. He wrapped the rope lightly around the pet's neck, knot-side down. He held the biscuit up just above Leo's puffing nose. As the animal strained to reach the treat, Ferret dropped it into his mouth, then, in a flash move, yanked the ends of the rope with all his might and shoved Leo down onto the concrete floor. Ferret placed his 180-pound frame squarely onto Leo's back, and tightened the rope further.

The dog pulled its head violently from side to side as it struggled to escape the death grip. But it was trapped. Leo's paws could scratch only the hard surface of the floor. Its larynx broken from the knot, the only sound that emitted from it was a desperate, but subdued, "kaaaaaack." Its tongue, bloated and black, protruded from its mouth. Blood sprayed from the dog's snout; most, however, entered its trachea and into its lungs, drowning the animal as it also suffocated.

Ferret, rigid and flushed, straddled the beast, now in its final death throes. Ferret's twisted face was a picture straight from hell. Eyes wide, nostrils flared, complexion vermilion, hair wild. His breathing was hard, sweat oozed from every pore. A fierce determination had taken possession.

Leo's body became limp. His reddened eyes bulged, yet were unseeing. As twitches of muscles and limbs faded into the stillness of death, Ferret let up on the rope. He rose and looked down at the slain pet. He again rubbed both temples. A thousand bloodied, chest-thumping barbarians bellowed atavistic victory shouts inside his ragged soul. Emotions out of control. Reason struggled vainly against the hordes that haunted him, who tugged him now firmly into their netherworld of wild freedom.

"The Evil," he murmured. "It is I. And I am it," he whispered, nodding in self-confirmation.

Without hesitation, Ferret left the dead dog and quietly slipped back into the house. He washed the blood off his hands in the kitchen sink, though spots and smears colored his shirt and trousers. He wasted little time. The barbarian hordes were on a relentless march. They carried him along.

On the kitchen table lay his brief case. He went to it and ever so carefully clicked it open. From the living room he heard Kenneth Clark deliver the concluding commentary on the PBS special on ancient Roman art. The children were sound asleep in their rooms. He reached down and slowly took the small sledge from out of the briefcase. He was a man determined. He knew what he had to do.

CHAPTER THIRTEEN

On the surface, Tulliver accepted Haley's congratulations with gentlemanly grace. Within, however, he loathed the military. He had managed, through his father's connections, to avoid the draft and, good God, having to serve in Vietnam. It wasn't on moral grounds that he did so. Oh sure, he participated in a couple of antiwar demonstrations at Princeton -- fortunately, not so vigorously as eventually to call the world's attention to himself for being a draft dodger, as Bill Clinton had done. Everybody protested something back then. It was just that the whole artificial atmosphere of strutting, saluting and sucking up left him cold. For a young man with a mission -- to get to the top as fast as he could -- wasting two years of his life playing soldier simply wasn't in the cards. And now, as he reached the next rung on the ladder of success, that of National Security Adviser to the President of the United States, he loathed the military more than ever, especially the U.S. Marines. He thought of them as tin-horned martinets. "Pit bulls with some vague awareness of the existence of a Constitution but otherwise unthinking, unoriginal, uneducated and unwashed," he was fond of sniggering to likeminded friends in the boardroom or at the country club.

"Semper fi, sir," Haley said as he shook his boss's hand with bone-crushing pressure and looked him squarely in the eye. He produced a beribboned box. "Karen always told me that I was entitled to put on a couple of pounds to celebrate each of my promotions. Her chocolate truffles are wicked. Enjoy." He handed the box to Tulliver with both hands.

"Mrs. Haley deserves a promotion too, Dan. How about if I make her Deputy National Security Adviser? By the time a new Administration rolls into town, they wouldn't be able to dislodge our fat asses out of the West Wing."

"That's one way to hold on to our jobs. I'll pass it along, but she's got a bigger job than that already: raising two wild boys and a girl and putting up with one badass Marine."

The two men shared a hearty laugh. There it was again, Tulliver thought to himself. That hypocrisy that only career men in uniform had. Paid to kill, they extolled family values to the rafters; as if to absolve themselves of the mortal sin of slaughtering or maiming other fathers. In this regard, the extent of Haley's hypocrisy went much further. He was Mr. Fix-it in an administration where the fix was always in. He got results every time. Tulliver usually didn't ask how.

"Dan, when I go up, you follow with me. I'll make sure you get that full bird quickly. Keep getting us results."

"Do my best," Haley said with ramrod directness.

True-blue American patriots like Haley made Tulliver queasy. Nonetheless, Haley was effective. He loved nothing better than fighting the bad guys in the trench warfare of policy-making. Since being decorated for his role on General Franks J-5 Planning Staff during the Second Gulf War, he won a fast promotion and an assignment on the White House staff. Tulliver was well aware that his subordinate's goal was to become a flag officer within five years. This was the carrot he held before the Marine's face.

"By results, I mean success. This Yugoslavia deal may be long in the tooth, but it has got to hold. With the way things are going in the Middle East and the near fiasco of the Sudan mission, it's more important than ever that the President's effectiveness in foreign policy not take any more hits. This morning, when the President fired Fennimore and asked me to take over the NSC, I assured him that I and my team would not let him down."

Haley nodded without comment.

"I plan to ditch most of Fennimore's people over the coming weeks. We don't need goofy academics to get in our way. That's why I'll be relying on you more. I won't be undercut like Fennimore was."

The last sentence hung in the air like a pregnant rain cloud. And in Washington, the passive voice was used a lot as a means of disguising one's culpability in a crime or a snafu.

"I thought we were humane," Haley said in a low voice. He sipped coffee from a styrofoam cup. His face was the picture of four-square rectitude; his eyes, however, were cold, almost indifferent.

"I never held anything against the man," Tulliver rushed to add. "He's pre-eminent among foreign affairs

thinkers. Trouble is, the university-think tank-foundation
types can't usually handle the rough and tumble of politics
once they're outside their ivory towers. Fennimore was
weak. He had to go -- uh, despite our bolstering him . . . at
various times."

Tulliver had been conniving against Fennimore
from day one. While going out of his way on the surface to
act the loyal deputy, Tulliver exercised tight control over
the information flow to Fennimore and President
Merriman. In the case of the Darfur conflict in Sudan, he
had managed to manipulate their attitudes by forwarding
the more upbeat intelligence and diplomatic reports while
withholding those -- reflecting the true situation -- which
painted a bleak picture of rising violence and genocide.
Behind the scenes, he had gotten Fennimore and leading
black figures to convince the President to undertake a peace
mission to Africa. At the same time, he clandestinely fed
the media inside information on the folly of such a mission.
The upshot was a policy disaster, one that Tulliver stepped
in quickly to "fix," thereby winning for him the President's
esteem and Fennimore's demise. Haley's role was to
carefully screen the reports, sending up only the relatively
few rosy ones.

"I like to think that we are realists," Haley said.
"After 9/11, the Marquess of Queensbury rules just don't
apply. The world knows when we act weak. The baddies
just lie in wait ready to pounce where they can, waiting for
the big ol' American lion to take a snooze. Weak leaders
invite disaster. It's up to us supporting cast to make the star
of the show look good and to keep the crowd feeling
content."

It occurred to Tulliver for the millionth time that
profundity was a trait alien to the U.S. Marines, or most

military officers for that matter. Those who affected intellectual depth appeared pathetic when sprinkling their discourse with mashed metaphors and trite homilies, a common trait among the intellectually challenged uniformed services.

"Keep things under control, Dan. Those two Croats almost did us in. The Croats told me that they were screening out the nutcases. What gives anyway?"

"State's supposed to take a good close look at them before they come here. State's falling down on the job, in my view."

"But those two guys. They're, um, under wraps now?" Tulliver asked disingenuously.

"They've been recalled, sir," Haley replied with no explanation.

Tulliver sat straight up in his chocolate leather chair and cleared his throat. "Eh, good. Good work. Recalled. Fine. That's fine." He nodded deeply and began to shuffle through the stack of paper piled in front of him.

Haley rose to leave.

"And those, those Africans we were supposed to bring in under CHASM . . ."

"Scratched, sir. Only a half dozen were brought here before the President's mission. After the mission, ah, didn't realize success, I called Goldman and told him to put a freeze on any further resettlements of Sudanese."

"That's good too. The very nerve of those people ordering the President of the United States to leave -- and during a peace mission -- simply goes beyond the pale."

Tulliver leaned back in his chair, folded his hands over his round belly, and stared out on to the South Lawn. Jutting his lower lip out and squinting, he took on a contemplative pose.

"You know, it just goes to show their primitiveness. We've got our hands full with our own after all. I never felt easy bringing in all those Liberians. Talk about risking blowing the cover on the program. Sorry to say it, but it's in the nature of the Negro--"

There was a tap on the door. Buckwheat Thompson entered. He instantly caught Tulliver's eyes and held them with a grave look. He clutched a bunch of papers in one hand and a fountain pen in the other. He did not acknowledge Haley's presence.

"Sorry to barge in."

There followed an awkward silence. Thompson stood still as a monument as he sought carefully his next words. Tulliver looked at him expectantly. Haley folded his arms and leaned forward from his perch on a window well.

"Well, what is it then?" Tulliver demanded.

"Big problem. Maybe. You know Win Ferret. Ambassador Goldman's guy who handles the Yugos?"

Tulliver searched his mind.

"Yeah. That fruitcake who mouthed off at the CHASM interagency meeting the other day. Until then he'd been a wallflower, taking notes for Goldman," Haley said.

A light of recognition flicked on inside Tulliver's head.

"That's the one," Thompson said. "Last Wednesday night, he went home from the office at his usual time, had dinner with the family, watched some TV, then proceeded to slaughter the whole lot. Including the dog." Thompson wore a wide-eyed stunned expression accentuated by large, horn-rimmed glasses. He carefully seated himself on the sofa in the middle of the expansive office.

Tulliver slowly sat forward and alert. Haley did the same.

"He methodically bashed the brains out of each of them. His 69-year old mother, his wife of sixteen years, and their three sons, Win, Jr., 14, Brandon, 11, and Jeremy, 5." Thompson spread out on the coffee table in front of the sofa a series of photographs. He then turned his head away and contemplated the Washington Monument which towered just beyond the South Lawn.

Haley, followed by Tulliver, got up and went toward the coffee table, cautious in their steps as if approaching a time bomb.

"Oh, Jesus," Tulliver said barely audibly. Before him lay black and white police shots of the crime scene and the victims. Laid out in accordance with the age of the victims, the first photos were of Cloris Ferret, the mother, with a large, blood-caked hole where her left eye socket had been; her hair was singed away and her clothing blackened ashes caked to her body. The next series revealed an unrecognizable young woman's burnt body; the parietal and temporal areas of the left side of her skull were missing. The rest of the photos showed the charred remains of the three boys. Their heads were likewise smashed. The kindergartner's head was wrapped in a knotted towel.

Tulliver looked up at Thompson aghast.

Thompson was nodding. He looked straight at Tulliver and said coolly, "The police say that he tied the towel around little Jeremy's head to keep the boy's brains from spilling out into the van."

"Van?" Tulliver asked.

"Oh, yeah. After he killed them. He loaded them into the back of the family minivan, covered them with a blanket, loaded a shovel and a filled gas can and drove three-hundred miles to North Carolina. Out in the middle of a forest, he dug a shallow grave, dumped the bodies in, poured the gas over them and set them on fire. Trouble was, five bodies piled on top of each other on a moist forest bed don't burn too well. A park ranger spotted the smoke from a distance and called in other personnel to check it out. By the time they arrived, Ferret took a powder."

Haley, though pale, had been taking it all in dispassionately. "Do the police have an idea where he is?"

"Not yet. They're looking. The FBI is rushing down. There's an APB out on him. I asked the FBI to keep the White House informed."

Thompson laid out additional photos of the Ferret household. The scenes were grisly ones of blood-splattered walls, chairs and the boy's beds. The photographer documented in pictures the dragging of the bloody bodies from their death spots, through the living room, to the front door and out into the driveway where the van had been parked. A final photo depicted Leo, the dog, in the garage with his legs splayed, jump rope around his neck and unseeing, open eyes.

"Why, why'd he do it?" Tulliver asked incredulously. "Was he having emotional problems?"

"Any leads on his whereabouts?" Haley added quickly.

"Never mind that for now," Thompson said as if giving an order to his superiors.

Tulliver raised his eyebrows in an expression that important men give when put into the unusual position of being commanded to do something.

"He's got documents. Lots of documents," Thompson continued.

"Documents? Of what?" the other two asked in unison.

"Two safe drawers of files . . . on CHASM."

"Oh shit! Shit! Shit! Shit!!" Tulliver's exclamations turned from the religious to the scatological.

Haley's jaw muscles tensed. His eyes blinked nervously. "Documents he took from where?" he demanded.

Thompson again shook his head slightly as if in disbelief. Yet he sported a strange Mona Lisa demismile. "From Goldman's office . . ."

"That's incredible. Don't, don't those weenies at State check--" Tulliver began.

". . . and from here," Thompson continued.

Tulliver fell silent. His face had the stunned paralysis of a deer caught by fast-approaching headlights just before impact.

"From the NSC. From our office," Thompson finished.

The other men could not speak. It was taking them a while to absorb the enormity of the news.

"Let me get this straight, Buckwheat," Tulliver finally said, his voice trembling. "This guy, this, this . . . nerd, Ferret, takes a bunch of compartmented top secret documents on a program virtually nobody's supposed to know about, takes them out of the State Department, out of the White House -- out of offices of such high security that they practically strip-search people on their way out, takes them home, or somewhere. He then massacres his entire family, including the pet dog, hauls the whole mess off to some woods in North Carolina where he unsuccessfully tries to incinerate it. Then he conveniently disappears . . . *presumably with hundreds of documents on one of this country's most sensitive fucking programs. And, and the goddamn FBI can't find the son of a bitch?!!"* Saliva flew from his mouth as he spluttered the last sentence.

"Yes. Except for the dog. He left the dog's carcass in the garage." Thompson still sported a stiff, nervous grin. It and his quick, flip reply further fanned Tulliver's ire.

In a movement almost too fast for the human eye, Tulliver kicked the coffee table over, sending the horrific photos flying in all directions. "You think this is funny mister?! You think this is funny?!! That lunatic, that, that Lizzy Borden with a security clearance is in a position to bring this whole fucking Administration down! Is that something that amuses you?!"

Haley inserted himself between the two, and placed his hands on Tulliver's shoulders. "It's okay, John. I'm sure Buckwheat here feels the same as we do. We all want him caught and quick," Haley said soothingly.

Thompson sat on the sofa dejectedly, his head bowed, but the weird little grin still in place. "Yeah," he said.

Ferret wended his way at a deliberate pace in his red convertible. Under a boundless blue sky warmed by a perfect sun, he breathed deeply of his newfound freedom. The scent of pine from the surrounding forest brought only pleasant thoughts, of family nature outings gone by -- Lynette, the boys . . ., of his days as a young army lieutenant in the 10th Mountain Division, of camping in Quebec with father and mother . . . mother.

The stark, dramatic land and seascapes of the Gaspé invigorated him, released creative energies. And the

French language. So mellifluous, soothing. Thank God that mother, born and raised in France, saw to it that he was fluent at a young age. An awkward, lonely boy. Mother. Not gentle like most. The way she punished. So much pain. And shame.

The traffic on Route 132, which hugged the undulating coastline of the broad Saint Lawrence, was sparse. Wide open spaces to liberate the spirit. He took it all in with a wide turn of his head and again breathed deep. He closed his eyes for an instant. The wind ran through his hair, caressed his head. So good. So free.

The cache of funds he collected by liquidating assets over a period of weeks and days before . . . before quitting work would keep him going for years.

But he would not be complacent. No. Though he had expunged the evil from within himself, he was too aware that it romped freely in villages of the Balkans, of Africa, of the Middle East, in military bases scattered abroad as well as at home, in the hardwood-clad, carpeted offices and conference rooms of the loci of power. Places he knew intimately. They, the powerholders were the evil and they must be stopped. Ferret nodded with great conviction. He would expose them, and protect himself, using that which he had taken from the dark, dirty recesses where the evil was documented.

"A man is not a man unless he has complete freedom and the means to *survive.* It is a primal urge." Mlavic's voice resonated.

Ferret put a CD into the player. *Freedom is just another word for nothing left to lose . . .* He smiled.

CHAPTER FOURTEEN

Gallatin missed Lauren terribly. Her aunt, Celeste's sister, watched over her at the clinic every day Gallatin was away and reported to him each day on his daughter's progress: none. After his encounter with Ferret, the leads had dried up. But he wasn't about to give up. Not in a million years. Ferret's words kept ringing in his brain. The Branko's were "taken care of. Out of the way." Were they dead? Or locked up in some military prison? "They got through, but shouldn't have." Got through what? Escaped from confinement somewhere? Got through with a mission? A mission launched by the federal government? Then there was the warning. "If you dig too deep, you'll get hurt. Seriously hurt." Too many questions. And the hint of answers was ominous. His only child was lost, huddled in the far reaches of some emotional bunker, having fled the terror of losing her mother to cancer, having experienced the fire bombing of her best friend's house and the critical injury done to that child. In the event that he, in his quest to get to the bottom of this tragedy, brought injury

or worse to himself, could Lauren ever expect to return
from that distant desert of her psyche? Her hope for
recovery lay in her sole parent being there for her. If he
were removed from the picture, what hope would there be
for his daughter ever to lead a normal life?

He had returned to Cleveland, and his office, after
ten days. He focused on his job, worked through the back
caseload, pleased his superiors with the results. But his
heart was not in it. And the nagging questions kept echoing
in his mind along with the teasing bits of revelation
provided by Ferret.

He sat by Lauren's bedside early in the morning,
sometimes during lunch hour, and in the evenings until the
hospital staff kicked him out. Like an angel fallen from the
stars, he pondered, as he gazed at the sweet, yet
expressionless, face. Her straight, light brown hair invited
frequent caresses from a distraught father. But most of the
time he sat hunched forward, elbows on his knees,
contemplating the only thing left in his life that had
meaning for him. As he recalled good times, the three of
them on vacation, at cookouts, playing ball with family
members and neighbors, at prayer in church, tears welled
up in his eyes. The tiny voice, now silenced. "When will
Mommy get better, Daddy?" she had asked over and over
again during the final, agonizing week of Celeste's life.
Without his girl, he could no longer go on. Gallatin had
concluded that their mutual survival depended one upon the
other. It was as basic as that.

Ferret's voice continued to intrude into his thoughts.
"Deep down in your male's rough soul. Did you not feel
. . . sense just a twinge . . . free?" A sick man. But that
sick man was his key to getting answers. Gallatin rushed to
a pay phone in the hospital lobby, fumbled through his

address book and punched 202 -- the Washington, D.C. area code, and the rest of the numbers.

A female voice answered equivocally, "Mr. Fer--, er, uh, Office of Special Admissions. May I help you?"

"Mr. Ferret please. This is Michael Gallatin."

Silence.

"Hello? Are you there? Mr. Ferret please."

"Oh. I'm very sorry. Mr. Ferret . . . is no longer at this office. Good day," Gerrie, the receptionist, replied.

"Wait!" It occurred to Gallatin in that flash of an instant that trying to get any kind of information even indirectly related to his personal investigation of the Suleijmanovic killings always seemed to be like attempting to catch snowflakes intact. "Can you give me a forwarding number please?" Gallatin's heart was pounding. He wiped the sweat off his forehead with his hand.

Silence.

"Ma'am? You still there ma'am?"

"Uh, yes. Of course. Mr. Gallatin, may I ask your relationship to Mr. Ferret?"

Now it was Twenty Questions time. His mind raced to seek a snap analysis of what was going on as well as an answer that wouldn't have this skittish functionary hanging up on him. It was evident that the woman was screening Ferret's calls and that Mr. Joe America had little chance of getting anything more than an assurance that she would "leave a message."

"I'm . . . I'm with the Nuclear Regulatory Agency. I've been working with Mr. Ferret on a . . . a special project. I'll be discussing this with him further by secure phone. But at this time, I need simply to talk with him about a convenient time when he could . . . come over here to meet with us." He blinked in astonishment at his own rabbit-out-of-a-hat imagination.

"I see. Well, Mr. Gallatin. A tragedy has occurred. Mr. Ferret, you see . . . his family was murdered early this week. And Mr. Ferret . . . he has not shown up."

Gallatin's budding pride in his mental and verbal legerdemain dissipated in an emotional vapor as the full impact of Gerrie's news made itself felt. It was a blow-between-the-eyes shock for which he wasn't prepared. And he struggled to comprehend it. It would take much more time for him to try to fit this grim development into the rest of the mystifying puzzle with which he was struggling.

"Why, I saw Mr. Ferret just the other day . . ."

"I suggest that you speak to the police, Mr. Gallatin. They may be interested in what you know about Mr. Ferret." Then, in a hushed voice, she said, "The FBI is crawlin' all over this place. And the *Post* too. They're runnin' a front page story on the killings. We've been in enough shock already, God knows."

"What do you mean?"

"Why, with Ambassador Goldman being removed and all. Tuesday he's running things like always. Wednesday he's fired. Well, he tried to hang himself at home last evening. Downstairs in the basement. And with his family upstairs watchin' TV. Poor man. If it wasn't for the creakin' of the water pipe he used as a gallows, he'd be dead too. His wife ran down and caught him before his neck snapped. We here guess that Mr. Ferret's killin' his family the way he did -- if he did kill them, mind you -- on top of his being sacked was just too much for him to handle."

"Ms--, uh, Gerrie. Who replaced Goldman?"

"Why, you musta heard through your office--"

"I've been away on a trip. Haven't caught up on things."

"Right. Well, it's Col. Maxwell E. Kaiser, U.S. MA-rines," she stated indignantly. "He's making big changes. Thinks we're all a bunch of kids in boot camp. You think this place was paranoid about guarding secrets before, you should see us now! Most of us civilians are sending out resumes. Ms. Hitz has also left. She's in the nuthouse. Just checked out. Poor thing. No family to take care of her--"

"Gerrie. Sounds like you've got your hands full. Thanks."

"I really think you should talk to the FBI. I'll get one over here--"

"Gotta run. Hang in there." Gallatin hung up.

The galactic leap from Wheeling-hick/fresh-out-of-grad school ingenue to junior staffer at the NSC was more than Lisa Valko could take in. But the meteoric jump to Director of Public Information after only a few months on the job was truly heady. In the rare moment she had to herself, Lisa would ponder her phenomenal success, but then stop. It was scary. If she allowed herself the luxury of navel-gazing, self-doubts about her abilities would surely arise. No. She would hang on to this career rocket for all she was worth and do her absolute best even if it did mean losing ten more pounds, adding wrinkles to her young face, and sacrificing anything resembling a social life.

Among the fast growing pile of yellow message slips which her secretary was neatly building on Lisa's upper left corner of her desk -- flush against a stack of unread, terse military analyses of the crisis du jour, just an inch away from a two-tiered in-box overflowing with memoranda, press guidance, cables and congressional correspondence, within an arms-reach of the half-eaten remnants of a cafeteria breakfast -- were three from Craig, the last one marked "URGENT."

She closed her eyes tightly and massaged her forehead with the fingers of both hands. "I don't need this!" she asserted through clenched teeth.

The phoned buzzed.

"Yes!" Lisa said impatiently.

"It's Senator Ballard's office. His administrative assistant, Mr. Stratham, wants you to talk with the senator about next steps on the Middle East situation," the secretary said.

"I'll call," Lisa replied tersely.

"Miss Valko, don't forget the 11:15 meeting with Amnesty International in the Cordell Hull room."

"I won't." She wanted desperately to hang up. Her energy resources were nil. Her coffee-corroded stomach rebelled. Her mind was suffering from information overload and chronic sleeplessness. She was running on empty. Just a few moments of peace and quiet. To collect her thoughts.

The phone buzzed again. She picked up the receiver, then dropped it promptly, cutting off whoever it was who was trying to reach her. Lisa grabbed a small bottle from her top desk drawer and quickly washed down two Advils with a stale diet Pepsi.

Amnesty International had become increasingly vocal in criticizing the Administration's less than vigorous pursuit of war criminals in the ex-Yugoslavia. Haley had

tasked her to neutralize their criticism by getting
sympathetic media to run stories favorable to the
Administrations policies. "Offer them exclusive
interviews, show 'em some classified analyses. Fix it," he
ordered.

The foreign relations committees of both houses of
Congress were clamoring for briefings on the status of the
Hague Tribunal's progress in prosecuting war criminals.
"Dazzle them. Nothing like a multimedia laser show with
dancing pigs to get their minds off the problem areas,"
Haley instructed.

Lisa had acquired a reputation for dealing
effectively with the press and non-governmental
organizations. Her slick presentations, deft handling of
government agencies and clever media manipulation made
the Administration appear scrupulous and responsible.
Over the months, however, she detected a change in her
character. No longer the recently graduated ingenue, she
became tougher, decisive, comfortable in pushing people
around who were twice her age and possessed decades of
professional experience. "Ballbuster," she'd overheard an
NSC staffer refer to her in a conversation with a colleague
in the cafeteria.

And now Craig.

In the weeks he had been calling, she couldn't
muster the nerve to tell him it was over once and for all.
The memory of catching him with her college roommate,
Kimberlee, giving each other a body wash in Lisa's shower
burned in her brain. Never mind that Kimberlee had as
much sexual discipline as Catherine the Great, and that
Craig, pleaing drunkenness, was sweet and touching in his
fervent apologies. But something tugged at her. Was it her
ex-beau's heart-stopping good looks and warm manner? Or

was it her growing sense of loneliness and emotional suffocation under a mountain of crushing work pressure? She realized that she was vulnerable. She was, after all, human. And though she worked hard to subliminate it, the right male company would be welcome right now. A man with whom to share confidences, laughter and tender contact

Lisa never imagined that she would ever envy the dead. But a *New York Times* article she had read while on the toilet -- it was becoming virtually the only time she could devote to leisure reading -- fascinated her. Scientists had uncovered the 7,000-year old body of an Indian princess perfectly preserved in glacial ice in the Northwest Territories of subarctic Canada. Her skin was smooth and unblemished. She wore a leather frock decorated with in-sewn stone and quartz beads. Her long, black hair was held in the back with a deer antler barette. Ivory bracelets still graced her arms which were folded on her breast, over which lay the remains of meadow flowers. Anthropologists speculated that the young woman had been interred deep in a mountain chasm by her grieving clan.

The eternal coolness and solitude that the young woman had found in death had a mystical appeal for Lisa. Of course, one did not have to be dead to find peace. It was just that life could become so taxing that peaceful contentment could sometimes seem an impossible dream.

Gallatin's call broke her fleeting mental escape.

He fumbled for words and was exceedingly solicitous and sincere. Again, just like men in West

Virginia. He thanked her for taking the time earlier to meet with him and point him to the right official -- Ferret. She had one eye on the clock.

"So, now I'm asking if you could give me the low-down on Ferret."

Lisa was only half-paying attention. The reason she didn't give him her well-practiced brush-off was her recollection of the tragedy involving the women in his life. She was proud of herself that she hadn't lost the very human trait of caring.

"Ferret?" she asked. "Oh, the State guy. What do you mean, the 'low-down'?"

"I mean, what's the story? Did he really kill his family, and, if so, why?"

Lisa learned quickly that people assumed that if you worked at the White House, you knew The Truth about everything, be it UFOs, POWs, the latest news headlines, Elvis, whatever.

"Uh, well. I believe they've concluded he's crazy. Flipped out." Her secretary placed several more message slips on her desk. Five additional unread emails rolled onto her screen. The President was to give a press conference in forty-five minutes.

"At your suggestion, I met with Ferret. Strange man. But he told me something which has been gnawing at me."

"Mike, can you give me the abridged version, please?" Lisa's eyes were fixated on her TV monitor. CNN had a special report on the succession struggle in China. The office clock buzzed as it struck the top of the hour. She brushed hairs from her eyes. *I must get to a hairdresser!*

Gallatin paused, restraining himself from shouting at Lisa, who was already acting like one of the Washington high rollers, supercilious functionaries who acted as if the universe revolved around them. No wonder politicians were constantly running for office by blasting the bureaucracy.

"It's like this!" he said, barely controlling his anger. "Ferret told me that the Brankos were 'no longer a problem.'"

"Well, that's good," Lisa answered absent-mindedly.

"What's so good about it?! Don't you get it? Listen to me!"

Lisa sat up with a start. This man was fast becoming an irritant. She simply didn't have the time.

"They *killed* the Brankos. Because those two got out of control; went on a rampage. They burned down the house of a Muslim family, with my daughter in it! They tried to kill me!"

"All right, so who's 'they' -- that is, the ones who killed the Brankos?" Lisa said, challenging him.

"Your employer. The government. That's why I'm calling you."

"Why me? Call the FBI."

"You're at the White House."

"That makes me employed, not divine."

"Lisa, there could be a conspiracy . . ."

That was it. Yet another fruit cake. Give him any more slack and he'll be railing about the Kennedy assassination.

"W-e-l-l, uh, look Mike, I really do have to run. Good luck. Nice talking to you." She hung up.

Ten seconds later her phone rang again. Against her better judgment, she took the call.

"I want to meet. It's terribly important."

"I don't think so, Mike. I'm really up to my eye-balls--"

"*Please*. I'm not a nut. My daughter's life depends on this. I've *got* to know. I've got to find the truth. I'll be back in D.C. on Friday of next week."

Lisa paused and rubbed her forehead. She hated to be thought of as "ballbuster." "Okay. At Chez Nous, on M Street, at 12:30, Friday."

"I'll be there."

CHAPTER FIFTEEN

Israel was on a rampage in the Middle East, bombing the hell out of Hizbollah and Hamas. Iraq and Afghanistan were getting no more peaceful. North Korea was launching yet more missiles. India and Pakistan were at it again, two nuclear powers beholden to no one. And the Taiwanese parliament had just passed a resolution to declare formal independence from Beijing, certain to have Chinese sabres rattling. The world seemed to be falling apart. And now, a cresting tide of violence in the Balkans threatened to derail the decade-old Dayton Peace Agreement.

Lord Braxton, the United Kingdom's Foreign Secretary asked for quiet consultations on the Balkan situation. Quickly filling a foreign policy-making vacuum which he himself had engineered, Tulliver wasted no time in upstaging Secretary McHenry by dashing off to London to meet with the Brits. He took Lisa Valko with him.

Lisa got no rest on the eight-hour flight. It was all work. Hone the talking points. Prepare contingency press Q's and A's. Keep the State Department, CIA and Pentagon in the dark, the better to achieve progress. Inclusion equated to policy inertia as each player vied with the others. Tulliver took his cue from Henry Kissinger, the master of the fait accompli. When Lisa went to the restroom, she refused to look at herself in the mirror. She had earlier noticed the bags under her eyes in the rear-view mirror of a White House limousine and was well aware that wishing them away would not do the trick.

Her one consolation was the inclusion of Buckwheat Thompson in the small delegation. Of the several dozen professionals on the NSC staff, he was the only one who, refreshingly, did not take himself too seriously. On this flight, however, Thompson appeared uncharacteristically sullen, sitting alone staring out the window of his seat in the U.S. Air Force Boeing 757. She sat beside him.

"Your enthusiasm is infectious," she said.

He cracked an anemic smile. "Matched only by your laid-back manner."

"God. Is it that noticeable? I've been telling myself to ease up on the throttle, but events won't allow it."

Thompson stirred his double vodka on the rocks. "Take a tip from Uncle Buckwheat. Idle the engines for a while. Look around you."

Lisa smiled at his signature comment. She looked around the cabin, then shrugged. "Well?"

"All these workabees. They all harbor illusions of becoming ambassadors, senior advisors, agency heads, Ivy League profs. The most any of them will achieve, however, is an empty life and a firm place on the treadmill of broken dreams."

Thompson raised the tumbler to her and downed the contents. He signaled to the flight attendant for another. "What are you having?"

"I'll pass. My body is suffering from enough ravages already without taking on another."

"You're a better woman than I, Lisa Valko." He took the second tumbler, again raised it to her and brought it to his lips.

"Woman?" she giggled. "Let me ask you something, Munro Bathgate Thompson III. What keeps you in the game? You seem to be so bitter and jaundiced against the system. Are you nonetheless happy? If not, why not just unhitch yourself and go your own way?"

A look of bemusement crossed his face. "Fair question. For a long time I thought that I could actually change the system, make it more responsive to the human condition rather than to the egos of self-centered individuals. But I've come to realize that the way policy is made in 2006 is little different from the way it was made in 1906: the 800-pound gorilla gets his way and a loaded .45 beats four aces any day." He ordered a third vodka.

Lisa eyed him wordlessly, trying to puzzle out this sensitive, yet embittered man. "So, answer my question. Why don't you leave?"

He put his drink down and pondered, then looked at her thoughtfully. "Family reasons."

"But you're not married. And your mother lives in Pennsylvania."

"It's my partner," he said with deliberation. "My partner is very ill and needs me." He held his gaze onto hers. "I haven't told anyone."

"Ohh," Lisa said, understanding. Her face was a study of feminine caring.

"And you? Is there a someone in your life?"

Lisa groaned. "What life?" She relented and asked for a glass of Chardonnay. "I went through a painful breakup. Now he wants to get back together. Trouble is, I have neither the time to think it over nor to pursue a normal social life."

"Take a tip from Uncle Buckwheat. Don't crucify your love life on the weighty cross of career." He winked and imbibed. Then, changing subject, he continued, "This Ferret business has been bothering me."

Lisa froze, looked at him intently.

"Something wrong?"

She shook her head slightly, as if shaking off an extraneous thought. "Uh, no. It's just that somebody else just mentioned that name to me."

"Who?"

"Michael Gallatin. Remember? You met him in my office."

"Yeah." Thompson leaned back and thought for a moment.

"He's convinced there's something fishy. He blathered on about a conspiracy. I have to be nuts. I'm actually meeting him next week over lunch."

"Love interest?" Thompson asked playfully.

She hit him not so lightly on the shoulder. "Don't be silly. It's just that . . . just that--"

"You're lonely . . . and he's a hunk maybe?"

She was unswerving. "So what exactly bothers you about the case?"

"Ever wonder what would drive a guy like that to murder his family?"

"He wasn't running on a full chip. Software crash."
She tapped the side of her head. "That's what they're
saying. Makes me shudder to think what he did."

"Maybe it was more. Maybe his conscience had
gotten to him. And don't speak of him in the past tense.
He's running loose somewhere as we speak."

"Conscience? For what? Resettling refugees? I
don't get it."

Thompson contemplated the ice in his glass and put
on his tight, nervous smile. He then looked at Lisa
squarely.

"Tell your friend, Gallatin, not to get close to this
case. His life could depend on it."

She looked back puzzled.

Thompson shrugged his shoulders. "Murder should
be left to the professionals."

Tulliver's favorite hotel in London was the
Dorchester. It was one of those classic British lodging
establishments where the elegance was unostentateous, yet
unmistakeable. Perfect for diplomats given to
understatement and discreet, sensitive liaisons, unofficial as
well as official. Neither baroque nor Hiltonesque
modernity fit his dry New England character. Victorian
came closest.

The meetings with the British had gone well.
Tulliver ensured that much of the discussion involved only
the British Foreign Secretary and himself -- and one
notetaker from each side; Lisa was Tulliver's. He was
eager to report the positive results immediately to the

White House. As his traveling retinue began shuffling out
of the suite, Tulliver signaled Lisa to stay behind as he
punched Lt. Col. Dan Haley's office number on the portable
STU-III secure phone. Tulliver held a much-needed, 4-to-1
crisp Martini in the other hand. He gestured for Lisa to
help herself at the makeshift bar in the corner.

As she fetched herself a Coke, she caught snatches
of conversation, though Tulliver had his back to her. He
gave a rundown on the consultations, then asked what was
happening at the other end.

"Fennimore? Wants to see me? I said goodbye to
the poor slob already--. He's angry? Well, that's tough
shit. The son-of-a-bitch should've . . . Wants to tell me
what? Aww, Dan! I leave town for a couple of days and
you start going soft on me. Fennimore's history and I have
you to thank for it. Tell Marge to take the calls but
otherwise to be non-committal. He's in therapy, right?
Have Marge send him a get well card from me. That's the
last I ever want to hear about that loser.

"McHenry. Hah! I didn't know he'd come out of
his coma," Tulliver said sarcastically. Dan, I'm looking to
you to make sure he's shut out on this thing. I don't care if
he does complain to the President. Send him over some
anodyne horseshit. Make something up. I'll deal with him
when I get back. Meantime, you keep State tied up in
knots, doing what they're good at: wiping each other's
asses."

Tulliver snorted gleefully and gulped his Martini.

"Goldman tried to do himself in? How? Jesus.
What is it with these guys anyway? I told you they were all
weak characters. The house cleaning came none too soon.
Kaiser's just the guy we need over at State. A kick-ass-
and-take-name Marine."

For the first time, Lisa got a glimpse of the real Tulliver, shorn of his official veneer. And she didn't like what she saw and heard. As she sipped her Coke, she pondered whether the absence of humaneness in her professional life came with the territory or emanated from this lone, power-driven figure. And what a contrast Buckwheat Thompson was in this sterile, testosterone-overdrive environment.

Tulliver stiffened. He looked around furtively, then cupped the phone receiver's mouthpiece with one hand and hunched like a beast over a fresh kill; the bold statements turned to muffled conversation. Lisa heard "First Lady" but nothing else. After a minute, he raised his voice again to issue last instructions, said a hasty goodbye and hung up.

Tulliver lowered himself into the reproduction Louis XIV desk chair and commenced to scribble notes, not acknowledging the presence of another human being in the room. Lisa felt uneasy. After several awkward moments, she rose quietly, took her purse and began to tip-toe toward the door.

"Lisa." Tulliver pronounced her name in the same stretched-out tone that her mother used when, as a little girl, she sought clandestinely to filch a cookie from a jar. Tulliver continued his writing, did not lift his gaze. "I'd like you to do something."

"Yes, Mr. Tulliver."

"John."

"Yes . . . John."

"Have a seat."

Lisa reseated herself on the sofa.

"I want you to write up the results of our meetings with the British. Make it 'Eyes Only - for the President.'"

"Right. By when do you need it?"

"You can draft it on the plane tomorrow. Give it to
my secretary to put in final. I want the President to have it
right after we put into Andrews. I don't want it transmitted
electronically. No one is to see it besides the two of us. *No
one*. Understand?"

Lisa nodded.

Tulliver finished his scribbling. He placed his notes
into a large envelope. Finally, he looked up at Lisa. A
slight grin formed; his eyes fairly sparkled over the half-
lenses of his reading glasses. He appeared as if the not-
inconsiderable weight of the work of state had magically
lifted.

He went to the bar and replenished his Martini. He
turned to Lisa and raised his eyebrows to solicit her drink
preference.

"Oh. I've got a Coke," she murmured.

"Ever been to Cuba, Lisa?"

"Why, no. Not exactly a vacation mecca for
Americans these days."

"They make a splendid refreshment called Mojito.
It was Ernest Hemingway's favorite. The best is still served
at one of his old watering holes in Old Havana, *La
Bodeguita*." Tulliver expertly threw together dark rum,
lime juice and ice in a mixer, shook the concoction and
poured it into a glass with seltzer which he garnished with a
mint sprig. He handed it to Lisa. "Salud!" He extended
his glass.

Lisa took the drink, clinked glasses and sipped the
Mojito. The ice-cold tartness went down well. She hated
to admit it to herself, but it was just what she needed on the
heels of non-stop work amid impossible deadlines and a
cardiac-inducing crisis atmosphere.

"You know, Lisa, we're very happy with your performance. A woman so young who has such a firm grasp on things is a rarity."

Lisa smiled at him.

"I'm convinced that you have squelched more criticism of the Administration on the Bosnia situation than otherwise might have been the case." He refilled her glass.

She'd been thinking long and hard about the punishing work pressure and her yearning to free herself from it. For weeks she had been rehearsing a request for lighter duties to deliver to Tulliver or Haley when the opportunity presented itself.

"The work is great, but I--"

"Sshhh," a clearly tipsy Tulliver expressed with one finger to his lips. "I propose a toast." He stood up and offered his replenished glass. "To peace in the Balkans."

Ever alert, Lisa rose instantly, though the rum had already affected her sense of balance, causing her to waver. She lifted her half-empty glass, which Tulliver wasted not a second in filling.

They again clinked glasses and drank. Hers was full yet again before her dulled brain could sense the action.

"And to the foreign policy successes of the President," Tulliver added.

They toasted and drank again.

Lisa fell back onto the sofa and let out a very deep breath. She took a long draw of her Mojito, which, on an empty stomach, shot like a comet to her benumbed brain. With her eyes shut tight, all of her senses seemed to concentrate on the tingling burn of the ice-cold Mojito wending its way effortlessly down her willing gullet. She kicked off her shoes and wiggled her toes. They were unfeeling.

By the time she sensed Tulliver's body next to hers, she had no idea whether it was a minute, five minutes or fifteen minutes later.

"And here's to another four years of President Merriman," he slurred.

To Lisa's unwarranted surprise, her glass was again filled, this time topped with a fresh sprig of mint. Without a care, she slugged it back.

"To . . . to peace in our time!" Lisa squealed as she rose uncertainly, raised her glass, took a swig, and dropped like a rock back onto the sofa.

Tulliver reciprocated and fell back with her, one arm around her shoulders.

The beneficent smile on Lisa's face would not go away. She hadn't felt so carefree since . . . since Craig and she went on the greatest erotic camping trip of all time in the Adirondacks. Her mind launched her back two years. Her eyes again shut tight, the vision of her and Craig making love, gloriously naked, shamelessly, for all of God's nature to witness, on the bank of a small lake returned to her, a long-dormant memory now uncovered, like a lost treasure.

The hand on her breast was not gentle like Craig's, but coarse and hurting. Through the mental light-years of Mojito-induced mellowness, her mind was vaguely aware that a male was partaking sexually of her body. She felt a warmness between her legs.

With effort, she opened her eyes to see the President's National Security Adviser nuzzling her left breast, one hand petting her inner thighs.

From deep inside her came a command. *Wrong! Wrong! Wrong!* This was not Craig. This was not love. This was not right. She ordered her brain to come to.

"No!!" She stood erect just as Tulliver was unzipping his pants. Her drink spilled onto the reproduction tapestry carpet depicting the martyrdom of St. Anne. The room spun. She caught herself from falling right onto the man who was trying to bed her. She placed one hand just over her brow and struggled with all her might to stay conscious.

Warm lips moved along her neck. She opened her eyes and turned her head to see Tulliver, naked from the waist down, caressing her from behind, tugging her unbuttoned blouse off. He pressed his groin against her. She was not in control of herself mentally nor, in this man's grip, physically. The more she resisted, the tighter he held her.

"I've . . . I've got to . . . to go," she mumbled. "Please . . ."

Tulliver's tongue licked her left ear. The resultant tingle combined with the Mojito buzz to make her feel weaker still.

"Lisa. Be with me. Live for this moment. It is our moment. To be together, alone. We've earned this pleasure," Tulliver breathed between kisses.

A flaming arrow of alertness shot through Lisa's core. She opened her eyes wide and went rigid.

"NNOOOOOO! Ayeeeeee!! H-e-l-p!!!" she screamed with all the force of which she was capable. Both elbows jolted backward, catching Tulliver in the solar plexus and right kidney.

The 195-pound Tulliver went flying backward and down onto the marble floor. He clutched his mid-section and turned crimson with pain. He couldn't breathe.

Lisa held her own breath as she feared she had caused Tulliver to have a heart attack or some other lethal

reaction. Adrenaline having overcome alcohol, she felt that
she should panic, but didn't know how and remained frozen
in place.

"Insane . . . bitch," Tulliver finally coughed.

Rather than feeling further threatened or even
insulted, Lisa felt relief -- that her boss was not having
cardiac arrest after all -- followed by shame. Then the
ridiculous sight of the President's top foreign policy adviser
writhing on the floor with his pants down, hair tousled and
stunned expression on his face was almost clownish, but
Lisa did not laugh. Instead she readjusted her bra, buttoned
her blouse and looked for the exit.

Firm knocking came from the entrance door.

Lisa and Tulliver looked at each other. The
knocking became louder, followed seconds later by the
metallic sound of a key entering the lock.

"Who is it?" Tulliver yelled with effort.

"Hotel security, sir," a male voice shot back.

With the second-nature speed of an Olympic
athlete, Tulliver had his pants back on and dashed down the
walkway to the door. He pushed his hair back, then opened
it.

A mustached gentleman clad in tweed greeted
Tulliver deferentially, but tilted his head to view inside the
suite. "Pardon, sir. But there was a scream."

"Yeah, right. It's my . . . my assistant here. She,
um, dropped a vase on her foot. She was moving it."
Tulliver kept the door half-closed.

"I see," the other man said doubtfully. "Shall I call
for medical help?" he offered. He leaned further to catch a
glance. "May I come in?"

Before Tulliver could respond, Lisa strode up,
paused for an instant for Tulliver to let her by and stepped

out into the hotel corridor graced with this sentinel of safety. She kept her eyes straight ahead.

"Yes, it's nothing. My foot is fine. And so is the vase." With long, deliberate strides, Lisa Valko gave herself as much distance as she could that night away from John Tulliver.

CHAPTER SIXTEEN

Lisa liked Chez Nous for its genuineness. The close-in, cozy French bistro remained at the same Georgetown location for twenty years, having undergone little remodelling during that time, a rarity in Washington's trendiest area. It was where she used to go with student friends when they wanted to splurge.

To Mike Gallatin, it was a nook in a world apart. For a man at home in gritty Shaughnigan's and familial Nostri Amici, a French bistro would take some getting used to, but not much. Its clientele consisting of the burnished Washington professional set, Chez Nous was, nonetheless, unpretentious, the service informal.

Lisa ordered a Kir. Gallatin took a draft beer. The waiter, young, clean-cut and fit, lingered nearby after serving the drinks.

"Come here often?" Gallatin began in an effort to break the ice.

Lisa took the place in with a slow sweep of her eyes. "Not any more. I used to before I-- my life changed."

"So, how have you, or, rather, has your life changed?" He looked at her intently and took a sip of beer.

Images of old friends sitting around cozily comparing job prospects, boys and dreams of the future flashed through her memory, followed alternately by the excitement and interminable work at the White House; her family's pride in her. Then the scene of her near-rape at the Dorchester ripped through her brain, causing her to jerk involuntarily. She spilled half of her Kir into her lap.

Gallatin jumped forward and patted her stained dress with his napkin. "If you get it to the cleaners this afternoon, you might be able to save it," he said.

The waiter came over with more napkins and some water. He said nothing. Again, he stepped back and acted busy with some paperwork near the cash register.

"It's okay," Lisa answered resignedly. "It's a goner. I just don't have the time."

"I must've hit a sensitive nerve. "

"You did. I mean I was thinking of something else. Rather it's like--," Lisa braced each hand against the sides of her head and closed her eyes. She took a deep breath, lowered her hands, opened her eyes and looked straight at Gallatin. "So, Mr. Gallatin, it's your nickel," she stated stiffly. She was all business.

Gallatin said nothing.

She followed his eyes as they took in every inch of her from her limp hair to her fidgety hands. His deep-blue eyes were sympathetic, gentle. The still-boyish face, topped by a shock of thick, light brown hair, put her at ease. His manner was one of frankness and concern.

"I'm Mike, remember? Not 'Mr. Gallatin.' Maybe it's not my place, but you look like you could use six months of vacation and some serious self-indulgence."

Lisa regretted her initial formality. She desperately did not want to be thought of as "ballbuster."

She finished what was left of her Kir with a long gulp. "I've been under a lot of stress lately, uh, Mike. I need more than a vacation. I need a new life." She forced a laugh which made her appear that much more strained. His soft, searching gaze eased her a bit. How long had it been since a man had looked at her so benignly and with so much understanding? With such gorgeous eyes?

"But you've come all the way from Columbus."

"Cleveland."

"Right. Cleveland. So, it must be important." She leaned forward on her elbows, challenged him with her eyes, smiled.

"It's like I said on the phone," he blurted; then restrained himself. "Look, I'm sorry if I came on a little strong when I called last week."

"Apology accepted."

"I'm not a nut. Really. Somebody burned down the house of an immigrant family. While my daughter was inside. She's in shock. Her best friend is covered with burns. The girl's parents are dead. The police have no leads. I'm a trained investigator. Does that paint a clear enough picture in twenty brush strokes or less?"

"Yes," Lisa said in a low voice. She was carried by his intensity.

"So, to recap: Two Croatians named Branko, formerly Brankovic, firebombed the house, ran off to Minnesota -- but only after shoving an assault rifle up my nose. They burnt down another house in Minneapolis, with the occupants inside, after torturing them. The big mystery is this: they were brought to this country bypassing the usual immigration procedures. Why? After they went on their rampage, they were hunted down and terminated. Why? Who? If you ask me, it wasn't Fedex, or American Express, or--"

"Get to the point, Mike."

"It was the United States government. I think I know some of the who's, the what's, and the where's. What I can't figure out is the why's."

A piping hot Alsatian bean and sausage *cassoulet* warmed Lisa's insides. Almost immediately, a rush of energy permeated her limbs and brain. Her body, deprived of proper nutrition for so long, seemed to be telling her that it liked three square meals a day.

"Win Ferret knows all about the Brankos. I was trying to get hold of him again when . . . well, you know."

"He's nuts," Lisa countered. "He butchered his entire family. Not exactly a reliable source, if you ask me."

"How can you be sure that he did it?" There was an edge to Gallatin's voice.

"Did what?"

"Kill his family."

Lisa opened her eyes and mouth wide in astonishment, as if she had just heard that Ralph Reed had replaced Jerry Garcia in the *Grateful Dead.*

"Just hear me out," Gallatin continued. He pointed an index finger at Lisa. His *étoufée de boeuf bourguignon* sat steaming and untouched.

"Say you've got some guys in the government who are operating outside the law. They're bringing in a bunch of war criminals for whatever reason. Those who buck their control are eliminated. Professionally. To keep the lid on. National security and all that. Meanwhile, one of the cogs in the wheel of this covert program starts to act strange, threatens the whole enchilada. They go after him, but the operation gets botched. They miss him and kill, let's say the mother. Other members of the family are witnesses. It doesn't take a rocket scientist to conclude that the witnesses also must be eliminated."

"You can't be serious." Lisa laughed contemptuously.

"I'm as serious as Ollie North. I'm as serious as G. Gordon Liddy--"

"I get the point, Mike. Occasionally, things, people, get out of kilter, but--"

"But what? Everything is hunky-dory in the Land of Oz now? Maybe it goes further than that. Maybe they were out to frame him. Kill the man's family. Pin it on him. He gets the death penalty."

"I don't have to listen to this nonsense." Lisa wiped her mouth and signaled for the check.

Perhaps too quickly, Gallatin's hand braced her wrist. He retracted it. "I'm sorry. Really. Please." He motioned for her to continue eating. He dug into his beef and baked potatoes. Neither spoke for the next five minutes.

Lifting her gaze but not her head, Lisa asked, "How's your girl?"

Gallatin shook his head silently.

"I'm sorry."

"Are you . . ." He paused to search for the right word. "Connected? Anyone special in your life?"

"Yeah."

"Is he good to you?"

"I don't know. I rarely see him."

Gallatin looked puzzled.

"His name's Merriman."

Gallatin got the joke and chuckled.

"Yeah. Well. The great love in my life these days is called the National Security Council. But the longer our relationship goes on, the more I'm thinking that we're not cut out for each other."

"Then quit. Get a less pressured job."

"You men are all alike. Here I'm looking for sympathy and you're offering up answers. Anyway, the divorce proceedings may come from the NSC. I've pissed off somebody important for refusing to do his bidding." She lifted the cup of hot herbal tea to eye level and carefully studied the delicate wafts of steam rising therefrom.

"I'll never understand why people stay for years in Washington," Gallatin offered. "It's like everybody's on this giant treadmill. The faster they run, the quicker they kill themselves. Life is empty here. A vast wasteland of the heart." He finished his coffee.

Outside the bistro, they stood for an awkward moment. Both were aware that Gallatin's business remained unfinished. But there was more, a sense of leaving a party too soon.

Gallatin stared at his feet, then looked up with those sympathetic eyes. "How about a short walk?" He nodded toward the Potomac.

Lisa looked at her watch, then up. A dozen sudden-death obligations intruded in her mind. Her immediate instinct was to make haste. But she thought again. An Indian summer sun shone brightly above as a gentle breeze carried crisp pre-autumn air. She savored it with a deep inhalation. She took in the tall, intense gentleman with the

gorgeous eyes who had just invited her for a stroll.
"Okay."

They walked at a leisurely pace on the Washington
Harbor path, hugging the slow-moving Potomac. Office
workers, ties loosened, shoes off, lazed in the brilliant sun.
Couples on wooden benches had arms wrapped around
each other. In a sea of self-absorbed workaholics, this
place was an island of tranquility.

"I have something I must tell you," Lisa said after a
moment of troubled thinking.

"I'm all ears."

"Remember Buckwheat Thompson? In my office?"

"Yeah, the preppy-looking guy."

"Well, he told me to warn you not to get close to
this case."

"Why?" Gallatin demanded.

"He didn't say."

"He must know. I want to talk with him."

"I don't think that's a good idea."

"Why not? He obviously knows. About the
criminals coming here, about Ferret--"

"He's going through a difficult time."

"You think I'm having the time of my life?"
Gallatin's voice cracked. He regretted again losing his
cool.

"What's his job?"

"Policy coordination."

"What the hell is that? Don't you get it, Lisa?
You're a dupe to all those phonies you work for. They've
got you putting out the perfect smokescreen through your
P.R. work. What better person to have doing that than
somebody who's not privy to the truth? You're lying for

them, but you don't even realize it. And Thompson's got to be in on it."

The strain of being pulled in different directions, of so many conflicting emotions was becoming too much to bear for Lisa. She stopped and stared at the cloudless sky.

"There's something terribly rotten. In the government. In the White House. You're sitting right in the middle of it, yet you don't even smell it." Gallatin almost tripped over his words. He spoke with the conviction of a religious zealot. "Lisa, you're helping in a coverup. It's wrong. *Wrong.* Join with me. We can expose it. We can . . ."

Lisa studied his face with fascination. All sound was blocked out. The carotid arteries in Gallatin's neck pulsed. His eyes bored into her. A river of emotions poured, raged from his heart to hers. She felt the intensity of this strong, principled man, was swept up by it. His voice became a hum. Like the fiddles the old men played back in West Virginia on warm, summer weekend nights. Like her mother singing a gentle lullaby when Lisa was a small girl. Like the buzz of bees and the chirps of birds in the woodland meadows around Cayuga Lake near Ithaca. When she was free. When she was . . .

A flash of heat from somewhere deep inside Lisa snaked soothingly upward, through her heart, to her head. An electric tingle relaxed her muscles and anesthetized her brain.

Lisa didn't give Gallatin any warning. Of the sensation of a female body suddenly pressed close to his. Of soft lips on his. Of the blush of a young woman's gentle cheek against his face. Initial shock gave way to reciprocal affection. He held her tightly and kissed her hungrily. All other sensation was negated. To each it seemed that beams

of renewed life radiated from the other's body and were
sent back again, stronger in intensity. Two lonely, love-
starved human beings had nothing at that moment but each
other.

Lisa eased back, a stunned expression on her face,
eyes wide, unbelieving.

"Oh. I . . . I'm--"

"It's, uh, it's okay," Gallatin said gently. His face
exhibited an identical expression of surprise and
contriteness.

"I'm sorry. Why . . . I don't know what got hold of
me." She swept her hair back with jittery hands and fought
to bring her breathing under control.

Gallatin let out a nervous laugh. "We've both been
under a lot of stress . . ."

He fell silent. They stood apart, the eyes of each
locked on the other's. A 737 taking off from National
Airport roared overhead. The sad wail of a boat's horn
from across the river echoed on the surrounding buildings.
A slow, damp wind lolled over them, carrying with it the
fecund, slightly nauseating smell of stagnant shore water.

Gallatin offered his right hand, palm upward. Lisa
placed hers in it. Gently, he pulled her back to him and
they kissed again, this time with forethought and no shame
and with all the time in the world.

Gallatin skipped toward his car, parked on K Street,
downhill from Georgetown center, near the river. His head
swam with emotions. Strong emotions. Conflicted

feelings. He felt light afoot and weighted down at the same time. So much to think over. So many questions.

He grabbed the door handle and readied the key. Then he withdrew. He returned to the river edge to think. He sat on a bench and watched the seagulls flitting over the water, darting down when they spotted lunch.

The questions lingered, but at least he was getting a clearer picture of them as well as a sense of priority in how to tackle them.

Gallatin rose, inhaled deeply and stretched. He lumbered back toward his rented Maxima. Half-consciously, he pulled the key out of his pocket. He looked at it. Attached was a small remote device. Gallatin marveled at the pace of technological change that was taking place in everybody's lives. Micro-chips were taking over the world. He pressed the unlock button.

The blast blew him seven feet back, the heat singed the hair on his face and hands. A fire ball surged to the sky from the remnants of the Maxima.

Yet another question confronted Gallatin.

Tulliver did some of his best thinking with a couple of scotches under his belt. If he wasn't off to some Georgetown dinner affair or White House reception, Tulliver liked to reserve Friday evenings -- the two-to-three hours of catch-one's-breath time after the normal work day -- to share a drink with Haley and to take stock of things.

With his feet propped up on his desk, Tulliver contemplated his glass of single malt as if it were a crystal ball. Haley sat attentively, ever the Marine, on the billiard-green leather chair directly in front. He took tiny, infrequent sips of his drink.

"Dan, what job do you want at State?" Tulliver asked without warning.

"Sir?"

"When I'm Secretary of State," Tulliver replied. He took his eyes off the swirling liquor and looked matter-of-factly at Haley. "What? Name it. Undersecretary for Political Affairs? A nice, juicy ambassadorship? What? Name your reward."

Haley never liked Tulliver, but he did respect the man for his candor. The White House adviser would see right through false modesty which, when one came down to it, had no role other than to ease the conscience of a schemer. Besides, In Washington, only naive fools lacking in ambition would exhibit modesty needlessly. Haley took up the gauntlet.

"Well, the wife has her commitments and the kids are placed in good schools, so I'd prefer to stay here." He scrunched his brow and pondered for a moment. "Yeah. Undersecretary for Political Affairs. Hmm. That would be nice. Are you offering it?"

"You've earned it, God knows."

"When?"

Tulliver again diverted his attention from his glass to his assistant. "McHenry's right on the edge of a precipice and we helped put him there. First the Africa debacle. Then this Ferret affair. And Goldman trying to hang himself, the poor, dumb son of a bitch. Those were merely embarrassing to the Secretary of State until the leaks about Ferret's taking 'top secret' documents came out."

"I've got the *Post* eating out of my hand," Haley said coolly. "We can put the word out that he's a spy -- for Moscow; worse, Iran. We can work the Hill. I can have everybody clamoring for a 'house-cleaning at State' in no time."

"I don't know. It's risky. Those horse's asses on the intelligence committees will next be demanding to know what documents he took. It's State we want to smear, not the White House. Besides, CHASM's too vulnerable already. Can't risk exposing it. Or we're dead."

"What then?"

"Just keep working at it. It's only a matter of time. Who knows? The old fart may just keel over from a heart attack, a stroke. In any case, I've got things wired with the President. The First Lady's been of enormous help."

Haley glanced at the ceiling to conceal a knowing look.

Tulliver poured himself another scotch. He offered Haley a refill, but the Marine indicated that he was still working on his first.

"How's Lisa doing?"

Haley was somewhat taken aback by Tulliver's abrupt switching of gears. He'd wondered whether Tulliver's interest in the fast-rising young woman was more than professional.

"She delivers," he answered carefully. "Especially on the P.R. side of things. She has a knack for it. And, of course, with those radiant green eyes and dimples, the media guys love her. They trust her."

"And CHASM? Has she gotten any inkling?"

"No. Not that I've seen. She's got the public convinced that we're out there beating the bushes to nail war criminals."

"I don't know, Dan. She's risen too fast, taken on too much responsibility for a kid her age." Tulliver rose from his desk and, with glass in hand, sauntered over to one of the high windows facing the South Lawn. The illuminated Washington Monument stood like a glinting excalibur against the crisp autumn night.

Haley restrained himself from reminding Tulliver that it was he who had been behind Lisa's meteoric rise, insisting that she be given more responsibilities, resulting in her being in closer proximity to and spending more time with Tulliver.

"She's proven she can handle it," Haley said.

Tulliver turned on his heel. "Just do as I say, Dan! Give her less. Watch her more!" he commanded.

Haley winced at Tulliver's verbal blast. He nodded.

"She's real chummy with that . . . that faggot who works on your staff," Tulliver spat with disgust. He knocked back another single malt. His face was flushed; he blinked nervously.

"Sir?"

"Stop sirring me, for Christ sake! Don't you military guys ever speak normally? That little lap dog. Works on CHASM."

"Thompson."

"Yeah. How in hell did you ever let a homosexual get into this program? How did he get cleared?" Tulliver demanded.

Haley's mind raced. "Well, uh, to tell you the truth, I didn't focus--"

"Well, now's the time to start, mister!" Tulliver slurred. He sloshed half his drink on the floor as he pointed reproachfully at Haley with his drinking hand. "He works on CHASM? All the nitty-gritty stuff? Who we're bringing in? Where they're being settled. All that?"

"He coordinates operations. He gets his hands into all of it." Haley, with his eye on the prize of higher office, was careful not to defend his exceedingly competent underling.

"And the . . . the Recall Program?"

"No. I handle that personally, through other channels."

"Good. Keep it that way. But you keep an eye on him too. Closer even than on the paperwork needed to become a full-bird colonel. Got me?"

"Understood, sir — John."

CHAPTER SEVENTEEN

Ferret's voice clanked in Buckwheat Thompson's ears like a spoon in a garbage disposer. Totally unexpected and certainly unwelcome. But it commanded his complete attention.

"I'm not responsible. They are. You must believe me."

Thompson struggled to come up with a course of action. Signal to his secretary to alert security. Hold him on the line until a trace could be put on it. Persuade him to turn himself in. Listen first. See what he had to say. A current of heat rushed through Thompson's body, up to his face and ears.

Ask a question, he ordered himself. "Who? Who did it then?"

"Your boss," Ferret replied.

Puzzlement combined with panic to render confusion in Thompson. Before he could ask for clarification, Ferret, in rushed speech, added, "They, all of them, are responsible for the evil. The evil killed my family. The evil. I . . . I loved my family. *Don't you see?"* Through the receiver came sobs, followed by uncontrolled weeping.

"Listen to me, Ferret--"

"Now I must go," Ferret interjected, changing moods as swiftly as a devil's wind. "You know they want me? It's risky for me to stay on the line. They have ways. I know. CHASM taught me. Sources and methods. Tradecraft. All that."

"Ferret, this is an open line."

"Fuck the open line, Thompson! Fuck CHASM! And fuck your bosses! Haley's the one. He ordered the killings of the Branko boys. Did you know that? Also a bunch of Liberians, a Guatemalan, two Rwandans, others. Because those criminals had killed innocent people. Innocent citizens, all over the country. Did you know that? Did you?"

Thompson fumbled with a pen and paper to write it all down.

"They got out of hand, totally out of control," Ferret continued.

There was a pause.

"Ferret? Are you still there?"

". . . and so did I," Ferret said barely audibly. "So, now they're after *me*." The last sentence he sang as a child sings a playground ditty.

"Listen carefully, Thompson. I'm going to give you some passwords. Write them down. Fast. Then check them out. HRACK. RAWFOLD, CPRESS, UPIRAN, NFRACK. Bye."

"Wait, Ferret. You need help. I can--"

A loud click ended the conversation.

TOP SECRET
ULTRA
DISTRIBUTION: CHASM -- EYES ONLY: NAT
SEC ADVISER/DEPUTY   NAT SEC
ADVISER; NSC: CHASM COORDINATOR;
DIRECTOR OF   CENTRAL
INTELLIGENCE; SECDEF; JOINT CHIEFS
SUBJECT: OPERATIONS PLAN II: CHASM

Executive Summary

Overall USG policy objectives re Bosnia
aim at restoring stability to the ex-Yugoslavia,
political and economic reconstruction of Bosnia,
creation of viable Bosnian armed forces, ensuring
Serbian adherence to the Dayton Accords,
safeguarding human rights, elimination of radical
Muslim influence. Key USG policy objectives are
addressed in NSDD-43 (Tab 1). OPS PLAN I,
dated December 29, 1995 (Tab 2) addresses the
program, with interagency agreement, to remove
intelligence assets and others from the ex-
Yugoslavia to the United States for a period of time
to be reviewed regularly by the CHASM
Interagency Task Force.

OPS PLAN II expands on OPS PLAN I
accordingly:

--   As a measure to ensure stability, U.S. forces in IFOR will suspend pursuing select persons named as war criminals by the International War Crimes Tribunal in The Hague;

--   As a further measure toward restoring stability, efforts will be stepped up to remove and relocate those cadre in the Bosnian Republic (BR), Serbia and Croatia who pose a serious threat to the accords by their disruptive activities; agreement by the concerned governments has been obtained;

--   In this light, special arrangements will be made within CHASM to relocate key staff of PM Karadzic, Gen. Mladic and other key officers of the Bosnian Serb forces; the particular sensitivity surrounding these cases dictates further compartmentalization within CHASM as well as total identity reconstructions on all individuals to be resettled;

--   Monetary inducements will be offered clandestinely to Karadzic, Mlavic, et al., to resign, with additional, ongoing support offered to those who agree to relocate outside of ex-Yugoslavia. CIA to administer.

--   As a contingency, in the event that the new Bosnian government proves to be non-viable, certain resettled CHASM assets will be repatriated and assisted in assuming positions of authority as intelligence assets of the USG. These repatriated assets would

pursue assigned USG policy objectives
aimed at ensuring a stable government non-
hostile to U.S. interests;

--   In order to expand U.S. influence with
Serbia, USG cooperation with that country's
security, intelligence and military forces
shall be established on a clandestine basis to
include training and provision of equipment.
By no means is the Bosnian government to
know of this relationship.

The passwords that Ferret had so hurriedly provided
to Thompson yielded from the otherwise impenetrable NSC
computer databank a veritable motherlode of information
on CHASM and related black programs which was
accessible to but a handful of high-level officials.
Information on which Thompson had been completely
blindsided. And he was not happy about it.

As usual, the call caught Lisa at a bad time. Haley
had been steadily reducing her responsibilities. But her
resultant workload had become anything but lighter. Haley
took her off the hot political issues and moved her into
Science and Technology. The new portfolio was unsexy
and dense, requiring many hours for reading in. Instead of
attending meetings chaired by the President, instead of
performing telephonic triage with calls from the nation's
media stars, Lisa now sat in on somnolent conferences of
dry, third-tier technocrats who droned on for hours about
"marine infrastructure redevelopment" and "enhancing

localized participation in rural capital improvement
projects." Maybe once a week she would get a call from a
cub reporter at *Scientific American.* Her career was taking
a sharp turn, and she suspected why.

Thompson's voice did not reflect his usual self-
confidence.

"Lisa. I need to see . . . um, can we . . . you free for
. . . for coffee?"

"Uh, sure, I guess. How about tomorrow at--"

"Like right now?"

Lisa detected that Thompson was struggling to
maintain a normal, even tone to his voice. "I'm supposed to
sit in on a teleconference of the Interagency S&T Working
Group, but the more I get involved in these things, the more
it feels like S&M. Downstairs in the cafeteria?"

"Uh, no. No. Meet me at the Seventeenth Street
exit in five minutes." He hung up.

Thompson was uncharacteristically silent during the
fifteen-minute walk to the Old Post Office, now a trendy
arcade of boutiques and food stalls. They each ordered a
cappuccino, Lisa taking hers decaffeinated.

Lisa paid close attention to Thompson's face. The
dark circles and drawn expression told her that something
indeed was bothering him. He suspiciously studied the
crowds of schmoozing yuppies, gold-bricking office
workers, pressured attorneys and aimless vagrants. He
sipped his coffee absent-mindedly.

"Hel-l-o?" Lisa called as she leaned forward with
penetrating eyes to try to get her colleague's attention.

Thompson stirred as if caught by surprise. A faint
grin glided across his face. "Oh. Sorry. Daydreaming. I
guess. Sugar?" He offered her a couple of packets.

"No thanks. I'm trying to become unwired. No caffeine. No sugar. No booze. I'm eating a lot of fruit. Trying to get at least six hours of sleep every night."

"Found religion, or something?" Thompson said with a half-hearted stab at humor.

"No. Just trying to re-find a life. I've been among the ranks of Washington's Undead for too long. You're aware that I've been consigned to the coal cellar of issues."

"Who'd you piss off?"

"*Don Juan* Tulliver."

"Shit. What happened?"

"Oh. He just wanted me to take a position which, shall we say, had nothing to do with our nation's foreign policy."

Thompson looked at her gravely. "You're kidding."

"You're so naive, Buckwheat. Do you actually think that all the young women on the NSC staff are here as part of an affirmative action recruitment program?"

"File a grievance, for crying out loud."

"Get real, Buckwheat. These guys are pros at manipulation. They'd simply lump me in the illustrious company of Gennifer Flowers and Paula Jones. Just another Bimbo Eruption on the part of another flaky camp follower. I'm already burned out to the max. I couldn't handle the added pressures, the prying, the pain."

"So, you're content to waste yourself on bugs, drugs and slugs?"

"Of course not. I just need to regain my bearings. Find something I like to do. And then move on. Trouble is, Haley isn't making it any easier. He keeps piling on the bugs, drugs and slugs. I think he's doing it on purpose to keep me distracted, preoccupied. What I can't figure out, however, is why."

"Because you're a threat. That's why."

"Huh?" Lisa looked at Thompson uncomprehending.

"It takes one to know one. From one Threat to another, I advise you to *be careful.*"

Lisa shook her head. "Buckwheat, I don't follow."

Thompson rotated his head slowly, searching the crowds in a paranoid fashion. He then focused again on Lisa. He leaned forward to within inches of her face.

"Listen to me, Lisa. There are things going on you wouldn't believe," Thompson whispered. "Bad things. Very bad things. I've been used. You've been used. Unwittingly."

"Bad Things. Like what?" Lisa insisted.

Thompson became agitated. "*Like murder! Now just shut up and listen!*" His unkempt hair fell over his forehead.

Lisa jerked back as if just ducking a bullet.

Thompson again studied the masses. He focused on a bum sitting three tables away who kept looking in their direction. Then to a Greek at a souvlaki stand who was leaning back with his arms crossed. A Brooks Brothers-clad gentleman nursing a Dr. Pepper had his black-leather attaché case pointed suspiciously at them.

"C'mon." Thompson shot up, grabbed Lisa's hand and yanked her toward the exit.

Out onto Pennsylvania Avenue, Lisa stopped in her tracks, and folded her arms across her chest. "What the hell is going on, Buckwheat?!" she demanded.

Thompson looked around almost frantically. A Metro bus pulled up to the street curb. He leaped to the open door and signaled Lisa to follow. "C'mon. *Come on!*" Lisa followed.

As the bus pulled away, Thompson looked out the
window. He untensed and eased into the seat. "You think
I'm crazy, don't you?"

"Wrong. I know it." Lisa's face indicated that she
was not amused.

"I had to be sure that they aren't onto us."

"Who?" Lisa asked dubiously.

"Haley's men."

Lisa gave Thompson a sidelong look. "Buckwheat.
Your partner. What's his name?"

"Huh? Uh, Gordon. Why?"

"How is he?"

"He's dying."

"You're under a lot of stress. I can see it--"

"Lisa, be still and listen!"

Lisa obligingly fell silent.

"Have you heard of 'CHASM'? 'Operation
CHASM'?"

"No."

"'PAPERCLIP'?"

"No."

"Otto Ambros? Wernher von Braun?"

"Von Braun, sure."

"Father of the U.S. space program, right? Also
father of the V-2 rocket used to blow up thousands of
British civilians. Ambros, director of I.G. Farben. He
decided that Zyklon B was the gas of choice to kill six
million Jews. He was found guilty of mass murder and
slavery at Nuremberg. Six years later he's carrying out
chemical weapons experiments on seven thousand GI's at
Edgewood Arsenal, Maryland. Just like at Dachau. Why?
How?"

Thompson had Lisa's full, wide-eyed attention. She shrugged.

"At least sixteen hundred Nazi scientists and their families were resettled in the U.S. after World War II. Under PAPERCLIP.

"Project National Interest. Project 63. Heard of them?"

Lisa shook her head.

"The CIA and the Pentagon used them to slip more war criminals into the United States to work for universities and defense contractors.

"The Ninth Proviso? The CIA Act of 1949?"

Again, Lisa shook her head.

"Loopholes to allow the Pentagon and the CIA to bring in Nazis, communist turncoats, revanchist killers from the Balkans, sordid, sadistic monsters of every stripe. CIA alien agents whose covers were blown, mad pseudo-scientists, intelligence assets, Fascist murderers who also happened to be anti-Soviet."

Two fit young men entered the bus and seated themselves behind Thompson and Lisa. Thompson fell silent. He grabbed Lisa by the arm, marched to the front of the bus, obtained two transfers from the driver. They got off at the next stop and boarded another bus.

"Come 1973. Bam!" Thompson clapped his hands.

Lisa jerked back.

"Watergate blows the whole stinking mess wide open. Congress is appalled and reacts swiftly. The programs are ended. *Twenty-eight years* after they began. Can you believe that?"

"Incredible."

"Well, get this. It *didn't* end. The good folks at DoD and the CIA -- with the White House's blessings,

simply resurrect the Monster Witness Protection Program
in a new form. Hence, Uncle Sam's new Rosemary's baby:
Operation CHASM. But this time, they shift the operations
and budget over to State. They bury it all in the most
innocuous bureau at State -- refugee affairs. So, while the
Congressional oversight committees and the *Washington
Post* scrutinize Defense and the intel agencies with a fine-
toothed comb year-after-year looking for nefarious, hidden
activities, CHASM goes unnoticed. Only now we have
new clients. Having sifted through all the best Nazis and
fellow travelers, they start tapping Latin American death
squad commanders, druggie informants, Cambodian
Himmlers, African mass murderers, Russian psycho-
torturers, East German Stasi agents and, yes, the most
effective practitioners of genocide from the ex-
Yugoslavia."

     "No."

     "Yes."

     "But, why--"

     "Never mind that for now. We haven't got enough
time. This is what I've been doing for the past six years."

     Lisa looked at him searchingly.

     Thompson turned his face to the window. "I don't
know," he said. "You know how it is. You come to
Washington all fired up. Got to make your mark. Become
a big shot before you're thirty. The secrets. The
clearances. The arcane, insider rituals of 'National
Security.' Proximity to power. The prestige. You sell a
piece of yourself every day in this town trying to grab the
brass ring."

     Lisa touched his arm. "So. Why now?"

     Thompson turned to her. His eyes were sad and
scared. He swallowed hard. "Because . . . because I didn't

know the full extent of what was going on until yesterday. Ferret told me."

Lisa blanched. "*The* Ferret?"

"Yes. By phone. Of course, he's crazy, but I'm convinced that it was CHASM that drove him over the edge. He coordinated the Yugoslav program. His key agent was a PAPERCLIP graduate, a former SS man now named Glassman.

"People are killed, Lisa. The criminals and psychotics they bring over here kill . . . kill your next door neighbors, vacationers, children. These people are pros. Most know how to get away with it. The serial killings of those college girls in Texas since last year? A Guatemalan colonel is responsible. But the police don't know it. CHASM shields them even as it tries to track them down and murder them. We, I mean the White House, kill the killers who get out of control. No embarrassments to rock the ship of state, you see?"

It was too much for Lisa to digest mentally. She rubbed the sides of her head as if she had a throbbing headache. Her eyes turned from side to side as she sought frantically to piece together the entire picture of what Thompson was describing. Her mind raced back through the months, examining her own role in the Administration.

"Me. How do I fit into all this? How?!"

Thompson looked at her gravely, silently.

"*How!* I need to know!"

"Lisa. You were the smokescreen. Haley fed you the substance. You turned it into pretty smoke and blew it into the collective eyes of Congress and the media."

The impact of his statement hit Lisa in the head like a steel I-beam. Now it all came together.

"I've . . . I've been the Josef Goebbels of . . . of an administration of murdering hypocrites. And I didn't even catch on. I didn't even catch on!"

Thompson placed his hand gently on Lisa's forearm. "No. You were used. Much more so than I was. I knew, I was centrally involved. Now I'm going to get back. Blow it wide open. I've got documents. I'm turning them over to the *Post* tomorrow."

"How far up the chain does this go? The President. Does he know?"

"He knows about CHASM for Yugoslavia. He approved it. The contract killings, I don't know. If he does and it gets blown wide open, he can assert 'plausible deniability,' claim he had no knowledge, make his underlings take the fall. Like Ollie North did for Reagan and Bush. But something tells me he's not aware, that it's Tulliver's show, at least that there's nothing in the files on the assassinations. Haley must run things out of his hip pocket."

Lisa stood up and ran for the exit, holding her mouth as if about to vomit. On the way, she yanked hard on the stop cord. Thompson followed. They found themselves as the only white people in the middle of Northeast Washington's most crime-ridden ghetto. Their office garb made them stand out that much more. They felt as if they had no clothes on.

Passersby studiously paid little attention to the visitors from Washington's other side.

Lisa and Thompson looked around for a Metro stop -- the oasis, the escape hatch for nice, middle-class citizens who find themselves in the wrong place at the wrong time.

Two young toughs with the hardened expressions of junkyard dogs took immediate notice of the pair. They trailed behind in the animated gait typical of their generation and milieu.

"Just keep walking," Thompson said through clenched teeth. They quickened their pace as they passed by pawn shops, fried chicken joints, tacky wig and nail salons. So did the young men.

"What do we do?" Lisa said, looking straight ahead. "I see no taxis."

"Look for a cop. There's got to be patrolmen in this neighborhood."

Lisa stole a glance over her shoulder. "Buckwheat! They're closing in!"

"Yo. Yo man. Wait up," a voice shot at them.

"Great. We don't have to worry any more about CHASM hitmen offing us. We're about to become D.C's 999th and 1000th victims of random, lethal violence this year," Buckwheat said. "We're fucked."

"Hey man!" the voice was louder.

Buckwheat swung around with his palms extended outward. "Hey, look. We made a mistake coming here--"

"You tellin' me!"

Lisa clutched her purse to her torso and shut her eyes, braced for the worst.

"Glad to have you here man. Ya'll come and join our block party." The men smiled beneficently. "Our church is sponsoring it. Great ribs and corn. I'm Ralph. This here is Jake." They extended their right hands.

R-e-l-i-e-f was spelled on the faces of Thompson and Lisa who looked at each other as would a pair convicts just spared from the gallows.

"It just goes to show once more. In this town where appearance is everything, what you see isn't necessarily reality," Buckwheat remarked to Lisa as they shook the locals' hands.

CHAPTER EIGHTEEN

Stille gleicht Tod. In all the missions he had carried out over the years, Fechtmann never lost track of the basics. After all, it was attention to the basics that ensured human survival just as it did in the animal world.

He kept an eye on everyone who entered and departed the grungy, old apartment building in polyglot Adams Morgan. His vantage point was a bench in a small park just opposite. He had scoped his target over a period of weeks, taking careful mental notes of his quarry's routine. Off to the office at 6:00 am. Return was more problematical. Could be anywhere from 7:00 pm till midnight. That was okay. He was careful. And the whores and junkies and bums who hung around the park ceased taking second notice of the lean, towheaded man in Levis and leather boots. Even down-and-outers were entitled to their privacy after all.

Buckwheat Thompson raided every NSC databank he could intrude into, stored the information on disks and stashed them in his apartment. Personnel records, funding transfers, policy formulation, black programs. Everything on CHASM.

"Operation Breathing Space" -- to channel cash to the Somali warlords. "Operation Pilgrim's Pride" -- CIA bribes to senior Indonesian officials to ensure that an American aircraft manufacturer clinched a huge plane deal. Contingency plans on whom to back as leader of Russia when Putin finally departed the scene. And on it went. Onto the discs. Until Wednesday. The passwords no longer worked. Something was wrong.

Haley appeared in Thompson's office like a specter in the night. The sudden realization that his boss was inches from him as he fruitlessly scanned the computer files startled Thompson.

"Looking for something in particular?" Haley asked.

"Oh, just cleaning the files out." Thompson hurriedly logged off.

"Cleaning out the files is a useful thing. So is OpSec. What do you think?" OpSec -- operational security. Acronyms are to the Pentagon crowd what Hershey bars are to a chocoholic. Haley paced slowly around Thompson's office, one hand in his pocket, the other examining bric-a-brac, awards certificates, framed photos and other personal office paraphernalia. He picked up a piece of driftwood bearing a brass plaque from the *U.S.S Thomas Paine*. "Hm. 'For Exceptional Loyalty and Service Dedication. Operation Just Cause, January 1990.'" He turned toward Thompson. You were part of the Grenada mission?"

"Briefly. I was a lieutenant serving on the *Thomas Paine*. Everybody was awarded something. The so-called 'Oh, fine. I Was There in Eighty-nine' medals."

"Doing what?"

"N-2. Intelligence."

"You were awarded the Bronze Star. You must have done something."

"I was tasked with obtaining TACINT on a hill where a bunch of armed Cubans were holed up. I climbed the hill, took pictures and notes and radioed data in. No great shakes."

Haley parked himself in front of Thompson's office window, now with both hands in his pockets, and gazed out on the gray courtyard walls and inner parking lot of the OEOB.

"Loyalty. So important in a line of work where lives are at stake. Where if just one weak link in the chain breaks, the walls come tumbling down and people get hurt. You agree?"

"Yeah. Sure."

"On that hill in Panama, you took the initiative, and with positive results. But you remained in the chain. A strong link in the chain." He turned and looked Thompson directly in the eye.

Thompson said nothing.

"The point is this. In this outfit loyalty is rewarded. Disloyalty is punished. Just as it is in the military." He tapped his temple with a forefinger. "Remember that."

Haley glided out of the office as silently as he had entered it.

As soon as he was gone, Thompson called home.

"Gordon?"

"No. Hospice for Dying Gay Attorneys. How can I help you?" the voice at the other end said in a bare rasp.

"Stop kidding around. How are you feeling?"

"I'm not taking the AZT any more, Buckwheat. The cost isn't worth it."

"Don't worry about the cost, damn it."

"I don't care any more. I'm not afraid. It's the agony of waiting. I dread it."

"Gordon. Listen to me. How about you and me leaving D.C. Go to Santa Fe like we always dreamed about? It's always sunny there. Warm. You'd like it."

"You're a sweetie, buddy. But what's the use?"

Tears streamed down Thompson's cheeks. "I'm quitting, Gordon. We're leaving D.C. Hear me? I'm coming home."

Gordon hung up.

So did the CHASM security man tapping the line.

"I'm going to get a cup of coffee," Thompson lied to the duty secretary. He left his office, in its usual disarray, for the last time. His suit jacket remained on the coat hanger. His father's leather brief case was open on the desk.

Thompson walked briskly three floors down the ornate marble staircase of the beaux arts building. He ducked into the cafeteria and purchased a coffee. Back out in the corridor, he looked around. Just the usual sample office population and blue-collar types moving supplies. Mindful not to rush, Thompson walked to the Seventeenth

Street exit, ran his building pass through the card reader and flagged down a cab outside.

He got out in front of Pollo Criollo, a Salvadorean chicken joint a block from his apartment house, and stood and observed. A half hour passed. Just the customary mix of Latinos, yuppies, strolling diners, African-Americans and African-Africans. A police van zipped by with its blue roof lights whirling.

Thompson strolled in a five-block circuit until he reached the rear of his building. Having quickly unlocked the door, he ran like an Olympic athlete to the stairwell at the end of the basement corridor, passed an empty laundry room, and scrambled up the stairs.

At the fifth floor, he paused inside the stairwell to catch his breath. He nudged open the exit door and peeked down the length of the hallway. Nobody. Nothing. Stillness.

He ordered himself to take stock for a minute. He was reasonably sure that no one had followed him. Everything else seemed normal. Certainly, by now, the duty secretary would notice that he was away far too long only to fetch a cup of coffee. *Shit! Why didn't I tell her that I was off to a late meeting? Shit!* He recalled Lisa's scolding him for being paranoid. *She's right. This job has turned my mind into mush. Time to get a life. Not much longer now.*

Thompson stood flat against the stairwell wall. He shut his eyes and breathed deeply. He saw his mother. She was smiling. She was stroking his hair. He was a little boy. Very sick. And she fawned over him. Assured him that he would get better. God will help you, she said soothingly. God helps all good, little boys. He wondered if God would help him now. He certainly had not been good.

Not since he was recruited into CHASM. Thompson made the sign of the cross.

He took his key out and slowly approached apartment number 5506 knowing that, one way or another, it would be the last time.

He paused. Cocked an ear to see if he could detect any telltale signs of Gordon. But all he could hear was the pounding of his heart.

As if he had all the time in the world, Thompson touched the key into the entry lockset of the deadbolt. He slipped it in silently one notch at a time. *Time to move!*

Thompson flung the door open, but was prepared to dash back. Just like he had on the hill in Panama.

The TV was on. Gordon never missed the evening news. He had always been a news junkie. Thompson left the door wide open. He stepped forward into the living room. Gordon was in his usual position in his usual house robe seated on his favorite easy chair watching Brian Williams.

Thompson came from behind. "Gordon," he whispered. "Get up. Time to pack up and get out of here."

Gordon didn't budge. Since he'd lost fifty pounds, Gordon tired easily. Sleep was his escape from the misery that wrecked health brought with it.

Thompson stood over Gordon. He placed a hand on his partner's shoulder. "Wake up, man! Let's get out of here!"

Gordon was stiff. Thompson shook again, harder. Gordon's head rolled back. The right temple was bashed in, the eye smashed. Brains, mixed with coagulating blood, fouled Gordon's robe, the arm chair and the carpet below.

All Thompson could do was to freeze. "No! No!"

He began to back away. The door slammed shut. It was too late.

CHAPTER NINETEEN

"Harder! Harder! Faster!"

John Tulliver felt he was too old for Olympic Sex. The worst of it wasn't so much that he lacked the physical stamina. It was just downright embarrassing for an already inhibited Yankee. A fifty-five-year old, overweight man boffing a forty-year old woman in contortions that would win the envy of Chinese circus performers was just plain ridiculous. At least the ambitious young women on the NSC staff were malleable. They let him call the shots. It was his nickel after all. Boss fucks subordinates. Boss rewards subordinates. That's the way it had been since the new republic's first diplomat, Ben Franklin, nailed every female he could lay his pudgy fingers on. Here the roles were reversed. Tulliver was the underling being fucked to earn a shot at promotion.

At least it wasn't in the Lincoln Suite this time. Screwing in Old Abe's bed went beyond embarrassment. It was sacrilege. The Rose Suite wasn't quite as burdened down with historical baggage.

"Now step up!" Manny Merriman commanded.
"Pull that ottoman over and stand on it." Her breathing was labored.

"Manny. Please come down. Can't we just . . . just cuddle. Or something?" Tulliver pled.

"I can't stay like this forever, goddammit! I'll lose my grip. Not to mention my desire. Now get up here!"

Tulliver sighed. He looked up at the First Lady, spread-eagled between the ceiling-high rear posts of the antique poster bed. Gloriously naked, except for spiked high-heels, and a coating of sweat.

Tulliver maneuvered the small ottoman to the foot of the bed. Gingerly, he stepped on it.

"That's it lover. Now come and get me. Get me!"

Tulliver held his now limp member as he struggled to maintain balance.

"Get it up! What the fuck is wrong with you? Get it back up!"

But fear of falling and sexual arousal don't work the same on all individuals. In Tulliver's case, the fear part overwhelmed the arousal part. He went crashing down to the floor. The Paul Revere silver tea set on the Townsend dresser crashed to the floor too. A troupe of girl scouts from Nevada participating in an awards ceremony in the East Room one floor below winced at the impact, certain that the ceiling of the old mansion was crashing down upon them.

A man and a woman of the White House service staff rushed to the suite and banged on the door. "Mrs. Merriman? That you in there? Are you all right?" the man shouted.

"Yes! Fine! Now go away!" Manny shouted back. She sat at the foot of the bed hugging her knees. She beheld the National Security Adviser sprawled naked on the one-hundred-year old silk Kashan carpet. "Oh, ho, ho, ha, haaa!" Manny squealed at the hillock of quivering, pink flesh which lay before her. She laughed uncontrollably for two minutes.

Tulliver pulled himself up with effort. He wanted to swat the First Lady. But career aspirations got in the way.

"Ooohh. Come here. Come to mama," she cooed, arms outstretched.

Tulliver obliged.

"Poor baby. Can't play mama's games? That's okay. I love you anyway." She stroked Tulliver's thinning hair. "Yes, we can cuddle. Come. Under the sheets."

Tulliver greatly welcomed the respite from sexual barnstorming. He lay with his head on Manny's breast.

"Manny. I'd like us to be honest with each other," he said after catching his breath. "Tell me frankly. What do you see in me? I'm hardly Antonio Banderas in pinstripes."

"Oh. Well." Manny played with her curls, her eyes searched for the answer. "Who my Antonio Banderas is -- that is, if I have one -- well, is my secret. You. You're fun. Yeah. You make me laugh."

Tulliver again wanted to swat her.

"Manny? Have you talked with your hus--, with the President about the Secretary of State job?"

"Oh, yeah. I did." Manny's mind was somewhere else. Her dancing eyes told Tulliver that it probably was with Banderas, or, at least, her own Banderas.

"And?"

"Huh? Oh. Yeah. Well, with this homosexual spy ring thing about to break at State -- why does State have all of these homosexuals anyway? And Buckwheat Thompson was right in the middle of it? With that slaughter machine -- what's his name?"

"Ferret."

"Right. That guy. Eeoow! Gives me the creeps!"

"Yes, Manny? And, what did, er, the President say?"

"Graham? I told Graham that he'd be nuts not to fire McHenry. Not a minute after the spy scandal is uncovered. I mean, it's been one disaster after another with that guy. He's sick and old, besides. Time to trade him in for a newer model. And do you know who I recommended as a replacement?"

Tulliver looked at her expectantly.

"Do you?" she teased.

"Uh, why don't you just tell me. I presume it wasn't Antonio Banderas." Tulliver barely held his sarcasm in check.

"John 'Flying Dick' Tulliver. That's who!" She poked his nose with the tip of her finger.

Tulliver embraced Manny and planted a fat kiss on her lips. He looked down at her, stroked her hair. "You're a remarkable woman. You have everything. Power, beauty, wealth."

"Brains?"

"Yes! Of, course. And with them, you always have the country first in your heart."

"But only in my heart. I reserve other places for other people."

Tulliver forced a laugh.

"Just think of it, Tully. If Graham does name you Secretary of State, you'll be able to fuck over the whole

country, the whole world, instead of just us girls in the lil'
ol' White House."

Tulliver could not force a laugh.

Lisa. It seemed that all of the women in Gallatin's
life met with tragedy, and that, as a result, torment was his
lot. His wife, Celeste, robbed by cancer of her beauty and
strength and, ultimately, her life. His daughter, Lauren, at
the wrong place at the wrong time, hurtled into deep trauma
and unconsciousness. Lisa. Against his better judgment,
he was falling deeply in love with her. Much faster than he
should. She, far into a lion's den of treachery, yet so
unknowing and innocent. Should anything happen to her,
he simply wouldn't be able to go on. He would give up.

He stared at Mr. Jameson straight in the eye. A
double, straight up, sat there, a mere foot from his lips,
beckoning Gallatin to loosen up, to let Mr. Jameson show
the way to fend off pain.

But Gallatin just kept staring Jameson down. So
far, it was a standoff.

Shaughnigan's was busier than usual for a Thursday
night. Working men often spent their paychecks the day
before they actually got it, and the onset of cold weather
tended to drive more of them to the bars.

The trio of musicians sang sweetly of lost loves and
homesickness. In due course, they would transition into
patriotic songs of battles lost and battles to be won. By that
time, the largely besotted bar crowd would be singing, or
slurring, along with them.

Gallatin reflected on his own battle. Over the well-being of Lauren. Months of personal investigation had gotten him virtually nowhere. The doctors told Gallatin that eventually Lauren would come to, but that her subsequent full recovery depended upon her ridding herself of the demons who put her in her present state. Gallatin needed to find those demons and strangle them. Only then Lauren would feel secure.

Jameson touched his lips to those of Gallatin. The old, familiar aroma of grain gone wrong wafted against Gallatin's face as seductively as a first kiss.

The glass fell hard on the oak bar and cracked, sending Gallatin's nemesis running in all directions. The bartender rushed over to wipe up the mess. He obligingly offered Gallatin a refill, on the house. But Gallatin declined, paid the tab, and marched to the phone as if his daughter's life depended on it.

"Lisa. I miss you."

There was silence at the other end.

"Lisa. Is something wrong?"

"I . . . need you, Mike. Please come." She was sobbing.

"I'm taking the first flight tomorrow. But I need to speak to your friend, Thompson, urgently. I've been thinking about it. He's the only link to Ferret. If he could help--, he's got to help. He seemed on the up-and-up. Ferret's the key--"

"Mike. He's dead."

"What do you mean?"

"Buckwheat. Murdered. Last night. With his partner. I'm afraid, Mike. But I know who's behind it. Come help me."

"I'm coming, baby."

News of the bloody murders of Buckwheat
Thompson and his roommate swept through the august
corridors of the Old Executive Office Building like a cold
wind. In hushed voices, NSC staffers strained to recall
encounters with the elusive deputy director of the Office of
Policy Coordination. A consensus was quickly building
among the overwhelmingly white, suburbanite NSC
professionals that such were the risks of living in high-
crime Adams Morgan.

The front office wasted no time in circulating a
memo from the National Security Adviser informing all of
the tragedy and containing Tulliver's own personal
condolences to the family. It suggested that donations be
made to Washington Children's Hospital in Thompson's
memory. Tulliver praised Thompson as "this most
dedicated public servant who devoted his life to the pursuit
of peace."

Haley's voice made Lisa's heart skip a beat. She
had no idea how long he'd been hovering behind her,
whether he had caught her conversation with Gallatin. He
leaned against the office shredder, arms folded across a
chest that did one-hundred push-ups every morning and
another hundred at the end of the day.

"Terrible news," he said in an even tone.

"Thompson," Lisa said.

"Yeah. He was a good deputy, at first. It goes to
show that crime touches everybody. I used to tell him he
was nuts to live where he did," he said, shaking his head.

Haley's professions rang hollow to Lisa. She held
back tears. "I've never had a friend killed before," she said.

"You two had become good friends, I gather?"

"Well, you work in the same office environment for months, you get to know people . . . a bit." She shrugged. "Do the police have any leads?" she asked, seeking to steer the conversation away from her friendship with Thompson.

Haley shifted from the shredder to the window. "Yes, as a matter of fact," he said with his face away from her. "Of course, we're being fully cooperative with the FBI."

"FBI?"

Haley turned around. "Yeah. Oh. You see. We've been investigating Thompson for some months now."

"Investigating? Why?"

Haley stood over her. "Espionage."

Lisa looked at Haley blankly, as if she hadn't understood.

"We shifted you over to science and technology in order to shield you from Thompson; to allow the investigation to proceed in secrecy and without undue interference. Now you can have an opportunity to get back into some of your previous stuff. Dealing with the press, which you do so effectively." He dropped a ream of papers on her desk.

"Here are the key results of our investigation on Thompson which we want you to draw on in briefing the media and congressional contacts."

Lisa glanced through the notes. The color drained from her face. "A homosexual spy ring? Centered at State?"

"Right. Thompson was in the middle of a growing circle of gay Foreign Service officers who had been recruited by Moscow to pass secrets to the KGB's successor, the SVR. Our preliminary findings reveal that

Ferret was Thompson's lover, that he killed his family first because he felt trapped in a heterosexual existence. Then he returned to murder Thompson after Buckwheat refused to break up with his partner. Same m.o. Ferret used a three-pound hammer to bash in the heads of Thompson and his boyfriend, exactly the same job he did on his family. Not very scientific, but effective. We've got the photos, but I figure it's best not to release them at this point. Not a pretty sight."

Lisa strained to try to follow Haley's tale of homosexual spy rings, lover's jealousy and murders. "So, um, tell me this. What's going on at State?"

"The FBI is rounding up a bunch of gay officers, including an Assistant Secretary of State and the deputy chief of Protocol. Based on our information. Oh, yeah. And McHenry's resigning at noon today. The President is appointing John Tulliver as Secretary of State. You can run with that too. We've got a complete bio package on John we want to disseminate as widely as possible." Haley formed a frame in the air with his fingers. "Contrast the drift over at State over the past two years with the positive results which John has achieved during that same period here at the NSC – on background, of course. 'Tulliver is the man the President repeatedly has had to turn to in order to save the Administration from terminal embarrassment, or worse.' There's the spin."

"Why me?"

"The press trust you." Haley paused. "Besides, we're all moving over to State. I'll be number three -- Undersecretary for Political Affairs. There could be something in the cards for you, Lisa. John Tulliver has his eye on you. Run with this one and, well, who knows?"

"These people at State who are being arrested. What evidence is there -- other than they're gay? I mean, courts need evidence, after all." Lisa's voice was strained. Her disbelief verged on sarcasm.

"Oh. They'll be fired. No trials." Haley looked at his watch. "Well, Lisa. I have a meeting in the Oval Office in exactly 25 minutes. You in?"

"Wait. No trials?"

"You're right. Courts need evidence. We have it, but, unfortunately, we won't be able to turn it over. It's highly classified. We'll invoke National Security. Remember Felix Bloch, the State guy caught spying for Russia in the late '80s? They fired his ass, denied him a pension. Wrecked that traitor's life. But, no trial. So, there's precedent. I'll await your answer tomorrow, at 0900 sharp." Haley closed the door gently behind him.

After he talked with Lisa, Gallatin sat alone in a booth with a cup of coffee. He tried desperately to piece together what was going on in Washington. In his mind, he painstakingly sorted through every piece of the puzzle, from the firebombing of the Suleijmanovics' house, to the rampages and subsequent killings of the Brankos, to a policy to bring dangerous criminals into the country, to Ferret massacring his family, to Lisa's unwitting role in a cleverly designed fabrication, to the booby-trapping of the car, now to the murders of Buckwheat Thompson and his lover. It seemed that the more pieces that entered into the equation, the less sense he could make of it. It was as if he were dealing, not with one picture, but several. At least the coffee kept his head clear. Jameson's would have numbed it.

His concentration was broken by a stirring rendition of *Wild Colonial Boy* by the trio. The beer was flowing, the spirits of the crowd were loosened. Gallatin frequently sought solace in the anchor of his ethnicity, in the comfort of familiar rituals. Subconsciously, he was returning to the womb, the womb of Eire in America. But many Irish-Americans lived a fantasy when it came to the old country. The nostalgia rooted half in myth, the Truth as forced by the political types, the denial that the world was changing as a new millennium unfolded, left a wanting, intolerant feeling inside Gallatin, intolerance with his own.

They began to pass the hat "for the lads." Half-drunk wage-workers tossed in amounts many could hardly spare. The hats filled. Noraid would be enriched still more by the New World to enable the Old World to fight its ancient battles. The money would buy weapons, ammunition, bombs. Should peace falter in Ulster, innocent civilians again would be blown to pieces, maimed for life, terrorized as they carried out their daily lives.

"Well, if it isn't the Prince of Orange," came a taunting voice as one of two circulating hats passed to Gallatin. "You can give, or you can get out," the tough-looking little man said.

Gallatin tried to ignore him.

Another man appeared, this one large and stupid-looking.

"Well, what'll it be then?" the small one said.

Gallatin had enough on his mind. His goal was to get on a plane to Washington in the morning. Local yokel Noraid shakedown artists were not on his agenda. Gallatin was more fed up than angry.

He got up and left.

Outside, the two men, plus a third, who appeared to be around 19 years old, blocked his way at the end of the block.

Gallatin stopped, looked at each defiantly and said, "I have no bone to pick with any of you. I'll be on my way."

"On your way down to the pavement," the little tough said as he charged Gallatin like a reckless, young bull.

Gallatin slammed his fist into the small man's neck. The man grabbed at his throat, at the same time gagging. Blood flowed from the sides of his mouth. He dropped to the pavement struggling to breathe.

Gallatin held the others at bay, swinging his fists expertly as he did in the boxing days of his youth. But his valiant defense came to an abrupt end as what felt like a grand piano came crashing down against the back of Gallatin's neck, from a fourth man, late to the melee, bearing a two-by-four.

CHAPTER TWENTY

Tulliver rearranged the Egyptian urns on a ledge for the ninth time. "No, no. It just doesn't work. You know what the trouble is?"

"What's that, Mr. Secretary?" Haley replied.

"This Department has no class. I mean, look at this office. The Danish postmaster general has better digs. I have to welcome foreign ministers and heads of state in this . . . pen? And we call ourselves the greatest democracy in the world?"

"That's the operative word."

"Which?"

"Democracy. Americans like the freedom without the flourishes. That's why we took such glee in throwing the Redcoats out. Remember when Nixon introduced liveried attendants and other royal trappings to the White House? That's about the time when the people practically went after him like mobs with torches."

"Funny. I seem to recall a little episode called Watergate," Tulliver said pointedly.

"Right. Watergate." Haley felt it was time to change the subject. "I'm afraid the press is devoting more attention to McHenry's leaving than to your accession to the office."

"Something is seriously the fuck wrong, Dan, when the media pay more attention to a loser on his way out rather than to a winner on his way up. Fix it!" Tulliver held his hand to his chin as he contemplated what precedence photos of him posing with a variety of kings, presidents and other potentates should take on his ego wall.

"Trouble is, there's a certain poignancy about an old cowboy like McHenry announcing stoically to the world that he has only six months left to live. The public laps it up. It's like movie of the week."

"Why the hell didn't we know he had liver cancer? We could've handled the PR differently. Hell, we could've gotten the son of a bitch dumped even sooner. As it is, if Merriman isn't re-elected, I'll have been Secretary of State for a mere eighteen months. Not enough time to make history." Tulliver threw the photo of him and Mobutu Sese Seko posing over the corpse of a freshly shot lion back into a box. "Wouldn't be popular with the PC crowd," he mumbled.

"He was just diagnosed. Even he didn't know." Haley looked at the ceiling impatiently.

"No excuse. We should've been getting hold of his medical records. Mark that for next time." Tulliver smiled at a large color photo of him shaking the Pope's hand. He put it in the middle of the wall. "We've got to do better with press relations."

"I'm afraid we've lost Lisa Valko."

Tulliver halted his interior decorating. "Lisa. Yes." A small smile was quickly replaced by a frown. "So?"

"I held out the prospect of a senior job for her here
at State. Gave her the line on the homo spy ring. Asked
her to run with it."

"And?" He placed an autographed photo from the
President of Israel -- "To John, My Partner in Peace" -- to
the immediate right of that of the Pope.

"She didn't bite. She announced this morning that
she was resigning."

Tulliver's jaw muscles tightened.

"There's more. Security has her on tape and in
photos with Thompson. Buckwheat clued Lisa in on
everything. On CHASM. Cases. Individuals. Recalls.
Now she's teamed up with Gallatin against us."

Tulliver strained to lift a huge, bejewelled scimitar
from the Sultan of Brunei out of a crate. "Where is she
now?"

Haley shrugged.

"Have her join the Recall Program then, and Mr.
Gallatin too, while you're at it," Tulliver said matter-of-
factly.

"We tried once -- with Gallatin."

"And?"

"And . . . it didn't work. Timing was off. But it was
ill-conceived. In any case, he's a civilian. He can't be
recalled. We should leave him out of this. If we start
going after non-government types, there's no telling where
it will lead," Haley said.

"Then cancel the son of a bitch. Annul him.
Revoke him. Use whatever euphemism you please! You
get the point!" Tulliver glared at Haley.

Haley bowed his head and sighed. "Yes, I do," he
said quietly. "But how can we live with ourselves?"

"We have no choice," Tulliver answered evenly.
He couldn't decide what he should do with the honorary
degree from the University of Indiana.

Lisa rushed up to kiss Gallatin, but stopped dead in
her tracks inches from his face.
"My God. What did you get into?" Tentatively, she
touched his swollen left eye. His physical pain reflected
itself emotionally in Lisa's face.
"I had a rendez-vous with destiny," he joked lamely.
"This time destiny outnumbered me." He lowered himself
cautiously onto Lisa's sofa. He looked around the neat,
single-bedroom apartment. The fresh flowers, dust-free
surfaces, tasteful knick-knacks and wall decorations
telegraphed femininity; the presence of woman which had
been so achingly missing from Gallatin's life.
"Mike. Look at you. You look like you fell into a
cement mixer. Maybe you should see a doctor."
"No. I'll be fine," he said with a grunt. "Remind
me to be born anything but Irish in my next life."
Lisa shook her head, not comprehending.
"I made the mistake of saying, 'I gave at the office,'
at a fundraiser for 'The Lads.'" He pronounced the last
words with angry contempt.
Lisa went to get a bottle of antiseptic and cotton
swabs. She sat with her thigh against his. Gently, she
removed the old bandage Gallatin had put on and applied
the medicine to his brow.
"Ow!" Gallatin jerked his head back.

She kissed his forehead. "Poor thing. Now be still."

He closed his eyes as she gingerly treated his wounds. At Lisa's urging, Gallatin related his latest run-in with Noraid. He opened his eyes to see Lisa's hands shaking.

"Lisa. What about Thompson?"

She told about the dual murders and the fantastical story being put out by the White House.

"I resigned yesterday."

Gallatin looked at her gravely. "You quit your job?"

"They've got to be brought down, Mike. The whole rotten nest of them. Haley, Tulliver . . ." Goosebumps paraded across her skin. She hugged herself as if bracing against a cold breeze.

"What is it? There's more."

Lisa turned her face away. "Mike. You need to know. In London. Tulliver . . . he . . ."

Gallatin touched her cheek and softly pushed her untrimmed hair back behind her ears.

"Oh, nothing happened. But almost did." She fought back tears. "I let my guard down. There. And in the job I had. I've been used. Like a--"

"Shh." Gallatin kissed her lips.

They kissed tenderly. The tensions in each lifted like a fog in the morning sun. They lay back on the sofa, Gallatin held Lisa firmly in his arms. Lisa stared intently into the darkness.

"They murdered Thompson, Mike. And his lover."

"But why?"

She shook her head. "It's only the tip of the iceberg. It goes further. They bring in criminals. War criminals and

others. Into the United States. Give them new lives, often
new identities. Buckwheat told me all about it before he
died. It's called CHASM. And I've got it all on these little
things." Lisa leaned over and grabbed her purse from the
floor. She pulled out a freezer bag containing computer
disks. "Some of these people the government sneaks in get
out of hand, criminal psychotics who murder. Haley sends
assassins after them to wipe them out. This program is
outside the law, not accountable to Congress. Nobody."

"It fits in with what Ferret had told me." Gallatin
sat up and struck his left palm with his right fist. "The
Brankos. That's how they got into the country. They
attacked the Suleijmanovic's. But then they were tracked
down and done in. Ferret. Ferret was a cog in the wheel.
But then it all got to him."

"Mike. They tried to get you. They wired your car.
It shows they'll stop at nothing."

They searched each other's eyes as they understood
the gravity of their situation.

"We can bring them down, Mike. Together." She
drew closer. "For Lauren."

"Yes. For Lauren." Gallatin braced her head gently
between his hands. Again they kissed, this time
languorously, back onto the soft-cushioned sofa, their
bodies together, creating one energy which, in turn,
invigorated their lovemaking. The whole evening lay
before them, just for themselves. In time, partly clothed,
they led each other, hand-in-hand, to the bedroom.

The freezer bag with the disks lay on the living
room coffee table.

He knew he shouldn't smoke. Not while out on an operation. The stench of tobacco risked spooking a target. Fechtmann took a long last draw on his Marlboro, then crushed the butt out under a black boot. Back before the Wall came down, Marlboros were gold. Traded in barter deals where the worthless East German D-Mark had no role. Fechtmann had enticed more than a few female countrymen into his bed using such simple bait as American cigarettes, Belgian chocolates and such. That was when he was somebody, with perks, a stake in the established order. Now he just didn't give a shit. Being just a tad sloppy would not land him in harm's way when stalking amateurs. Besides, one or two more operations with big payoffs like this one would put him where he wanted to be. A fairly wealthy man with enough resources not only on which to live comfortably, but which he could use to invest in a legitimate business. Like a bar in the Keys. Another immigrant success story.

He didn't like the area, a "transitional neighborhood" on Capitol Hill. Why did these yuppies insist on living in such places? He turned against a wall and deftly inspected his silent pistol. Six polished rounds lay snugly in the clip.

But he packed the silent pistol for self-protection this cold, late autumn evening. In a small tote bag slung over his shoulder, Fechtmann carried the actual tool of lethality for this operation: a three-pound minisledge which he picked up at Sears for $13.99.

The floodlit Capitol dome shone brilliantly several blocks away against a cloudless, star-filled sky. On the dome's crown, Lady Liberty stood looking down, ever alert, on the nation's capital.

Fechtmann took pride in being an assassin. As with any proud professional, he held himself to high standards. Ending human life was not pleasant. Therefore, clean and fast were his guidelines. He was morally opposed to making his targets suffer and he felt even the most loathsome deserved a modicum of dignity in death. It was with tremendous misgivings, therefore, that he took on this operation. Haley had provided him a complete file on Ferret's massacre of his family, including the photos not only of the abattoir that Ferret's house had become, but also of the autopsies on the two Ferret women and the three boys. His instructions were clear and simple: duplicate the murders against Buckwheat Thompson and his lover; and now against Lisa Valko and her lover. It was essential that Ferret's m.o., such as it was, be replicated unto the finest detail.

The file contained small glasine envelopes. One contained strands of Ferret's hair, obtained God knew how. The second held fibers from the same clothing Ferret had worn on his last day in the office, the day he murdered his family. Fechtmann surmised that CHASM personnel gleaned the fibers from Ferret's work cubicle. Plant the hair and the fibers in Lisa Valko's apartment after the deed was done were his instructions. The White House could then fortify its lie of Ferret the serial killer.

As he approached the iron-gated front of Lisa's apartment complex, Fechtmann felt a sudden queasiness in his stomach. He thought of the bloody mess he would create and felt shame. For weeks he had been telling himself, $200,000 for the Thompson job plus another two-hundred grand for doing in Valko and Gallatin. On top of his earnings from previous operations, all carefully invested in growth mutual funds and Treasury notes, the money would give him the ticket to retirement. After this job, the only things he would kill would be flies at his Florida bar.

The wrought-iron gate filled an imposing archway of red brick, the motif for the entire complex of twenty modern units. Fechtmann walked past the gate at a leisurely pace. Private security lights combined with light from street lamps to illuminate the high brick wall enclosing the apartments. Fechtmann turned the corner on Seventh Street, low branches of maples hovering around the city's lamp posts rendered the area darker. Late Sunday evenings were the deadest of nights in Washington. The street was deserted.

Fechtmann reached into his tote bag and pulled out an aluminum grappling hook with a light, yet strong, black, knotted nylon rope. Quickly, he scanned the street again, then swung the hook up. It caught the inner edge of the concrete slab top of the wall. He scaled the ten-foot structure nimbly, lay for a moment on top to view the courtyard of the complex, then jumped down, landing on his feet with a light thump. Fechtmann winced as pain shot up from his left knee to his pelvis. At 47, the ex-Stasi officer just wasn't as lithe as he used to be. He knew exactly where he had to go.

"Are we in love?"

"I don't know. Are we?"

Gallatin propped his head on his hand and looked down on Lisa. With his free hand, he stroked Lisa's forehead, cheeks and neck. She closed her eyes in pleasure.

"Are you afraid to be?" she whispered.

"Not any more. You?"

"Not any more either."

A long silence passed as they took in the afterglow of lovemaking.

"Say that we *were* in love. Where would it lead us?" She leaned on her elbow and smiled warmly. Her eyes were at the same time affectionate and challenging.

"A thousand points of light, a shining city on a hill, to quote a couple of presidents."

She held her smiling eyes unwaveringly on his. "Now be serious," she said.

"A lifetime with each other, I would hope. But, Lisa . . . I have to tell you that I'm afraid."

"Of what?" Lisa's face expressed puzzlement.

"That, having been starved for love, I might rush into it, not ready, unable to leave the past behind me."

"You mean your wife?"

Gallatin nodded.

"Oh, my darling. Take your time. Take your time." She leaned forward and kissed him. Again they were in each other's arms. They resumed their lovemaking. Lisa took the initiative. Her hair enshrouded Gallatin's head as she pressed her lips hungrily against his, her arms holding her lover's large shoulders with all their might.

A waft of cold air chilled Lisa, causing her to wrap herself and Gallatin more tightly in the blankets.

The sudden movement stopped Fechtmann in his tracks. He remained frozen until he was certain that his targets were in deep sleep. He mentally cursed himself for taking so long to slither into the apartment after picking the door lock. A cold draft risked alerting the pair. He indeed was getting too old for this line of work.

In carefully measured movements, without a sound, he laid his black tote bag on the carpet at the foot of the bed. He knelt down. Without taking his eyes off of the snoozing lovers, Fechtmann slowly reached into the bag and took out the mini-sledge. He gripped the tool firmly in his right hand.

His disciplined mind coldly calculated distance, force and timing needed to accomplish the mission. Another part of Fechtmann's brain, however, was sending different signals. Fechtmann fought off shame and self-loathing as he stared dispassionately at the slumbering lovers. Most of his previous victims had deserved to die, having played a bad hand in the international espionage game. Fechtmann told himself that he was a highly skilled technician in the art of assassination, not a bludgeoner. He was being brought down to the level of the madman Ferret.

Fechtmann closed his eyes and breathed deeply. *Just this one last mission.*

He concentrated on sounds, smells, movements. Every audible traffic noise, distant radio music, overhead aircraft registered in his ears. No foot steps, no active neighbors, no police sirens, no stirring from the bed. The green light to move in for the kill blinked inside his head. He exerted every muscle to raise himself as silently and strongly as a cobra. Every movement was programmed and carried out with the utmost caution. A black-clad, golden-haired avenging angel he was.

Fechtmann neared the right side of the bed where Gallatin lay face-up, snoring. It was vital that he eliminate

Gallatin first since he potentially would pose the greatest threat. A swift, powerful chop between the eyes would finish him instantly. He had envisioned that Lisa would awaken at the impact of the hammer crunching bone, would look up terrified and remain petrified long enough for him to bash her face on the upswing. It might, in fact, take two swings, or more, to finish off Lisa. Fechtmann just wanted it to be over, the best outcome for all.

It took him a full minute to reach the head of the bed, to position himself precisely where he should be for the coup de grace. The German hovered over Gallatin, breathed methodically; he raised the hammer over his head. His brain made last-minute homings and projected into his eyes the correct trajectory. He held his breath. The arteries of his right hand bulged as the fingers gripped the sledge's handle like a vise. Down. Down. Down.

The warm, sticky spray which settled instantly on Lisa's face felt comforting in her subconsciousness; perhaps it was prenatal memories of being in her mother's womb. Within seconds, however, it felt cold and slimy. She opened her eyes.

The loud pop caused Gallatin to jump reflexively half out of the bed, muscles tightened even before he could consciously make out what was going on.

The lethal end of a silencer-equipped Glock 17 nine millimeter met his eyes. The muscles remained taut, but his body froze in place.

At the other end of the Glock was a tallish, unshaven white male sporting an evil grin and alert eyes.

Lisa yanked the blankets up to neck-level in a gesture of futile self-protection. She barely aborted a scream.

The man, still smiling, put a forefinger to his lips. "Shh."

He took a step forward, still pointing the weapon alternately at Gallatin's and Lisa's faces. He indicated with his left hand for them to remain still.

In a quick motion, he looked downward, aimed the revolver toward the floor and squeezed off a round. Fechtmann's body jerked. The man resumed his threatening posture toward Gallatin and Lisa.

"I do not kill you," he said in accented English. "Him I kill." He dipped his chin slightly. "I save your lives. You understand?"

Gallatin, eyes wide and unblinking, nodded slowly.

"From you, I want documents. You know?"

Gallatin shook his head in confusion. The man caught Lisa's eyes steal a glance at the coffee table in the living room.

The man took a quick look behind him and shifted position. "They are in there. Yes?"

"You want the disks," Lisa said.

"Yes. Computer disks. From White House. Yes?"

Lisa nodded. "On the coffee table."

"Good. Now you go on floor. Both of you. Face down." He gestured impatiently with his gun. "Now!" He pointed the barrel at Gallatin's forehead and tightened his grip. The message was clear.

Gallatin placed his hands behind the back of his head, knelt beside the bed and cautiously lowered himself down to the floor. Lisa followed suit. Gallatin glimpsed a pool of blood emanating from the dead Fechtmann's head at the foot of the bed. He could hear Lisa reciting the Lord's Prayer.

stay like that," the man commanded calmly.
backward toward the living room, weapon still
couple.
natched the freezer bag, backed up to the door,
revolver, then ran into the night.
fied, Lisa and Gallatin remained motionless
the floor. Assured that the intruder had fled,
wly, amazed at still being alive.
atin ran to the door and looked out into an
courtyard. He rushed back, bent over
and took a pulse that wasn't there. "This man's
id.
ook Lisa into his arms. Lisa shivered as if half-
latin gripped her shoulders and took a close

you all right?"
took a quick moment for a systems check of
he nodded that she was okay.
you sure?" Gallatin rubbed a finger down her
howed the redness to her. She clutched her

atin pointed his chin at the corpse. "That man's
t in the back of the head. Never knew what hit

e gleicht Tod.
leapt to the bathroom to wash her face. She
o the sink. She wiped herself with a towel.
aining her composure, she said, "Mike, do we
e--"
call the police," he said.

CHAPTER TWENTY-ONE

One wouldn't know by Anne Haley's rambunctious boosterism at a daughter's soccer match that she was a quiet, shy woman by nature.

"Go Panthers! Go! Go! Go!! Kick Leslie! Kick the goddamn ball, Leslie!!" she whooped as her 14-year old husbanded the ball uncertainly between her feet, just ten yards from the goal.

Dan Haley was proud of his wife, a rare female who juggled a career as an residential housing architect with raising three children and looking after a hard-to-please husband.

He caught her eye as she lowered her face, one hand shielding her brow, fearing the worst. For one instant the game was the furthest thing from their minds as their locked gaze crackled with the electricity of love.

A thunder of applause erupted as Leslie's grand slam successfully made it past the opposing side's goalie and into the net. Dan and Anne Haley jumped up and down, arms around each other's waist, as if they were teenagers themselves again.

"God, I'm thirsty," Anne exclaimed, out of breath.

"I'll get a couple of Cokes," Dan said. He negotiated his way down the bleachers in the direction of the snack stand.

As he paid for the drinks, a man sidled up next to him and smiled. Haley returned a polite grin and about-faced to return to the game.

"Colonel Haley." The man mispronounced the title as "Co-*lo*-nel, in the manner many non-English speakers do.

Haley stopped and took in the slim, stubbly-faced man with a shock of dark hair over his forehead.

"I wish to talk to you please," Mlavic said politely, yet firmly.

"Do I know you?" Haley asked.

"Not yet. But we have common acquaintances. For example, Mr. Ferret, of State Department; Miss Lisa Valko. Chaim Glassman, maybe you also know him?"

Haley stiffened.

"This is urgent matter, Co-*lo*-nel. I need only some minutes. But someplace private."

Haley took careful stock of the Serbian. A twenty-three-year career specializing in dangerous situations told him that he was not likely in any peril with the stranger. The latter could have offed him easily without alerting him had that been his objective.

"The car," Haley nodded toward the parking lot.

They climbed into the front seat of Haley's 1999 Volvo station wagon. Haley set the icy Cokes on the dash.

"Not to waste time, Co-*lo*-nel. My name is Mlavic.
Co-*lo*-nel, formerly of Special Forces of Bosnian Serbian
Republic."

"CHASM," Haley said.

"Yes, CHASM. I come to make proposal."

"What kind of proposal?"

"I need job."

"Glassman will help you--"

"*No!*"

The unexpected outburst, thrust at Haley like a
sharp knife, gave him a jolt.

"No more work in . . . in brewery. Or factory. Or
even laboratory. No. No." Mlavic shook his head
vigorously.

"Then, what do you want?"

"I wish to work for you."

Haley shook his head with incomprehension.

"To replace Herr Fechtmann."

A knot tightened in Haley's stomach.

"Oh. You did not yet hear?" Mlavic sneered with
malicious glee. He is dead. I killed him. Last night."

"I don't know what you're talking about. I never
heard of anybody called Fechtmann." Haley looked
straight ahead through the windshield.

"I see. Perhaps you have bad memory, such a busy
man in White House." He tossed a thick manila envelope
in Haley's lap. "These will no doubt refresh your bad
memory."

Haley hesitated.

"Go ahead. Open. You must see." Mlavic sported
his trademark eerie grin.

Reluctantly, Haley tore open the envelope and
pulled out a stack of documents. He scanned them, all

marked TOP SECRET and compartmented through codenames, mostly CHASM. Virtually the entire history of Operation CHASM was laid out, with heavy emphasis on the Yugoslav segment. Restricted memos from Haley to Tulliver were there, as were bio sheets on some of the war criminals brought into the country. At the bottom of the pile was an extensive bio sheet, complete with a photo, of a smiling Fechtmann. The sheet merely referred to him as a "sensitive asset."

"You are in receipt of stolen government documents. Don't try to blackmail me, mister. You'll be arrested and these things will be confiscated." Haley fought to remain cool, despite a heartbeat that made the throbbing veins in his neck and face betray his anxiety. He knew that he was very close to being at the end of his rope. But maybe he could find some last trick up his sleeve.

"Oh, my dear co-*lo*-nel." Mlavic shook his head. "Please do not play games with me." He dropped another envelope into Haley's lap.

Haley tore it open in slow motion, as if he were ripping out his own guts. He pulled out dozens of bank transactions, sums in the tens of thousands of dollars wired to an unnamed account at the Royal Grand Cayman Bank. At the bottom of that stack lay a single sheet listing codenames on the left side, assets' real names on the right.

"Please look down to middle. You see 'GERookie?'" Mlavic helpfully indicated the name with his forefinger. He moved the finger across the page. "See. 'Fechtmann, Martin A.' Now, here. These memorandums by you. '$45,000 paid to GERookie for completion of mission, 3/05/03.' And this one, same date, 'Col. Javier Gonzalez Mendoza, recalled by GERookie.' What does this mean, 'Recalled?' It is on many memorandums."

Mlavic feigned the air of a curious neophyte. He waved his hand dismissively by an ear. "Oh, well, your Congress can try to piece together. Also newspapers."

"What do you want?"

"*Now* you understand."

"Cut the bullshit! What the hell do you want?"

"Like I said, I want job. I replace Herr Fechtmann. Same work. Same salary. I am good. Very discreet. I assure you. I am professional soldier. Perfect fit!"

"How do I know I can trust you?"

"You do not. But this is not important."

"What do you mean?"

"You - have - no - choice. Co-*lo*-nel. I want $100,000. Now. As retainer. Each time you question my trust, I demand more money. Understand?"

A defeated Haley lowered his head. "Yes," he whispered.

Another eruption of cheers emanated from the bleachers. Perhaps Leslie had scored another goal.

Haley gave Mlavic a steely look. "First assignment, colonel."

Mlavic smiled expectantly.

"Lisa Valko. Recall her. And her lover."

Chaim Glassman was as proud of his grandchildren as any grandparent. There they were, all four, captured in framed photographs, neatly lined up on his desk. But kids grow fast and Glassman went about replacing old photos with newer ones as methodically as he collected stamps. And, God willing, a new grandchild would be more welcome than a hundred Black Honduras stamps. His youngest daughter was still young enough to bear another child. He prayed that she would become pregnant just once more before . . . before he died.

The employees of Glassman Engraving Co. had returned home for the day. Soon Glassman would tidy up and also drive home to Greta's *Jägerschnitzel,* and *Kirschstrudel* for dessert, his favorites. The old man might not have many days before him, but they were sweet days.

He turned to the bookcase behind the desk and reached to fetch a bottle of *slivovitz.* Just a short one, for the road.

The sweet days almost came to a premature end right then and there as he turned around to be confronted with an unexpected guest. The bottle dropped to the floor, but did not break.

"Where's your hospitality? No *Prost* for old times?" the apparition said. He wore a large, dark green rain coat, Alpine hat and dapper, pleated trousers.

"You!" Glassman gasped.

"Old friend."

Glassman remained frozen in place behind the desk, his eyes wide, futilely refusing to accept the image before him.

"May I have a seat?"

Glassman nodded uneasily.

"Please sit down. Your standing there makes me nervous." The man reached down, picked up the bottle, and set it on the desk. "Glasses?"

Glassman slowly lowered himself into the desk chair. He produced two shot glasses. "Where have you been?" he asked, still transfixed.

"Let's just say that I've been on sabbatical." He poured two glasses, presented one to Glassman. "*Prost*. Or should I say, *lachayem*." He slugged back the potent drink. "And now I'm back."

"You are one of the FBI's most wanted. You are taking a big risk being here," Glassman said.

"I have unfinished business," Ferret replied.

"What?"

Ferret stared at the old German silently.

Glassman cringed.

"Don't worry, Chaim. You're my friend. I would never harm you."

"Your family?"

"Betrayed."

"I don't understand."

"Why doesn't anybody get it? Buckwheat Thompson reacted the same way."

"You killed him."

"I did not!" Ferret banged the desk with the flat of his hand.

Glassman jumped.

"Betrayal. The White House did him in. Don't you see? And they're pinning the blame on me. It's clever. Just like the way they did in my family."

Glassman shook his head, indicating he didn't understand.

"Oh yeah. I didn't do it."

"Who then?"

"The Evil."

Glassman furrowed his brow.

"The Evil System did it. CHASM. The program is evil. And I became the Evil. Don't you *see*?"

"I see," Glassman said as he focused on Ferret's trembling lips and overearnest eyes. He really didn't see.

"Do you have any snacks?" Ferret slugged back another *slivovitz.*

"What?"

"You know, chips, pretzels, stuff like that."

"No, but there is a store around the--"

"Never mind. I came here because I need your help."

"My help?" Glassman's heartbeat doubled.

Ferret reached inside his coat. Glassman watched closely.

"Here." He set a small box on the desk.

Glassman cautiously picked up the box and opened it. Inside were a half-dozen computer disks. He looked up at Ferret for an explanation.

"Hundreds of documents on CHASM," Ferret said.

"And?"

"And, two things. First, it's sound insurance in case they try to betray you as they did me. Second, in the unlikely event that you acquired a conscience, you could, you know, blow the lid, expose the Evil."

"Indeed," the old man said. He pondered for a moment, rubbing his white beard. "Why me? CHASM and PAPERCLIP have been good to me. My God, I would have been hanged, or jailed for many years, had your government not rescued me."

"Chaim. How old are you?"

"Eighty-three, next month."

"As a young man, you were responsible, directly or indirectly, for the violent deaths of, what? Thousands? Tens of thousands? You've lived a lie for the past sixty years. A Nazi murderer posing as a Jew. But you've been a quiet, law-abiding citizen, raised your kids here, your grandkids. Will you go to your grave loving Adolf Hitler?"

"Of course not!"

"Will you go to meet your Maker being proud of having massacred so many people."

"I never--"

"Don't lie to me, Chaim! Will you, on your death bed, tell your family how well you served your adopted country by caring for war criminals like yourself?"

"Stop it!" Glassman slammed down a ledger and stood up. He pointed an arthritic finger at Ferret's face.

"You. You killed your own family! Slaughtered them like pigs! How can you . . . How can you . . ." Tears streamed down Glassman's face. He fell back into his chair and covered his face with his hands as he wept uncontrollably.

Images, grainy black and white images, flashed in Ferret's mind. Corpses at Auschwitz. Lynette's dead eyes staring emptily back at him. The mass graves at Babi Yar, at Novi Sad. Win, Jr., Brandon and Jeremy sprawled, twisted like broken dolls on their beds, soaked in their pooled blood. Tito's partisans hanging from street lamps. Cloris, mother, half her face torn away. The ovens at Dachau; the smoldering bodies of his family in a makeshift ditch. A melange of portraits: cold, unsmiling Heinrich Himmler, smooth, mendacious Radovan Karadzic, Ferret himself. Ferret clamped his eyes as tight as he could, vainly wishing the jarring images away.

"Ferret. Ferret!"

The women placidly watching TV. The minisledge swiftly coming down on their heads, in turn. The boys soundly asleep. Screams. The large hammer again falling down, repeatedly, like an ax. Anguished pleas. Stifled terror. Blood.

Glassman shook Ferret. "Are you all right?"

A cascading, train wreck-like screech along with a vast chorus of pathetic screams pierced Ferret's brain. He could not bear it. He reached in his coat and pulled out a snub-nosed .38 revolver and pressed it hard against his temple.

Glassman charged at him.

Bang!

In the dead stillness that followed, Glassman did not know whether he lay atop a corpse or a 39-year old ex-athlete bent on counterattack. Either way, he was afraid to open his eyes and find out.

"Get off me, you old Kraut!" Ferret pushed the old-timer off of him. He sat up and shook his head. He looked down at an out-of-breath Glassman. "Why did you stop me? Why?"

"I've had enough blood on my hands for one lifetime. I do not need yours as well." Glassman put his fingers to his lips. "Sshh." He listened intently, then rose and peeked out the windows. "Apparently, no one heard. Now go. Leave, immediately."

Ferret, head bowed, picked up the gun, stared at it for a brief moment, then tucked it into his coat. As he reached the door, he looked at Glassman. "Chaim. Expose the Evil," he said intently. "I, uh, lack credibility."

"And I do not?" Glassman said.

"As an act of contrition. It's not too late for you."

"Please go."

Ferret disappeared into a heavy, spring downpour.

CHAPTER TWENTY-TWO

"You didn't kill him? Who did then?" the reporter asked.

"We told you already!" Lisa implored.

Gallatin squeezed her hand, and signaled her to hush.

"A man with a foreign accent. He shot the intruder in the back of the head--," Gallatin began.

"While you slept," the reporter rejoined.

"The gun had a silencer."

"The police say that it's your gun."

"How can it be my gun? I don't--"

"Your employer says you're licensed to carry a handgun."

"Not a Glock! And certainly not with a damn silencer! My God, my fingerprints weren't even on the gun!"

"The police say you rubbed them off."

"Why would I do that?"

"Because this particular weapon was unlicensed and in the District of Columbia, that's a felony." The reporter held his notebook, still unopened.

"I don't believe this!" Lisa interjected. "We went to the *Post* first. We thought you guys would run with a story like this." She rubbed tired eyes.

"We did."

"Yeah. A two paragrapher on page three of the Metro section as a local crime story," Gallatin said.

"Okay, okay," the reporter, Jason Tealy, said calmly. His youth and utter self-confidence lent an air of arrogance to the *Post's* most junior political affairs reporter. "What evidence do you have of a . . . 'secret program' to bring war criminals into this country?"

Lisa sat with her legs crossed in the small boarding room Gallatin had rented. With one elbow on her knee, she propped her head at the brow and looked exasperatedly at the floor.

"How many times do we have to tell you? The intruder--"

"Which one? I'm losing track," Tealy interrupted.

"*The second one!*" Lisa shot back. "He took the disks."

"Of which you had made no copies."

"Right! Stupid move on our part," Lisa hissed.

"So, it's your word against the White House's."

"At this point, yes," Lisa said.

"I'll let you in on something," Tealy said, full of himself. The President's Chief of Staff told Howard Chumley -- our editor-in-chief -- that there is no such program, that you didn't have the clearances to know about one, had one existed and that, well . . ."

"Well what?" Lisa demanded.

Tealy let out a long breath. "That you were asked to leave the NSC staff because of, what they termed, 'moral improprieties.'"

"Moral improprieties?! Like what?"

"It's really not for me to say, Miss Valko. Just look at it from our perspective. Here we have a young ex-NSC staffer, recently dismissed from her job, shacking up with an AWOL insurance investigator from Cleveland. You live in a high-crime area. A thief breaks into your apartment while you two are--. Well, anyway, Mr. Gallatin here, described by his employer as hard drinking and increasingly paranoid, grabs his unlicensed handgun and pops the burglar in the head. The cops arrest you, Mr. Gallatin, for keeping an unlicensed weapon and using undue force against an intruder. Now you are out on bail. And, Miss Valko, your landlord throws you out.

"You claim that the government is harboring war criminals from a number of countries, but you possess no evidence, not to mention a logical reason why the government would be doing so. The White House tells us that you're making it all up to get back at them for having fired you."

"What about my car getting blown up?" Gallatin demanded.

"Ah, yes. Well, my sources tell me that you've pissed off a lot of people. Could be some personal vendetta stemming from one of your insurance investigations. I hear it could even be the IRA. Now that could be a different story."

"Then you don't believe a word we're saying," Gallatin said.

"It's not that. Uh, remember when President
Reagan met with Gorbachev the first time? He said, 'Trust,
but verify.'"
"What's that got to do with us?" Lisa asked.
"I'm trying to trust and I definitely need to verify. I
mean, we're talking journalism 101 here. If we weren't
careful, we'd be running every latest conspiracy theory on
the Kennedy assassination, every Elvis sighting. We'd be
no different from the *Enquirer*."
"Sounds to me like the *Post* has lost its edge.
You're in bed with the White House. Just another Old Boy
in the Power Establishment," Lisa said, the edge in her
voice now razor sharp.
Tealy got up. "If you're ever able to back up your
story with anything solid, give me a call." He proffered his
card. Neither Lisa nor Gallatin made a move to accept it.
Tealy left it on a small side table and showed himself out
the door.

Lisa stood with her arms folded, staring out the
window onto busy North Capitol Street.
"Mike, what do we do now?"
"Try the *New York Times*?"
"Forget it. We'll get the same treatment. You have
to understand, these people all went to the same schools,
they play squash with each other, they intermarry. They
rock the boat only when they have it in for somebody.
Everybody hated Nixon. They went after him like a mob
after Frankenstein. Merriman is a different kettle of fish.
He may be feckless, but he puts on a good face. The media
haven't been so taken in by a sitting president since JFK."

"So, then we try other papers, TV, radio, till somebody bites."

"Mike, you're so naive. Don't you see what's happening? Tulliver and Haley have planted stories about us that effectively paint us as the Slut and the Nut."

"Don't call me naive!" Gallatin rejoined. "I may not be some hot shot Washington know-it-all, but this backwoods baboon isn't as dumb you think."

"I didn't call you dumb. Just naive. Look at what Tulliver and Haley have accomplished. They've successfully planted stories that I was 'fired' for having carried on an affair with a Romanian known intelligence officer -- of all things -- and that, after I was reprimanded, I went on a nymphomaniacal binge by sleeping with the entire diplomatic corps. You, they paint as a booze-swigging, gun-crazy conspiracy theorist become half-mad over his wife's death. Who's going to believe us -- without some real evidence to back us up? Tealy was right. If we're lucky, maybe some sleazy tabloid will take our story and run it next to the latest UFO fantasies and Paris Hilton's love life. That's exactly what Tulliver and Haley want. It would nail us once and for all as fringe fruitcakes."

Gallatin picked up the phone and began to punch a number.

"What are you doing?" Lisa demanded.

"Calling the *New York Times*."

"Are you crazy?!"

"No. I'm not naive, and I'm not crazy. I believe in fighting back."

Lisa went over to Gallatin, snatched the receiver out of his hand and put it back in its holder.

Gallatin grabbed her arm hard and threw her down on the floor.

Lisa sprang back up. "That does it!" She rushed across the room, threw her suitcase on the bed, opened a couple of dresser drawers and proceeded to toss her clothes willy-nilly into the bag.

"What are you doing?" Gallatin asked.

"What's it look like, lover boy?"

"Where are you going?"

"Back to Wheeling. Away from Cloud Cuckooland. Back to normal folks. My family. I'm retiring to my brother's farm to keep company with a lot of farm animals for the next sixty years. At least they don't lie and don't push me around."

Gallatin sidled up to her, reached his hands out to touch her, but couldn't bring himself to do so. "Look, I'm sorry. The pressure on both of us has gotten way out of hand. Let's just talk this out--"

Lisa swung around. "Mike. I'm sorry. I really am. But I need time to get my head on straight. I'm afraid that if I stay here, I'll . . . I'll become just like Mr. Ferret. I just can't risk it."

"And us? What about us?"

She shut the suitcase and struggled with the zipper. She rose, put her face close to Gallatin's, placed one hand gently on his cheek. "Oh, Mike. I don't know. Just give me time. I just don't know." Lisa heaved her suitcase around her shoulder by the strap, opened the door and rushed out to the street to hail a cab.

Win Ferret's favorite radio talk show host was Cy Lauer which he used to tune into every morning as he

drove to work. It was one of his fantasies to host such a
show. Ferret was always ready for "Say It Louder" Lauer.
But, on a slow early Monday morning, was Cy Lauer ready
for fugitive Ferret?

The topic of discussion was "Do you hate your
spouse, and what are you going to do about?"

"Oo-k-a-y. It's Win Ferret from . . . where're you
callin' from?" Lauer crooned.

"Up north."

"Uh, right, sure. Whatever. So, Win, do *you* hate
your wife -- we're talkin' wife here, are we? Not 'partner,'
'companion,' 'life mate'?"

"I'm straight."

"*Damn* straight, I'll bet too. Ha, ha, ha! So, Win,
do you and the missus get along? I don't care how lovey-
dovey couples are, there're times when you're tempted just
to haul back and let 'em have it. Don't deny it, Win. What
d'you say? Ever feel like it?"

"Yes."

"And how do you deal with it?"

A radioman's worst enemy, silence on the air, hung
in the ether like a radioactive cloud.

"I . . . I . . ."

"You what?"

"Killed her."

"Huh." Another pregnant pause as Lauer sought his
bearings. "Right, Win! What'd you do? Fantasize the
whole thing in your sick little brain? Mental release is
what the shrinks call it," he said, valiantly struggling to
maintain a lighthearted atmosphere amid panicky doubts
about this caller.

"No. I really killed her."

"Heh, heh." Again silence. "Okay, Win. I'm game. You knocked off the old lady. How'd you do it?"

"With a hammer. A small sledge, to be exact."

"Yeah?" Lauer's verbosity was drying up. "When and where?"

Seven weeks ago. In Bethesda."

"Wait a minute. There was a murder. A multiple murder. Are you, my friend, claiming to be that guy?"

"I *am* 'that guy.'"

"Right! Well, thanks for calling, whoever you are. Next caller is Fred, from Phoenix! Take it away Fred--"

"Wait! I can prove it!"

Lauer hesitated. "Yeah? How?"

"The . . . the pajamas my sons were wearing. Win wore striped ones, Brandon had red, solid red -- no buttons; and little Jeremy had on a single-piece job with Mickey Mouse's face on it. None of this appeared in the papers. Check it out."

"Uh-huh. Let's assume for a moment you are who you say you are. Why'd you do it?"

"I couldn't take it any more."

"Take what any more?"

"The evil I was forced to carry out on behalf of the White House. Operation CHASM. A program to sneak war criminals into this country and settle them in normal communities -- like the FBI's witness protection program."

"Name names."

"John Tulliver."

"Sure, everybody knows who he is."

"Col. Dan Haley. He's CHASM's overall coordinator. Buckwheat Thompson. They murdered him because he was about to blow the lid on the program."

Lauer bolted upright and hurriedly scribbled a note -
- *Get the FBI. Now!* -- and pressed it against the glass of
the sound- proof recording cubicle. He signaled double
time with his hands. A studio assistant immediately got on
the phone.

"Milan and Zlatko Brankovic, shortened to Branko.
They went on a killing spree across the Midwest until the
White House had them assassinated . . . I've got to go now."

"Wait! Ah, you're on a roll. We're lapping it up--"

"They'll trace my call. I've got to leave."

"Just one more question, Mr. Ferret! How. How
could you do it. Kill your wife and kids, your mother. Was
it temporary insanity, or what?"

"I ask myself that question a thousand times a day."

Click. Ferret hung up.

The rabbi recited the *kaddish* as he tossed a handful
of soil onto the coffin. Few of the deceased's family could
pray along with the rabbi, having been brought up with
little in the way of religion, though several of the younger
members knew at least parts of the ancient Jewish prayer.

The passing of an unassuming eighty-three-year old
normally attracts little, if any, public attention. The news
crews which jostled at a respectable distance to record the
rites, however, showed that this funeral was for no ordinary
man.

Upon the rabbi's final blessing and the last farewells
by family and friends, the newsmen broke out of their self-
confinement to launch themselves into the funeral party
like a barbarian horde waylaying peaceful villagers.

"Mrs. Glassman! Did you know you were married to an ex-Nazi? Were you born Jewish, Mrs. Glassman?"

"Were any of you aware of Mr. Glassman's secret work for the government?"

"Rabbi! What compelled you to perform services over an SS officer?"

Glassman's heirs and friends maintained a stoic silence as they strode hurriedly to their vehicles. Several of the older men and woman paused to confess that they were perplexed by the *Plain Dealer* cover story with its fantastic allegations about a long-time friend and business associate, a quiet immigrant who had shown generosity and compassion toward his community and his synogogue for a half century.

What made the whole account especially perplexing was that the *Dealer's* story was fed to it by the dead man himself. On his death bed, as his heart weakened by the hour, Chaim Glassman turned a package over to his attorney with instructions that it be delivered to Cleveland's newspaper upon his death.

> *I am Gruppenfuehrer Rolf*
> *Schleicker, formerly of Adolf Hitler's*
> *Schutzstaffel, or SS. For the past 60 years, I*
> *have lived a double lie. The first is that,*
> *since coming to America, I have been Chaim*
> *Glassman, a Jew. The second is that I have*
> *been, since 1947, a secret agent of the*
> *United States Government charged with*
> *resettling more of my kind in this country. I*
> *have clandestinely assisted scores of war*
> *criminals of many nationalities. I write this*
> *testament, hoping that Yahweh will forgive*

*me of my sins, though I know that I deserve
to burn in Hell. From my dear family, I also
ask for forgiveness, if not understanding. I
bequeath half of my considerable estate to
the Simon Wiesenthal Center, that it may
bring to justice many of the persons whom I
aided.*

   *Upon the fall of Berlin in April 1945,
American troops arrested me. Their
intelligence officials were impressed by my
specialized knowledge and my contacts in
Eastern Europe. They recruited me . . .*

Enclosed in Glassman's package to the *Dealer* were
over six decades of diaries and papers documenting his
roles in the SS and in Operations PAPERCLIP and
CHASM. Along with Cy Lauer's conversation with Ferret,
it was viewed by the White House as a torpedo that had
slammed broadside into the Ship of State.

CHAPTER TWENTY-THREE

The girl whimpered as the President touched her.
Christ! Where did LaFontaine find these little tarts
anyway? They seemed to be getting younger and younger.
As his hand explored her, a chill ran through him, bringing
the proceedings to an abrupt halt.

Merriman bolted upright on the bed. He looked
down at the girl. "How old are you?"

"Ah'm, Ah'm twunty yeahs old, suh." Her wide,
midnight eyes revealed fear and vulnerability, a
combination that normally piqued the Chief Executive's
sexual arousal.

But he knew she was lying. And while the
American people would judge him harshly should it ever
come out that their President slept around, they would
throw him in jail if they found out that he did it with
underage girls. Add to the volatile mix that he had a
particular penchant for young black girls, and anything was
possible.

Merriman took another close look at the girl. She modestly covered herself with the bedsheet. If anything, her eyes became wider.

Merriman pondered, wrestled with his emotions. God, how a good lay before a press conference stimulated him, got the juices flowing, bolstered his self-confidence. Orgasm, the riskier the circumstances the better, acted as a narcotic for Graham Merriman. And he needed a double dose two hours before announcing a major White House shake-up.

I'll have to talk to LaFontaine. In the meantime . . . He lowered himself on top of the girl.

Just as he had with every adversity during his adult life, he would take it like a Marine, Dan Haley repeated to himself as he cleaned out two years worth of some memorabilia and a lot of junk from his desk and file cabinets. He should have shredded all papers relating to the Recall Program long ago, but that made no difference now that they were all printed verbatim in the world press, thanks to Buckwheat Thompson and Winford Ferret.

Anne had told him that he was nuts to take the fall for the President and for Tulliver. He'd replied that he had no choice but to do so for the President. He had sworn to Duty when he came into the Marines and he had every intention to live up to his oath. Semper fi. He had a keen sense of history. Presidents may have their foibles, but, good or bad, they held the Republic in their hands. Dan Haley just felt too much loyalty. It was for the country's sake that he'd take the wrap for CHASM. Sacrifice for

one's country. That, after all, was what soldiers were paid
for.

Haley paused as he saw his in-box -- the last time
he would plow through it. The *Washington Post* lay on top,
crisp and untouched. There he was on page one,
photographed leaving the West Wing, stiffly erect, wearing
his uniform, smartly holding a brief case.

President Fires White House Aide
Marine Colonel Ran Rogue Operation, President Says

"Rogue operation!" Haley harrumphed. "Who says
you can't fool all of the people all of the time? And they'll
actually get away with it."

Billy Jaspar McGrew had wasted no time in
offering himself up as Haley's defense counsel. A
flamboyant lawyer, McGrew specialized in the obviously
guilty, celebrity malefactors who had all the evidence
stacked against them. McGrew was a magician with the
law; almost all of his clients walked. He would defend
Haley for a cut of the book and movie deals. He even
offered to help him launch a political career.

Tamara stuck her head in the office guardedly.
"You want something Dan? Can I help you?" the attractive
blonde secretary asked.

"Huh? Uh, no. I'll be fine. You're wonderful, as
always, Tami."

She looked furtively behind her, closed the door,
and went up to him.

"I think you should see this. They haven't gotten
around to cutting us out of the loop yet. It simply landed
on my desk with the morning take." She handed him a
document bearing the presidential seal.

TEXT - PRESIDENTIAL STATEMENT

Embargoed till 20:00, April 21

On April 19, I learned that an operation was being run out of the National Security Council and the State Department which had no authorization from me and of which I had no knowledge whatsoever. This operation, called CHASM, placed persons in our refugee resettlement program who had no legitimate claim to refugee status. Moreover, from preliminary indications, many of them may be guilty of war crimes in various countries racked in recent years by internal conflict.

I have ordered the immediate dismissal of the official on the NSC staff who ran this rogue operation, and I have ordered an immediate and vigorous investigation, the results of which will be disclosed fully to Congress.

Be assured that your President will do all in his power to right this wrong and to ensure that all of those who abused their office by taking part in it will be prosecuted to the fullest extent of the law.

Finally, it is with deep regret that I accept the resignation of John Tulliver, an energetic Secretary of State and my good

friend. That this rogue operation carried
over into the State Department, without his
knowledge or approval, should in no way
blemish his great accomplishments as a
loyal public servant. The decision to resign
is his alone and I will miss him.

Haley handed the press announcement back to his secretary, shook his head and resumed packing out. Tami backed deferentially out of the office, closing the door silently behind her.

"I'm taking no calls," he said after her.

Haley opened the bottom drawer of his desk. A black leather pouch sat snugly in the rear. He paused, then reached down, picked up the pouch and placed it directly in front of him on the desk. He pulled himself up and put his hands, palms down, on either side of the leather satchel. He did not flinch as he sat and stared.

Carefully, he lifted the pouch and held it edgewise on the desk, while, with his other hand, he slowly unzipped it. The pouch fell open like a book. On one side lay a weighty, black firearm. On the other, a dozen brassy bullets were strapped neatly in a row. The Colt .45 Model 1911 had been his father's, a Marine officer who had risen quickly to the rank of brigadier during the Korean War.

He picked up the gun and held it lovingly with both hands, then set it on the desk. Haley proceeded then to load bullets methodically into the gun's magazine. He stopped at two.

He thought of his father's heroism, and he pondered his own shame. His career, to which he had devoted his heart and his life, ended abruptly, aborted. He pictured the faces of his children. How could he ever face them? What

would he tell them? That he was really not acting outside
the law? He, of course, was. That the President told him to
do it? No proof of that; besides, the Nuremberg Trials
showed that following orders in the name of evil was still
evil, and also criminal. Finally, he told himself, he had
ordered people to be killed. Not in combat, but gunned
down like mad dogs. *The shame. The shame.*

Col. Dan Haley raised the gun to his lips. He
opened his mouth and stuck the barrel in, touching his
palate. He shut his eyes.

"Put your clothes back on. Oh, Tully, you're such a
pill. Truly precious." Manny Merriman sat on the edge of
the bed with her legs crossed. She was shaking her head as
she put out a cigarette.

"Are we through too?" Tulliver asked. He stood
before her naked but for a bath towel which he held with
both hands in front of his crotch.

"Well, I'd certainly say that one of us is definitely
through. I've got to meet some Eagle scouts or something
in the Rose Garden in twenty-five minutes." She looked at
her watch.

"I thought you wanted to see me to . . . to . . ."

"Fuck? Uh, no thanks, Tully. I'm getting it
elsewhere these days. I just wanted to tell you that we're
through. That's all." She stood up and primped herself in
the bedroom mirror.

"Can we at least talk?" Tulliver reached for his
underwear and trousers on a vanity chair.

"Nothing to talk about, sweetie. Unless you wish to discuss your recurrent problems with potency. Have you had yourself checked out, as I suggested months ago?" The First Lady struggled to keep a bang in place.

"Well, I have something I want to ask you." Tulliver almost fell over as he got one foot stuck in his trousers.

"Make it quick. You always were quick, lovey."

"This resignation business. I was wondering if you, well, might convince your hus--, that is, the President to reconsider. To refuse to accept my 'resignation' and insist that I stay on. After all, all those shenanigans were going on at State under my watch, but I didn't even know about them. The real culprits, Goldman, Ferret, Haley -- they're out of the picture now--"

"Stuff it, Tully! I'm not some jerk-off citizen watching the evening news. If you intend to peddle yourself as some noble public servant falling on his sword in order to take the heat from his president, go and do it in Peoria." She swung around. "You Washington power studs are all the same! Screw over the women around you. Screw over the public. Get them to buy your line, do your bidding. Well, mister, it all catches up with you sooner or later."

"But, Manny, I thought we had something--"

"We used each other, Tully. In Washington, everyone is a whore. Don't you get it?!"

She picked up her bag and strutted out of the room.

CHAPTER TWENTY-FOUR

The crowd at Shaughnigan's was light. Perhaps it was the fickle spring weather of northern Ohio, or maybe it was the entertainment that week -- a young girl with a guitar who sang wistfully of lost love, unrequited love, and impossible love. The music was neither the foot-stomping kind nor patriotic.

The color TV over the bar offered the only entertainment till the girl came on at eight. The bar had only four denizens: Gallatin, Lisa, Ray D'Angelo and Pat the Bartender.

"Jameson's?" Pat, proud of his recall of clients' favored drinks, asked Gallatin.

"How about Ocean Spray, aged one month in a glass jar?" Gallatin replied with a smile.

"Gotcha." Pat pointed his finger at his head. "I'm reprogramming the data bank. From now on the screen will pull up the correct input." He let out a hearty laugh.

The local station was running the sports news. Figures of baseball players scrambling on a slushy field were followed by highlights of some soccer match somewhere the names of whose players all ended in a vowel; this, in turn, was replaced by a middle-aged golf star taking forever to putt one into the eighteenth hole.

The buxom waitress swung around the bar with a tray poised up on one hand and her order pad and pencil in the other. She paused before the klatsch at the bar and said, "Just thought you'd wanna know--"

"Don't tell me," Gallatin interjected. "That The Lads will be comin' by to collect," he finished in a mock brogue.

"No. That the special tonight is shepherd's pie. Comes with a side order of salad or a choice of vegetable."

Gallatin appeared flabbergasted. He looked at D'Angelo.

"Oh. Yeah. I went around to all the Irish joints to let them know, on behalf of the Cleveland police department, that allowing unlicensed solicitation of funds is punishable by a fat fine and that I had it on good word from the State Attorney General's office that collecting funds for a foreign conflict constituted a violation of the neutrality act. I added we might have to close some establishments which turned a blind eye to such activities on their premises."

D'Angelo took a sip of his beer. "Oh yeah, ICE swept through here the other night. Guess what? They nabbed four illegal aliens. All micks. A short, ugly guy, a big, stupid one and two other bozos. They've been deported. Seems they were facing charges of freight hijacking, extortion and loan sharking back home."

Gallatin raised his glass. "I always said the Cleveland cops were the best in the business. Good work."

"Can't do our job without friends," D'Angelo said.

They all drank to Gallatin's toast.

"Speaking of justice for all, let me raise one to you two. To a wonderful life together and to vindication," D'Angelo reciprocated.

"Vindication isn't ours yet," Lisa said. "Nothing's happened to Tulliver -- yet."

"That one guy blew his own brains out. Tulliver's next in line," D'Angelo joked lamely.

"Haley," Gallatin said, shaking his head. "He may have saved the country a trial, but his testimony against Tulliver and others would have been invaluable. He could've copped a plea, gotten off with twenty years. Schmuck."

"You think Tulliver can wiggle out of it?" D'Angelo asked.

"No," Gallatin said. "The DA for the District of Columbia, a guy with limitless political ambitions himself, is pulling out all the stops to nail Tulliver and company. It looks like this CHASM thing goes far and deep. Anything but a 'rogue operation.'" He looked at Lisa forlornly. "It also looks like we'll be busy testifying before grand juries and congressional hearings for months."

Lisa rolled her eyes. "Oh, God. Why couldn't I be a refugee on my brother's farm?"

D'Angelo fell silent. He looked up at Gallatin. "How about Lauren?"

The Greyhound bus arrived at Chester Avenue station, two hours behind schedule. The rumpled passengers spilled out into the grungy area of decrepit buildings, marginal businesses and crossed humanity. The wet, empty streets glistened in the cold drizzle. Off of the bus, Mlavic lit up a cigarette and rubbed his four-day growth of beard as he surveyed the scene. He picked up his army surplus duffle and walked past the waiting cabs. He turned left for no special reason.

He walked for blocks, just heading for the lights of what he assumed was downtown. After fifteen hours on the bus, Mlavic had a gargantuan thirst and considerable hunger. He checked out a diner; it didn't have a liquor license. He continued on, black boots scraping the moist sidewalk. He ignored the panhandling winos and twenty-dollar whores. A modest neon sign announced, "Red's." He went in.

Mlavic ordered a draft beer before choosing a barstool. A couple of men were shooting pool off in the rear. The nearly deserted place had a scattering of clients, all seated at tables. In the corner of his eye, Mlavic saw a lone youth seated near the bar nursing a drink. As he took a long draw on his beer, Mlavic took a closer look around. Something was different about this bar. By no means upscale, it also was bereft of the familiar raunch and functionality of a blue-collar establishment. He ordered a second beer, with vodka chaser.

As the alcohol lightened his head, Mlavic pondered his situation. No work. No sponsor. No long-term plans. No identity. No papers. Little money. Far from home. But the mission at hand, likely his last, obsessed him.

The youth rose, carried his drink to the bar and sat down, one stool removed from the Serb.

Mlavic ordered a cheeseburger with fries.

"Some game, huh?" the young fellow said cheerily.

"Huh?"

"The game last night. The Cavaliers clobbered the Bulls."

"Oh." Mlavic tried to ignore the kid. He plunged into a bowl of popcorn on the bar.

"From out of town, huh?"

Mlavic looked reluctantly at his neighbor. "How do you know?"

"No living male in Cleveland doesn't know about the game. Besides, you don't look like you're from here. Or this country, for that matter."

Mlavic shrugged.

"I'm Norm." The young man extended his hand.

Mlavic perfunctorily shook hands, but avoided making eye contact.

"And you?"

"Peter," Mlavic lied.

"So, where do you come from? Let me guess. Uh, Hungary. We've got a lot of bohunks in Cleveland."

"What do you want?" Mlavic asked point-blank.

"Nothing special. Just breaking the ice."

More people began to flow into Red's. They were all males.

"What do you do?" Mlavic asked.

"Oh, I work at one of the hospitals. I'm a software guy."

Mlavic looked quizzical.

"You know, systems. Computers."

"I see. Which hospital?"

"Cleveland Clinic."

Mlavic suddenly felt sociable.

"Is that so? Tell me about this clinic." Mlavic leaned closer to Norm; he had all the time in the world.

Stimulated by Mlavic's stream of questions, Norm described at length the sprawling health complex, where he worked exactly, how he got there, what he wore, the key internal checkpoints. At Mlavic's request, he took out his work ID.

"And this little plastic card gets for you access to any place?"

"Well, most places. After all, I have to service systems gear, sometimes on very short notice. Lives could depend on it."

"You are very important, I think," Mlavic said.

"No. Not important. Maybe essential though." Norm held Mlavic's gaze.

Mlavic didn't flinch. "You are also very interesting."

"Thanks," Norm replied, his eyes still locked onto Mlavic's. "What do you plan to do in Cleveland?" he said in a soft voice.

"You tell me."

"I can show you around."

"I would like that."

"I'd be delighted." He looked at the door.

Mlavic got up. Norm followed. They left together.

Norm took Mlavic to his apartment, just ten minutes by car. He offered Mlavic a drink and invited him to make himself comfortable. Mlavic's eyes took in every detail of the place with cold precision. He accepted the drink with a wicked smile. At this point, conversation was replaced by body language. Norm rose from his chair and proceeded slowly to the bedroom. Mlavic finished his drink, got up and followed.

His eyes needed time to adjust to the dark. He heard the sound of clothes coming off, followed by the rustle of bed sheets. He stood motionless.

"Peter?" Norm said.

"Yes."

"I'm here. In the bed."

"Of course."

"Don't be nervous, Peter. We can take it easy, if you'd like."

"Yes. I would like that."

"Come then."

Mlavic removed his leather jacket, then took off his shirt. He seated himself on the edge of the bed.

Norm's hand touched Mlavic's neck.

Mlavic leaned down and placed one hand on Norm's forehead, as if to caress his hair.

Norm let out a long sigh. He closed his eyes.

Mlavic placed his other hand gently on Norm's throat.

The two men remained still, Norm relishing every delicious second.

Mlavic's hand on Norm's forehead tightened. Norm's head sank deeper into his pillow.

"Peter?"

"Norm." The serrated blade ripped through Norm's neck with the violent rudeness of a train wreck. Speed and brute force brought stainless steel hard against cervical vertebra faster than Norm could contemplate that his life was coming to an abrupt end.

Mlavic positioned himself over the dying man so that both hands were on the knife, pushed forward by the

Serb's full body weight. A final, desperate breath gurgled from Norm's throat. His arms, hands, fingers stretched outward, then fell limp. Mlavic slid the knife across, ensuring that his victim's jugulars were completely severed. Death came almost immediately. The blood flowed seemingly by the buckets, infusing the bed, the floor, the walls, Mlavic himself, with a sickening, thickening morass of life's essence.

Mlavic took off his pants and undershorts. He showered the blood from his body, then shaved. He found Norm's work clothes and donned them along with the dead man's work ID, then turned off the lights and departed, quietly closing the door behind him.

Mlavic drove Norm's car the few miles to Cleveland Clinic with the help of a city map he found in the glove compartment. This, most likely final, mission was driven by pure rage and blood-red vengeance. Just as he had secured for himself his dream job, just when he was assured a substantial income, two citizens brought it all down, virtually overnight, in turn, rendering Colonel Dragan Mlavic a nobody, a zero. Lisa Valko and Michael Gallatin would be lucky to die as quickly as Norm. No. He would see to it that they suffered, would watch each other die at his hand. But he would start by making them irrational and furious, by getting the child first.

"Here, he's coming," D'Angelo said as a news anchor appeared on the TV screen over the bar.

"I don't know if I can watch this," Lisa said. She slumped onto her folded arms atop the bar.

"Why? You write the speech?" Gallatin quipped.
Lisa sneered.

A smugly self-confident network news anchor on
the TV screen announced a special address by the
President. He gave a brief round-up of the scandal that had
broken out in the Administration's national security
apparatus, giving center attention to the bloody suicide of
Colonel Haley earlier in the week and the serious criminal
charges being brought against Secretary of State John
Tulliver.

President Merriman, seated at his desk in the Oval
Office, came onto the screen.

"My fellow Americans," he began. "It is with a
heavy heart that I must address wrongdoing within my
Administration. As you know, an individual working in the
National Security Council . . ."

President Merriman's handsome face appeared
pained as he recounted the White House's version of recent
events. A single official had carried out a mission without
his or the Vice President's knowledge. Unfortunately,
certain misguided officials in the State Department went
along with the rogue operation. Three officials were
unstable individuals; one took his own life; another is in a
mental asylum; the third killed his own family. The
operation to bring in "illegal aliens" did not have the
approval of Secretary of State Tulliver. But because it took
place on his watch, he insisted on assuming responsibility
for the events and turned in his resignation. This
Administration has launched a "vigorous investigation" and
will cooperate fully with the appropriate committees of
Congress to get to the bottom of . . . blah, blah, blah.

Ten minutes later, President Merriman penetrated
America's television soul with his brilliant, sincere eyes.

"My fellow Americans. Rest assured that no stone
will remain unturned as we vigorously seek the truth and
impose measures to ensure that this kind of thing will never
happen again."

Merriman formed a well-rehearsed avuncular smile
cum twinkle in his eye.

"I am reminded of a young girl I met recently, an
African-American girl, who, visiting the White House,
looked up at me and related how she had traveled all the
way from southern Mississippi to see the President and to
work under him . . . to assume a higher position . . . in the
service of her country. I told that girl -- Fanny was her
name -- that in today's America, there is opportunity for all
because there is truth and justice for all. Therefore, my
fellow Americans, as throughout our history, truth and
justice will prevail now as well."

"Pat, turn it off. Please," Lisa implored. She
looked at Gallatin. "Mike. I can't stand it. Let's go."

"I promised Lauren I'd tuck her in," he said.

"She's come out of it?!" D'Angelo asked.

"No," Gallatin answered.

Mlavic pulled into Cleveland Clinic's employee
parking garage, sliding Norm's ID through an electronic
reader to gain access. Clean-shaven, clad in Norm's pale-
green hospital uniform and with the victim's work ID
pinned on his chest, Mlavic easily blended in as he
sauntered confidently through the corridors and up the
elevators of the prestigious hospital. A directory at the
entrance listed the various wards. Children's trauma ward

was on the ninth floor. As he left the elevator, Mlavic paused, waiting until no one was around, then scrutinized a floor plan mounted on the wall. It was too confusing. He saw a nurse seated behind a counter further down the hallway.

"Hi. Patient named Gallatin please. Female." He flashed a pleasant, professional smile, then glanced at his watch with the air of a busy staffer making the rounds.

The frumpy, middle-aged nurse examined Mlavic over her reading glasses. "And you are?"

"Maerkel, Norm Maerkel. Systems."

"I'm not aware that there's been any systems equipment problem in that ward." She shuffled through the papers on the counter.

"It's software. A software thing. Not equipment," Mlavic answered.

The nurse examined him closely over her reading glasses. "I see."

"Is it this way?" Mlavic asked with a benevolent smile, pointing to his left.

"Uh, yeah. Um, 9012. We'll be putting the kids to bed in thirty minutes. Please make it quick."

"Sure. Thanks."

Mlavic walked briskly down the corridor and through an access door. While his movements were studiously easygoing, his eyes scanned the horizon mechanically to register key physical points as well as any signs of potential danger.

A double door led to the children's trauma ward in room 9012. Mlavic stood and peeked through the glass in the doors. No movement. He pulled the right door open and calmly entered the ward. There were ten beds, all occupied by very young patients. The walls featured

Disney posters; get well cards were pinned to the wall over children's beds. Boys and girls hugged their favorite teddy bear or doll. Other paraphernalia of kiddies' entertainment -- model airplanes, coloring books, assorted toys -- lay scattered in and around beds. The TVs had been turned off in preparation for bedtime. The children all were entering the lethargic state of oncoming slumber.

Mlavic checked the medical charts at the foot of each bed. He spotted an unconscious girl at the end of the ward. She had short, brown hair, and a delicate, thin, impassive face. The chart read "Gallatin, Lauren -- Shock."

Mlavic moved to the head of the bed. He placed a hand on her cheek and nudged her head. No response.

"She never wakes up," a small voice said.

Mlavic wheeled around. A boy, perhaps seven, lay on his side staring at Mlavic. His head was shaven; he was gaunt and very pale.

"Oh?" is all Mlavic could bring himself to say.

"Yeah. She's been here a long time. I've never seen her wake up. She's in shock," the little boy said.

"I see. Well, go to sleep. It's late."

"It hurts too much." He pointed to his head.

"Close your eyes. It will go away."

The boy stared at Mlavic. Mlavic pretended to check out the wiring on a nearby monitor. The boy's eyelids became heavy. He nodded off.

Mlavic placed his arms underneath Lauren and lifted her. Steps in the corridor became closer. One of the double doors swung open. Mlavic quickly put Lauren back and strode business-like toward the exit. He passed a visiting couple.

Gallatin and Lisa barely took notice of the departing hospital worker.

They stood next to Lauren. Gallatin caressed her head and kissed her forehead. "Baby, I'm back," he said. "I brought Lisa with me. We have an important announcement. We're going to get married. Won't it be nice, the three of us together?"

"She's beautiful, Mike," Lisa said.

"I'm taking her home. Soon. They can't do anything more for her here. She'll come to. I know it. Familiar surroundings and lots of love will do it."

They were silent for several minutes. A nurse entered the ward. "Visiting hours are coming to an end," she whispered with a smile.

Gallatin again caressed his daughter's face. He said a silent Hail Mary and crossed himself, then bent down and kissed Lauren good night.

Gallatin and Lisa left the ward.

Thirty seconds later, Mlavic reappeared. He looked at the boy with the shaven head. The boy's breathing was deep and regular. His eyes moved actively behind their lids.

He looked down on Lauren. He did not see an innocent girl in repose. He saw a Muslim. A target for his vengeance. A convenient victim through whom to channel rage and by whom to lure his ultimate targets to their deaths.

Mlavic looked about furtively. No hospital staff. The children were all asleep. He reached into his tunic and took out a black, folding stiletto. A swift slash across the girl's tender throat would do it.

He placed the tip of the silvery blade ever so tentatively below Lauren's chin; her smooth flesh yielded to the blade, but he did not apply pressure. He looked the girl up and down. Slowly, he drew the blade from Lauren's throat and languidly traced a line on her skin, across her larynx, down into the small valley above her collar bone, until the steel met the cotton whiteness of her nightgown. A drawstring at the top was tied in a bow. Mlavic placed the blade under the string and jerked upward. The razor-sharp stiletto cut the string cleanly in two. He reached down with his left hand and pulled one side of the gown away, revealing an adolescent's small, white chest. Mlavic grinned evilly.

The double doors swung open.

Gallatin walked briskly back to Lauren's bed. He reached inside his breast pocket and pulled out a silver crucifix on a delicate chain. He brought it to his lips and kissed it, then placed it around Lauren's neck. The cut drawstring, put back in place by Mlavic before he ducked under the shaved boy's bed, did not move.

"This was your grandmother Bess's. I almost forgot about it. It'll bring you blessings. Don't worry, baby. God is looking down on you." He kissed her again and exited the dark ward.

Springing out from under the neighboring bed, Mlavic knew he would have to finish the job quickly and run. He took a deep breath, hovered over Lauren and directed his knife just below her right ear. With a slight yank, he effortlessly severed the crucifix chain.

Lauren's eyes opened. She focused on Mlavic.

Mlavic was stunned. *Plunge the blade in!* he told himself.

Lauren popped up and completed the scream she had stifled on that cold night when she flung her best friend's burnt and scarred body out the window of the Suleijmanovics' home. It was powerful and piercing. The adrenaline surge it induced in Mlavic made him jump back.

In sequence, one high-pitched scream after another sliced through the air as each child awoke terrified. As instructed in case of emergency, they pressed their bedside call buttons. Mlavic could hear fast-paced footsteps approaching the ward. His eyes shifted back to Lauren. Oddly, she held his gaze with sober, unafraid eyes while, at the same time, screaming at the top of her lungs -- as if what she was doing were calculated.

"Who are you?!" demanded a large-framed nurse at the other end of the ward.

Mlavic spat. He lunged ahead to the double doors, shoved the nurse against the wall and sprinted down the corridor to the nearest stairwell. He threw himself into it and frantically leaped down the steps three at a time.

The children's screams coursed through the hospital's hallways like an electric current.

As he was about to enter an elevator with Lisa, Gallatin stopped dead in his tracks. "Lauren," he said. "Come."

They ran back in the direction of the children's ward.

The rattled nurse pointed at the stairway. "A tall, dark man. That way," she said.

Gallatin turned around and followed in Mlavic's wake. Lisa was right behind him.

As Mlavic approached the seventh floor exit, a uniformed security guard was bounding up from the sixth floor, night stick in hand. They caught sight of each other. The guard raised his club. Mlavic flew out the exit door. Gallatin was right behind him, followed by the guard and Lisa.

Mlavic crashed into an empty gurney in the hallway, spilling assorted metal and plastic medical equipment onto the floor. As he got up, his Glock nine millimeter fell onto the floor and in the direction of his pursuers. He continued his run. Astonished hospital staff ducked out of his way as he plunged forward.

Mlavic barged into an intensive care unit, shoving equipment out of his way and into that of his pursuers. Monitors beeped and flashed as ICU patients were startled out of their rest. A male orderly stood menacingly in Mlavic's path. He turned left, broke through a metal and glass door with his shoulder and found himself in a room with elderly patients. There was no egress. He turned around, but his way was blocked by Gallatin, the orderly, the security guard and Lisa.

Mlavic, pouring with sweat, looked around frantically. He brandished the stiletto back and forth.

"Give yourself up man," the guard said calmly, his black skin also glistening with perspiration. He held one hand up to urge calm; the other gripped the nightstick tightly.

"*Rrraahh!*" Mlavic roared, threatening them with the knife.

Gallatin stepped forward, his eyes locked onto Mlavic's face. "Put it down. There's no escape."

More people came into the ward and formed a semicircle to shield the elderly patients. One by one, they were evacuated.

Gallatin faced off with Mlavic. He squinted. Gallatin knew the face. "The bedroom. That night. It was you. You shot the intruder. Took the disks."

"I should have shot you both. In the back of the head," Mlavic snarled back.

"It wouldn't have been the first time, would it? You're from over there, aren't you?" Gallatin asked. "Which? Serbia? Croatia?"

Like a cornered beast, Mlavic bounced from side to side, seeking even a tiny weakness in the wall of hunters crowding around him. Gallatin met his every move.

"CHASM. You're one of those," Gallatin said evenly.

"I am Colonel Dragan Mlavic. Special Forces commander," Mlavic huffed proudly. "I am *not* criminal. I am soldier."

"What was your mission here, Mlavic? Kill my daughter?"

Mlavic grinned without letting down his guard. He pointed the knife at Gallatin. "You."

"Me?" Gallatin said.

"You and her," he tilted his head at Lisa. "You brought it all down. You brought me down. You must pay. I should have killed you then!"

"You're a kid-killer, Mlavic" Gallatin taunted.

Police sirens approached the hospital.

"You were going to kill my child first, weren't you? That's what you did over there. Killed children."

A wave of children's plaintive screams filled Mlavic's head, those of the youngsters in ward 9012 supplemented by scores of Muslim children, now long dead. The growing police sirens intensified the cacophony to an unbearable level. Mlavic hit his own head with an open hand as if to try to knock the deafening sound from his brain. He shook his head vigorously, but the hellish noise only grew in intensity.

"Drop the knife now," the guard commanded. He and Gallatin closed in on Mlavic.

Mlavic looked left, then right. No escape. Within seconds, the police would arrive. The screams of children enveloped his brain like a rogue tumor. Mlavic lunged at Gallatin, his knife ripping Gallatin's shirt, but only grazing the latter's abdomen. Gallatin threw himself on the Serb's back. He tried to put an arm-choke on Mlavic, but was thrown off like a bronco-buster. Again, Mlavic made a swipe with his blade, this time wildly. The tip of the silvery weapon sliced open the shoulder of the guard, who crashed to the floor in pain. Gallatin prepared to drop himself to the floor and throw himself across Mlavic's feet to knock him over.

Mlavic sidestepped, then grabbed a metal swivel chair from against the wall. He heaved it above his head. His pursuers instinctively backed away. Under the exertion, Mlavic's face was a contorted, ugly grimace.

Mlavic spun around and hurled the chair against the room window, smashing it into countless shards. A stiff, cold wind blew into the ward. Papers, plastic utensils, pieces of linen and clothing flew in all directions.

Gallatin stopped in his tracks as the Serb climbed onto the window ledge and braced himself uncertainly.

"Get down from there. Get down. Give yourself up--" Gallatin began.

Mlavic gave a stiff military salute, then leaped into the air as he would off a diving board over an outdoor pool. Gallatin and the others ran to the window to see the Serb crash head-first onto the parking lot seven floors below.

CHAPTER TWENTY-FIVE

The Empire Builder raced across the final mile of
the northern plains, just west of Browning, Montana.
Before the speeding Amtrak train loomed the Continental
Divide like America's own Great Wall. In the distance,
against a brilliant sky soared the snow-capped peaks of
Glacier Park.

Lisa Valko sat staring out at the changing
landscape, grateful that the monotonous flatness of the
Great Plains was finally giving way. She was glad. The
billiard table land had deepened her gloom.

"Why so glum?" Gallatin asked. He rubbed her
shoulder soothingly. "Look. Mountains Majesty. We're
finally leaving fields of waving grain. Cheer up."

"I don't know, Mike. It's this whole CHASM
business. I just can't get it off my mind."

"That's precisely why we're on a house-hunt out
West. Make a clean break. Start new lives and all that."
Gallatin studied Lisa's worried face. "Lisa. We've got to
start looking ahead."

"It's just that . . . if only I were convinced that things will turn out right. That the truly guilty will get theirs. I'll never feel vindicated until that happens. Especially Tulliver." Lisa shivered.

"The guy's been forced to resign in disgrace. The Attorney General has convened a grand jury. His fingerprints, so to speak, are everywhere. I'd guess they'll throw the book at him. Five-to-ten in the slammer at the very least."

Lisa looked warmly at Gallatin and tucked a hand inside his arm. "Mike, before I called you naive. It's not that. But Washington is hall of mirrors. And you have to have been inside it to understand it. First, look at Merriman. He not only knew everything concerning CHASM, but approved it. I know. It slipped out during a cabinet meeting I attended. That means that the CIA Director, Defense Secretary, Chairman of the Joint Chiefs at the very least were also involved, not to mention God knows how many bureaucrats working for them. It's major cover-your-ass time in the nation's capital. It all rolls downhill. To those who can't defend themselves. The dead. Thompson. Glassman. Haley. Driven over the edge -- Goldman. The so-called 'Rogues.'"

Lauren walked down the aisle, precariously balancing several burgers, fries, soft drinks and cookies. A broad smile beamed on Gallatin's face.

"I got everybody the same thing. It's easier that way," Lauren said. She distributed the goodies and sat down opposite her father.

Gallatin leaned over and gave her a peck on the cheek. "Thanks sweetheart," he said.

"Real food! After all that time being fed by tubes. Ugghh! Time for me to pig out," Lauren said with a big smile. She plunged into her quarter pounder.

Lisa leaned forward. "Lauren, do you remember anything from that time?"

Lauren took a half minute to gulp down her first bite. "I think I dreamed of Dad, and of Nura."

"Did you call her yesterday?" Gallatin asked.

"Yep. She's doing great. Plastic surgery is no fun, but she says she's feeling better about herself. She also loves her foster parents in Minneapolis. They're Bosnian Muslims too."

"We'll swing by there on the way back and you two can catch up on things," Gallatin said.

Lauren fell instantly sullen and gazed forlornly out at the increasingly hilly terrain flitting by.

Gallatin took her hand and rubbed it. "What is it, honey? You're with us now. Open up."

Lauren looked at her father with tear-filled eyes. "I also dreamed about Mom. Do you think that she . . . she woke me up?"

"Oh, baby. Your mother will always be there. In your thoughts. And that's good."

"So, why did I wake up at that moment? Just when that evil man was about to hurt me?"

Gallatin looked reflective, gathered his thoughts. "Early on, after we had you in the hospital, all the specialists could tell me was that you were in shock and that it was anybody's guess when you would come out of it. But one doctor, Dr. Benjamin, had a more concrete answer. He said that only by confronting the demons that sent you into shock would you be able to recover. Mlavic was one of those demons."

Lauren was silent as she pondered this. She stared out the window, a hand caressed the silver crucifix her father had placed around her neck on the last night of her long slumber. The chain was whole now.

Lisa whispered sweetly into Gallatin's ear, "I love you. And I love your daughter."

Gallatin returned her affection. His brow then furrowed and his eyes squinted.

"What's bothering you, Mike?" Lisa asked.

"One missing piece in the puzzle."

Lisa looked at him inquisitively.

"Ferret."

CHAPTER TWENTY-SIX

Dozens of svelte sail boats whisked across the Riddarfjarden as gracefully as Olympic skaters on ice. Stockholm was in the full bloom of summer. The northern sun basked the city's deep green parks, red-hued ancient buildings and chrome and glass skyscrapers in a rich, natural glow. Those Swedes not out of the country on vacation moved about leisurely at a pace more akin to Latins than to Nordics.

The panorama from the Mosebacke Cafe, perched high up on the southward island of Södermalm overlooking the Swedish capital, was magnificent. Most of the Floating City's fourteen islands were within view. Clients nursed drinks and munched on *grillad oering* as if they had all summer to do so. Such is the brevity of the northern warm season that natives seek to relish every precious minute of it.

William Winford Ferret III enjoyed the view and the warm breezes as if he had been born and raised a Swede himself -- rather than an American fugitive on the FBI's ten most wanted list. His face was the picture of contentment as he slumped down into his chair and stretched his long legs. He raised his glass to a waiter for a refill of Aquavit.

"I will give you a *krona* for your thoughts," the pretty young blonde woman said to Ferret in her liltingly accented English.

Ferret placed both hands behind his neck and looked out over sprawling metropolis. He focused on a point due north. "That's the *Gamla Stan*, isn't it?"

"Yes. It is the Old City. And may I compliment you on your learning Swedish?" she said. "You have a knack for languages." She leaned over and kissed him.

"Oh, sure. I've traveled a bit. But, to collect on that *krona*, I'm thinking that I'll never return to the United States."

"Never?"

"Yes. Never. I'm fed up, Sonja."

"Fed up?" she asked with an uncomprehending shake of her head.

Ferret took a deep breath. "America isn't what it was when I was growing up. People trusted and helped each other. Citizens had faith in their government. Neighborhoods were safe. Now . . . now, it's too . . . too violent. One cannot raise a family safely in America." He knocked back his Aquavit.

"So, we raise a family here. In Sweden. *Ja?*" Sonja said.

Ferret reached over and held her hand. His eyes fixed on hers, yet betrayed neither warmth nor reassurance nor hope. "One day at a time, dear. One day at a time."

At 35, Kevin Hanlon was an up-and-coming
Department of Homeland Security lawyer. He'd raced up
the promotion ladder to attain senior rank at a young age.
His forte was program management and his talents were
sorely needed at chronically dysfunctional Immigration and
Custom Enforcement. Constantly saddled with new
programs, the overburdened agency could barely cope.

Hanlon burst into his new office in an annex on the
Federal Triangle, just two blocks from the White House.
With styrofoam coffee cup in one hand and a rain coat in
the other, he quickly greeted his hand-picked staff, plunked
himself down behind his desk and paused one moment
before digging into the stack occupying a heretofore virgin
in-box.

*Deputy Attorney General. Before forty. Do all that
it takes, Kevin. Make this program work. The President is
watching.*

He pulled from the top of the stack a red-covered
folder marked TOP SECRET - ROVER CHANNEL NO
DISTRIBUTION. Finally, his marching orders.

FROM: OFFICE OF THE NATIONAL
SECURITY ADVISER
SUBJECT: TERMS OF REFERENCE:
OPERATION MARIPOSA

Reorganization of refugee operations entails
new responsibilities for the Departments of
Justice and Homeland Security.

Operation MARIPOSA directly addresses
the need to accommodate resettlement of

selected individuals with close association
with the USG whose continued presence in
their home countries has been deemed
counterproductive at the present time. The
parties to the civil conflict in the Congo
have reached a peace agreement . . .

Kevin Hanlon had his hands full. No time to read
that day's paper. The *Washington Post* sat untouched on
his coffee table, its page three story on CIA involvement
with Congolese military officers who allegedly raised
millions of dollars selling illegal drugs channelled into
America's inner cities, remaining unread.

Printed in the United States
69530LVS00006B/70